Skin Hunger

A RESURRECTION OF MAGIC

Skin Hunger

KATHLEEN DUEY

Atheneum Books for Young Readers
NEW YORK   LONDON   TORONTO   SYDNEY

Atheneum Books for Young Readers

An imprint of Simon & Schuster Children's Publishing Division

1230 Avenue of the Americas

New York, New York 10020

Book design by Mike Rosamilia

The text for this book is set in Meridien.

Manufactured in the United States of America

First Edition

2 4 6 8 10 9 7 5 3 1

Library of Congress Cataloging-in-Publication Data

Duey, Kathleen.

Skin hunger / by Kathleen Duey.—1st ed.

p.   cm.—(The resurrection of magic)

Summary: In alternate chapters, Sadima travels from her farm home to the city and becomes
assistant to a heartless man who is trying to restore knowledge of magic to the world, and a
group of boys fights to survive in the academy that has resulted from his efforts.

ISBN-13: 978-0-689-84093-7 (hardcover)

ISBN-10: 0-689-84093-4 (hardcover)

[1. Magic—Fiction. 2. Fantasy.] I. Title.

PZ7.D8694Ski 2007

[Fic]—dc 22   2006034819

FOR GARRETT AND SETH

Skin Hunger

~1~

Micah's breath scraped in and out of his lungs; his feet were clodded with road-mud. He labored past the agate-eyed cows in the apple orchards along River Road; then, at the edge of town, he climbed Mattie Han's rail fence. Running heavy-legged, he cut between her thatch-roofed house and her market garden. Going down the long hill toward the square, his chest aching, the downward slope shoved him along and he let it, barely managing to stay upright. Every step was a jerking effort not to fall face-first into the dirt. On High Street, he finally stumbled to a stop.

Hands on his knees to ease his gasps, Micah scanned the close-packed crowds below him. There had to be a magician here this market day. There nearly always was, sometimes two or three. Micah's eyes blurred with tears and sweat. He wiped them clear with a balled fist.

There?

He straightened up, staring. Beyond the tangle of wagons and carts in the pasture below the stock pens, he caught a second glimpse of swinging black robes and went on, down the steep bank that separated High Street from Market Street, sliding the last few feet into the road. A cart horse shied and a Gypsy in indigo shouted and raised his tattooed fist. Micah found his feet and ran again, going straight into the maze of tents and farmers' booths, pushing past fruit carts and women selling bolts of bright cloth.

The magician had drawn a little crowd. Micah lurched toward her, the sound of his own rushing breath muting her voice as she spoke to the people gathered around her. She was holding up a deep blue vial for all to see. Micah wriggled through the crowd and stood before her, staring up at the drawing of a slender-stemmed herb on the paper label.

"My mother . . . ," he managed, then had to stop, his chest heaving. "My moth—"

The old magician glared at him. "Hush!"

"You . . . you have to . . . ." Micah stopped again. He had meant to shout. It came out a whisper. He tipped his face upward, aiming the words. "Please. Come. *Please*."

The old woman smiled. "Once I am finished here. These good people want to buy my tonics."

"No, you have to come *now*," Micah said, finding his voice. The magician didn't even glance at him. She had raised the blue bottle and was talking over his head. He grabbed at her sleeve. Annoyed, she jerked it free, stepping back, and dropped the bottle. It shattered on the cobblestones. Micah stared at the shards of blue glass. Only the stopper was whole, spinning in a slow circle. He looked up. The magician loomed over him, her hand lifted high. Micah flinched and raised one arm to protect his face.

"What's wrong with you? That boy needs help!" a woman shouted. "Can't you see that?" Micah heard more angry voices. The magician's face softened abruptly and she reached to pat Micah's cheek, then grasped his hand, hard. She leaned close. "Make one more sound and I won't come. Do you hear?" He nodded, staring at her hand on his. He would remember, all of his life, her yellowed fingernails, rimmed in black—little half moons of filth.

— 2 —

When I was eleven years old, my father decided to get rid of me. I don't think he gave a crap if I lived or died—he just wanted to stop looking at me. Waiting for the carriage that morning, I stared westward through the steam rising off the river mouth. Beyond it, across the delta and the still-water marshes on the other side, the night-torches in the South End slums of Limòri were being snuffed out.

Once the eye-burning stench of the greasewood was gone, the beggars would swarm back to the boardwalk. But by then the shopkeepers' dogs would be off their leashes. Most were half wolf. All were underfed. Some nights, when I knew my father was angry enough to hurt me, I crawled up the tree outside my window to get to the roof. I could usually hear them barking from up there. Once in a while, I heard someone scream. It always gave me the shivers—how could people live there? Aben went up to the roof with me once. Not to hide from our father, but for the adventure. My brother never had to hide.

"Hahp?" I turned. My mother was wearing one of her dim little smiles. She was holding herself straight, moving with exaggerated, fluid grace, looking vapid, which meant she was frantic with worry over me. And fear of my father.

"Are you all right?" she asked in a near whisper, as though the sound of her voice would be enough to ignite my father. He was faced away, but I knew by the set of his shoulders that she was right to be careful. He was not far from one of his rages. I nodded, then looked past her at the house. If the stories were true, I might never see it again.

The expansive slate roof angled in every direction, covering the three wings of the old house, all its eaves dripping in the mist. It was a whole world, that roof, and I knew every inch of it, every broken slate, every patch of slick moss. I would miss the brittle smell of the wet stone when it rained. The salt pines on the far side of the grounds were gray-green in the early light. I would miss them, too. I had often played there. My father rarely walked that way.

There was a cold-fire lantern shining from a window in the servants' wing. I counted. Fifth from the tower—Celia was awake. She was always up early. She sang softly, almost constantly, as she fed fires, kneaded dough, ground herbs, made pies. No one ever made better griddle cakes. No one ever made me feel as safe. All my life, she had let me hide in the kitchen beneath the stone pastry table. My mother was cold to her, always finding fault with her work, but I loved her.

I caught a glimpse of movement behind the sheer window drape. Celia was dressing. I blushed and turned away. The sea-gravel that paved the carriage path grated beneath my boots and my father glanced at me. I stared out at the water like I hadn't noticed. I was used to missing Celia and her cooking. I was used to being hauled off to schools. I usually liked it. I *liked* living away from my father. But this time was different.

"The carriage is ready, sir!"

The stableman's call made me look; it was the little white stallion this morning, of course, harnessed in black leather. He was pulling a carriage I had never seen before. There were silver vines curling over the dark wood, the leaves and thorns wrought in great detail, polished bright. I glanced at my father. Had the carriage been *made* for this occasion? How long had he known?

I watched the driver pat the pony's neck—Gabardino handled horses gently, and I was glad. I had loved the white colt, had often watched him racing around the pasture with the rest of the spring foals. He was a Malek-Cross—a careful braiding of three ancient breeds. They were small, trained well, and had no fear of height. Malek Farms had a stable master of great skill—my father. He sold the Malek-Cross colts for what he called a filthy profit, all but the rare white ones. He was keeping those for himself—he had this stud, one mare, and a barely weaned filly now. In ten years he would have a herd of the small, elegant ponies.

The stallion was immaculate, of course, his dark hooves

rubbed with beeswax. He never got dirty anymore. Rainwater hadn't touched his skin in three years. His neck was arched and he tossed his mane. But his eyes were opaque—dead. It always happened with the training.

Pulling the pony to a halt, Gabardino leapt down to help my mother. Her beaded slippers barely touched the mount-step. Her silk dress shushed against the polished wood. Father climbed up after her and made an impatient sound as she took a moment to arrange the billowing fabric of her skirts. I sat on the rear bench, across from my parents, fighting the fear crawling inside me. My father had made it very clear; I had no choice. I looked north toward the bay. It was silver-gray this morning, the flat color of a parlor mirror before the lamps are lit.

I shivered and glanced at Gabardino. He was unwinding the reins from the silver cleat, holding them loosely, giving the pony his head. The carriage began to roll forward The little stallion trotted, then cantered, his milky tail streaming out behind. Then, at a command from Gabardino, the pony leapt upward, pulling the carriage into the air.

"Hahp," my father said. "Sit up straight."

I stiffened my spine and bit at my lower lip, feeling the pain anchor me to reality. I did not want to go to the academy. But what I wished, what I feared, didn't matter a crap to my father, and it never had.

"Sit up *straight*," he repeated. My mother made a little gesture of protest and started to say something to him. He lifted one hand and she lowered her head.

In that instant, I hated him more than I ever had.

— 3 —

"My mother needs help," Micah said. "Birthing."

The magician leaned closer to his ear. "Six pieces of silver." Then she patted his head with one bony hand and straightened, smiling at the little crowd.

Micah stared up at her. "Five," he whispered back.

The old woman shook her head, a tiny movement meant for no one but him. She was still smiling. Her teeth were long and yellowed. Micah could smell her. Her robes were stiff with sweat and road dust.

He felt his eyes sting and refused to cry. "Five is all we have."

She looked down at him, tilting her head, then spoke to the crowd. "A woman in need calls me away," she told them. "So you must buy quickly and—"

"Micah?"

He turned.

"Micah, what's wrong?" Mattie Han's plump face was flushed as she made her way through the crowd.

"My mother," he began hoarsely. Then his throat constricted, and he couldn't force out even one more word.

Mattie gripped his shoulders, bending to look into his face. "What is it? The babe?"

Micah nodded.

Mattie rounded on the crowd. "Clear off!" Her big hands were closed into fists. "Be off! Go!" She began to load the magician's crates into the wagon. The bottles jangled. The old woman scowled. "Have a care with those!"

Mattie's eyes flashed. "That boy's mother is my friend. Hurt her and I'll have your ears." She slid the next crate into the wagon. "You should be ashamed. Selling bottled-up mint tea."

The magician drew herself taller. "That tonic is made from a rare mountain moss that grows only—"

"Hush," Mattie hissed. She jabbed a thick finger at the driver's bench. The magician hesitated, then gripped the handhold and climbed up. Micah scrambled up on the far side, then waited, trembling, as the old magician made a show of arranging her robes and unwrapping the reins from the brake cleat.

"Mind what I said," Mattie shouted at the magician. Then she looked at Micah. "Tell your mother I'll come tomorrow, midmorning. I'll cook and help with the babe."

The magician raised her arm to snap the whip. The

rack-boned cart horse leaned into the harness and the wheels creaked into motion. Micah swallowed hard as the wagon tilted, coming up onto the rutted track that led back to the cobblestones of Market Street. He dug his nails into the worn wood of the bench. He had never been alone with a magician like this. He had never been this *close* to one.

The old woman turned to pat his shoulder. "Five, you said? You sure of that?"

Micah nodded and shifted from beneath her hand, sliding to the outside edge of the bench. She laughed. Micah refused to look at her. He sat still as stone as the bony old horse ambled along. An hour passed, or more, as Micah sat with his thoughts spinning, his mouth dry. It felt like a year.

When the wagon finally creaked to a stop in the farmyard, Micah jumped to the ground and ran toward the house, shouting for his father. The door banged open.

"Come quickly," Papa called. "I'll tell her you're—"

"I'll need the five silver," the magician said. She had gotten down quickly and was pulling a leather bag from beneath the driver's bench.

Micah saw his father's face harden, but he turned back to the house. The magician glanced around, her eyes crossing Micah's. "My horse?"

Micah nodded. "I'll see to it. Just hurry."

The old woman's face creased into a smile. "Give her some hay, will you, dearie? But don't unharness her."

Micah nodded and watched her smile widen when his father reappeared, holding out the pouch that held his mother's inheritance, all of their savings, and next year's seed money. She loosed the drawstring with her yellowed teeth, then bit down on each coin to prove the softness and purity of the silver. Only then did she walk to the porch and go up the steps. "Show me where she is."

Micah watched them go in. He heard his mother cry out, once, and his whole body reacted. Then his father closed the door. The sound of the hinges somehow freed Micah's feet from the ground, and he walked back to the cart horse. He led the old mare to the mossy wooden trough, wagon and all. The pump handle was warm from the sun. He knelt and drank with the mare, and the cold water steadied him a little.

When the mare lifted her head and stood slack-jawed, her muzzle dripping, Micah brought an armful of hay. He knew his father wouldn't like it—not after the way the magician had been about the coins. But it wasn't the mare's fault.

Micah heard a muffled cry and stiffened. The old mare nosed at him, wetting his shirt. He tied her reins to the oak that shaded the chicken coop and tossed the hay on the ground beside her. Then there was nothing to do.

The air felt heavy; it clung to Micah's skin as he walked toward the house, his eyes fixed on the front door. Lifting his foot to climb the porch stairs, he heard his mother scream. He stopped midstep, off balance, then twisted around like a snared rabbit and ran across the yard, then downhill, toward the barn.

His heart pounding, he shoved at the heavy door and

inhaled the warm smell of livestock and hay. Gripping the smooth, worn wood of the pitchfork handle, he filled the hayricks. He worked stiffly, listening for another scream, but it did not come. He milked the goats and walked the bucket to the creek to cool the milk. When he came back up the hill, his father was in the barn, looking for him.

"It's all quiet now. I heard the babe's first cry."

Micah felt like laughing, like crying. His father lifted him and swung him in a circle, then embraced him. They walked back up the hill and sat beneath the oak tree, fiddling fallen twigs in their hands, scratching lines into the dirt, listening to the old mare switch her tail at the flies.

When the door opened, Micah scrambled to his feet.

"Is she all right?" his father asked.

The magician smiled easily. "Of course. The babe is a girl."

Micah's father shot him a glance, and they grinned at each other.

"Mind you both, let them alone," the magician said sternly. "It was a very hard time." Micah watched her walk, leaning outward against the weight of her bag, talking to his father over her shoulder. "You risk your wife if she doesn't get proper rest."

"She won't lift anything heavier than a spoon," Micah said, and his father nodded. The magician hoisted the bag into the wagon, then untied the mare and climbed up.

"Thank you very kindly," Micah heard his father say. "Thank you for coming."

The magician turned. "Rest will mend her. Just leave her to sleep until tomorrow and she will be fine."

"She won't lift a finger for weeks," Micah called back. "We'll see to that." His feet felt light, dancey, silly. The magician stung her old horse with the whip, and the wagon swayed and creaked as it rolled across the farmyard, headed back toward the road.

"A girl," Papa said. "Your mother wants Sadima for the name, after her great-gran." He ran his hands over his face. "I like it well enough."

Micah smiled. He liked the name too. Sadima would be rosy and beautiful and sweet, not a bit like Brahn's pale, weepy little sister Tarah. As they walked toward the house, Micah straightened his shoulders. He was ten years older than tiny Sadima. He would protect her.

"Micah?" His father gripped his shoulder as they went in, startling him out of his thoughts. "You're a good boy, Micah. No father ever had a better son."

Micah stared up at his father, astonished at the praise.

"Let's get the eggs in," his father said quickly, looking back out the door at the sky as though he was just now realizing that evening was near. "When she wakens, we'll want to feed her more than yesterday's soup."

Micah got the basket from its hook. The hens were fussy and quarrelsome; they were used to him bothering them in the morning, not when the afternoon sun was slanting through the planks. Coming back, he opened the door to see the hearth fire crackling. His father had piled on the wood, warming the room.

"Here, then, Micah," his father called, ladling a bowl of thick soup from the iron pot. "Good enough for you and me."

They ate in silence, both of them glancing down the hall every few seconds.

"I'll just go peek in," Micah's father said when his bowl was empty. "If she's half-awake, nursing the babe, maybe she'd like some broth." Micah followed his father down the hallway, wondering if little Sadima would have light eyes like their mother's, or brown like their father's. "Be still now," his father whispered, turning the door latch. Micah smiled as his father eased the door open. He thought he could hear the faint whimpering of the baby.

His father leaned in, then stepped forward. Maybe, Micah thought as he followed, they should take Sadima back into the sitting room and hold her while his mother slept. Maybe they should—

A wordless cry from his father severed Micah's thoughts. He stared, blinking. The linens were stained with an ugly, deep red. No. Not red. Red-brown. The blood had dried. His mother lay with her eyes fixed open, one crooked arm stiff upon the blankets.

Micah stood, helpless, as his father dropped on his knees beside the bed, mouth twisted open as he patted his wife's face, gripped her hands. Micah heard him whispering, pleading with her to waken. On the floor, naked and unwrapped, lay the newborn infant, her skin blue-gray. Micah stumbled sideways, his eyes crossing his mother's dresser, the wall, the window. Nothing looked right. His mother's dresser was bare. The pewter candlesticks were gone. So was the little cut-glass wedding vase from the windowsill. The top dresser drawer hung half-open. The rest were askew, shoved closed.

The baby whimpered, and Micah jerked in response. He turned and picked her up. She was ice-cold. He opened his shirt to press her against his bare chest. His father lay across his mother's body now, shaking with sobs.

Micah carried the baby to the sitting room and stood by the fire, warming her. Then he went outside to put the sound of his father's grief behind him. Holding his sister close, without a single human thought in his mind, he walked toward the barn. His father did not look for him until morning. It took him an hour to find his children, burrowed into the haystack, asleep, Micah's body curved around his sister, still keeping her warm.

– 4 –

As the pony pulled the carriage higher, I was sweating.
I could smell my own fear, sour and sharp, seeping
through the scent of rose-soap on my skin. My tunic was
damp around my neck, even though it was chilly. I
inhaled slowly, fighting the nausea I always felt at the first
steep ascent, and the uneasy churning in my gut. Then,
to keep from looking at either one of my parents, I
watched the house shrink as we went higher—the lawns
faded with distance and the slate roof dissolved into the
gray mist. I squinted. It was gone. There was nothing
behind me.

"Stay east of the river for as long as you can," my father
ordered the driver. Gabardino's shoulders lifted a notch,
then fell, to indicate he had heard. I glanced at my mother

as the carriage tilted again. I was instantly sorry. Her eyes caught at mine.

"Will you be all right, Hahp?"

"Of course he will," my father snapped.

I turned away, staring down at the river. The water widened and slowed as it ran past the rows of shacks and rough-stone shops. The docks were full of ships, and I could easily imagine the death-stink of the wet holds. It didn't bother my father. It made me vomit.

South End. The crap-end of Limòri was coming awake. The cobblestones were dark and slick with fog-drip. The big-wheeled carts and the rough-coated ponies that pulled them were crowded against each other in the narrow streets. The lice-headed drivers were shouting, snapping their whips. I leaned forward and counted the blue and red pennants on the ships. Eleven. There were only eleven Malek ships in port. Most of the fleet was out, then.

"Higher, please," my mother said softly. She hated South End. Even distant glimpses of the packs of ragged children and skinny dogs made her sad and uneasy.

"Higher," Father repeated for Gabardino. The driver nodded.

My mother was smiling at me. It was a false smile—most of hers are. She straightened her rings, touched her hair, smoothed her skirts, then did it again: straighten, touch, smooth. This whole time, her eyes were fastened on me. "Perhaps you will like it," she said quietly. Her smile warmed. "When you were little, you always followed them around when they came to the house."

I looked down without answering. The South End slums were receding into the fog behind us now too, smells and all. The pony was still pulling us upward. This high, everything was scented by wind and stars. We passed over Middle Park, then Ferrin Hill, the ancient estates canopied with spreading oaks and tall sycamores brought in from the forests to the north. I wanted to live there— the days were long past when you had to be related to the king; all it took was gold, but my father could not stand the sight of a neighbor's house. He hated most people— and most people hated him.

Gabardino guided the pony into a gentle curve. My father always liked to pass over Malek Gardens, with its ponds and the hundred little waterfalls fed by streams that ran in circles, the water flowing obediently uphill, then cascading down again. Before the waterfalls, there had been year-round blue roses and blood-red lilies. As soon as other people began to have waterfalls, my father would pay for something new.

Twice a year children from South End were brought here and allowed to play for a few hours, like puppies let out of a filthy run long enough to air. Then they were carted home again to tell stories of magic waterfalls and fish as bright as flowers and all the rest. I had gone, once, when I was six or seven. I had cried, watching the stick-thin children run in circles, half-mad with delight. Aben had not. The next year Father left me home.

I stared down at the maze of lawns, paths, streams, and woods. The families of Ferrin Hill paid to have the pavilion or the amphitheater to themselves for weddings and memorials. My father rented the woods to the Criers Race and the gazebo to the Lutist Guild. The Eridians rented the entire park for their annual Celebration of Birth.

My father had to know that the four long nights of ritual made the people on Ferrin Hill uneasy. But he didn't want to slight the Eridians, even though I had heard him laugh at the rumors about them many times.

"You might know a few of the boys," my mother said, and I could tell from her voice that she was desperate to end the silence.

I glanced at her and nodded. I might. Application to the academy was kept secret; my father had threatened me with a whipping if I told anyone, even Aben. But there had been whispers at school among those of us who were second and third sons, not heirs, and who weren't needed at home.

I had tried so hard to fail the stinking test. I had never tried that hard at anything in my life. I heard my mother's silk skirts rustle.

"Hahp?"

I turned to meet her eyes.

"Just do your best." She whispered the words like a bashful child, glancing aside at my father. I nodded and looked away again.

She cleared her throat. "Some of your friends will surely be—"

"Be still, Anna," my father interrupted.

I saw her flush and knew she was close to crying. I

wanted to tell her the usual things, that I'd be fine, that I would write letters, that I'd see her at Winterfeast. But I wouldn't.

I loosened my collar slightly and rubbed my palms on my trousers, staring at the dark cliff that filled half the sky as we got closer. Gabardino was guiding the pony downward. I could see the entrance ledge halfway up the cliff, the enormous doors—and the ancient steps cut into the rock. They were rounded with time and moss, slanting across the stone face in a long crisscross pattern. There was a boy about halfway up. I couldn't imagine climbing those steps—but I knew that messengers did, every day.

I looked away from the cliff, back out over the city. The copper roof of the Eridians' Meeting House on the other side of the river shone orange-pink in the early light. The windows on Ferrin Hill sparkled like diamonds. I imagined standing up, leaning over the side of the carriage slowly, a half inch at a time, pretending to look down at something. My balance would cross some invisible point and the weight of my body would make the decision. But I would have to be careful. If I did it too slowly, my father would stop me. If I leapt, my mother would never be able to believe it was an accident. Did I have the nerve to do it? Would I die instantly? Was the carriage still high enough for that?

I wished I could ask my father.

He would know.

He knew shit-everything.

"Hahp. Sit back," my mother said urgently, and I sat down without thinking.

So there it was.

I was a coward.

— 5 —

"You'll do barn chores?" Papa's voice was flat, heavy with weariness.

Micah nodded, eating with one hand, holding a wad of Sadima's nightshirt in the other. She was sitting astride his right leg, watching him chew his square of hard brown bread. At least she had stopped crying. There was precious little food left, and they were all hungry. He ruffled her wispy red hair.

"You sure?" his father asked sharply, rolling up his pallet.

Micah nodded again. "I will," he said, around a mouthful of bread. "She'll nap soon." Sadima patted his chest and reached toward the bread. Micah tore off a bit for her to chew.

Papa stood at the door. "Don't let her drop that. Turn that last round of cheese in the spring house and make sure it doesn't mold, or we won't make it to planting time."

Micah said nothing. Papa rarely strung that many words together, and grim as they were, it was better than silence—or the flares of anger he had so often now. Micah heard the door squeak, then bang closed. He listened to the unevenness in his father's step as he left, crossing the planked porch. Papa had twisted his left knee plowing last year and had been laid up all summer.

Micah had tried, but the harvest had been thin—he'd managed planting by wearing a sling his father had stitched, carrying Sadima along with him. This year she was too old, too heavy, and she wriggled like a fish when she wanted down. Planting the house garden, they had tried weaving a cage of willow wands, lining it with blankets. Sadima had screamed and wept, and neither of them could stand to leave her in it. Mattie Han had wanted to help. Papa was too proud to accept anything from his neighbors. None of them had known he was hurt until the summer was nearly gone. He had forbidden Micah to tell anyone.

Micah touched his sister's cheek and watched a smile spread across her little face. She was thin. They needed a good year. He waited until the sound of the cart and the hoofbeats of the cart horse had faded to silence. "I will make you a bargain," he said, looking into Sadima's eyes. She smiled and put two fingers in her mouth. He gently pulled them out and tried to look very serious. "You can come to the barn with me if you play quietly in the hayrick and let me get the stalls cleaned."

Sadima's whole face lit with joy. She swayed back and forth on his hip. Micah grinned at her and felt his throat tighten. She was, in many ways, a miniature of their mother. She got joyously silly over the smallest things—a glimpse of a red-tailed wren flying over the house, the scent of clover blooms. Maybe, when she was older, she would clear off and plant their mother's abandoned flower beds. Micah inhaled the scent of his sister's hair, wishing he could take her outside more often.

He was supposed to leave her in the house this morning and every morning, locking her in what had been his parents' bedroom. It was fixed up for Sadima now, carpeted with blankets, her rag dolls in a low bin. The bedstead was gone, bed and bedding burned to ashes the day after the burial. The dresser was out in the barn, the drawers full of tools and bits of twine and wire. Papa slept in the sitting room on a pallet on the floor.

The room was big without the bed and dresser in it. If Micah was in there with Sadima, she would crawl around happily, pulling herself to a standing position on the doll box. But she cried hard when he went out and closed the door. Her sobs tore at Micah's heart.

"Let's go then," he said, adding his plate to the rest of the dirty dishes in the wash basin. He'd clean up later—Sadima would nap midmorning. "Don't tell Papa," he warned her, smiling. She talked all the way to the barn, using the musical not-yet-words that meant she was delighted and grateful to be coming along. He could feel her tiny hands as she patted at his shoulder, then gripped the folds of his tunic when he started down the slope to the barn.

Micah walked slowly, letting his sister absorb the cool morning air, the color of the sky, the rustling of the willow leaves when songbirds moved in the branches. When he pushed the slide bar back with one hand and went inside the barn, Sadima made a little sound of glee. Micah stepped onto the lowest rail of the empty stall so he could lift her high over the vertical slats of the cart horse's hayrick, then lower her gently into the feedbox. She laughed and sat down happily. Micah gave her a pile of cracked corn to play with, then started milking.

There were three goats, all nannies. He milked Dunny first. Her sweet, creamy milk they kept for the household— to drink and to make their own cheese. She was at the scant end of her cycle now, it was time to breed her again. Tock and Lolly's milk went into a different bucket. Papa sold it to Mr. Hod. His wife clabbered, salted, and pressed the cheese that half the folks in Ferne ate. The Hods paid on the nose, in struck coppers. Milk money would buy barley seed come spring.

Micah looked at his sister. First she swept the grain into a pile with her hands, then patted it, smiling. He heard her singing to herself, her voice high, sweet, and tuneless. When he glanced at her again, she was sucking at the corn. She made a face, turning to look at him, her cheeks puckered. Micah laughed and she smiled.

By the time Micah was on the third goat, Sadima was dropping bits of corn through the slats of the hayrick, one by one, giggling when they landed on the stall floor below. He poured Mrs. Hod's share of the milk into a cloth-covered cooling tin, then hoisted the bucket of Dunny's milk to carry to the house. Sadima was still absorbed in her game, laughing at the growing pile of corn on the stall floor.

Micah walked past her slowly; then, when she didn't look up, he hurried out the barn door and started up the path to the house. He would just pour the milk into the cooling jars on the sideboard and run back to the barn. Sadima couldn't get out of the hayrick, and she wouldn't have time to get restless and cry.

Micah walked fast, holding the bucket out to one side, careful not to slosh the milk, slowing only when he got to the porch steps. In the kitchen, he set the jars into the basin of cold creek water, then poured the milk with the grace of long practice. He grabbed a piece of bread for Sadima to chew on while he finished the chores, then slammed out of the house and ran down the hill.

When he came back through the barn door, he saw that his sister hadn't moved. She was still sitting down, and he could hear her happy voice. Micah exhaled and smiled as he walked toward her. He had to talk to Papa, convince him that she needed to . . .

Micah stared. There was a rat perched on Sadima's shoulder. She was babbling a stream of baby words as it leaned forward, its snout nearly touching her mouth. It could probably smell the corn on her breath, Micah thought. He stood uncertainly. It might run if he startled it, but he would have to go through the stall gate, then reach through the slats to shoo it. Sadima might stand up suddenly and startle it first . . . and rat bites often got infected and left scars. What if it hurt her eyes? Horrified, Micah watched the rat stand on its hind feet and place its paws on Sadima's ear, the light touch tickling her into laughter. If *she* tried to shove it away, if she grabbed it and squeezed . . .

Micah took three quick steps and vaulted the stall gate, whirling around to face the hayrick—and then could only stand stock-still again. The rat was rubbing its cheek against his sister's. Sadima reached up with one hand and touched the rat's fur. It responded by coming back onto all fours and ducking its head beneath her fingers. Then it looked past Sadima at him.

Micah stared. It was sick or something—no rat ever acted like this. He glanced around, spotting a stall rake outside the gate, just in reach. Sadima turned and stared at him. Her eyes narrowed, then went wide. Her face flushed as she began to cry. The rat touched her cheek with its forepaws, then turned and jumped to the stall floor.

Micah lunged for the rake. He swung it upward, over the stall gate, and killed the rat before it could run any farther. Sadima screamed. Micah jerked back round to look at her, terrified that she had hurt herself somehow, or that the rat had bitten her in that last instant. But she was staring at *him*. Her face was contorted, angry. Her hands were tiny fists.

Micah reached to lift her out of the hayrick, and for an instant, her body was rigid. Then she dissolved into tears and pressed against his chest for protection as she always had. He held her close and told her, over and over, all the way back to the house, that he would never let any harm come to her.

— 6 —

When the carriage wheels touched stone and began to
turn, I felt my stomach clench. Gabardino reined in,
pulling the stallion to a halt when my father told him to.
The wheels gritted against the rock as the pony sidled in
the traces, shaking his long mane. I sat, frozen, my arms
crossed over my uneasy belly.

"Hahp," my father said, leaning close enough that I
smelled the scent of the soap on his skin. "*Sit up.*"

I straightened. Gabardino was opening the carriage gate,
pulling the hinged steps out for my mother. I stood, my
ears thrumming with the sound of my own fear. I had seen
the iron doors a hundred times from the carriage and had
never realized how big they were. I had never seen them
open. A ship could have sailed through them. It took me a

moment to see the wizards standing on either side, their backs against the dark stone. Their black robes hid them like moths on bark.

My father cleared his throat. I climbed down, then helped my mother, my hands clammy with sweat. I stepped on her hem. She pretended not to notice and smiled at me. My father came last down the carriage steps and gathered himself, his shoulders back, his head high, looking around. We were the first to arrive.

I stood still, scanning the sky. I could see three tiny dots, carriages coming this way. I would fail at the academy. Why not? I had failed everywhere else I had been sent. My father's donations had always bought me lenience, and, in the end, a provisional letter of recommendation to the next school. I could not imagine the wizards allowing that.

What happened to boys who walked inside those doors? No one knew. But the white pony's eyes reminded me of the cold, strange eyes of the wizards. I stared at the cliff's edge. It was high enough ten times over. If I ran straight out and jumped, I *would* die. I glanced at my father. I would never again have to hear how I disappointed and shamed him, how fortunate he was that Aben was the older of his sons, the one who would inherit. My mother would weep, but she would understand, I thought. Surely she had thought about it at least once, about escaping my father forever. And it would be better for her if I were gone. She stood up for me against him sometimes—and she always paid for it in bruises.

Trying to think, I looked past my mother at the sky again. The carriages were getting closer. I glanced at my father, then back at the edge. I had missed my first chance. This might be my last. Did I want to die? I tried to answer that question and could not.

Then I saw the messenger boy. He was coming to the top of the ancient stairs. I watched him appear in little upward jolts, his head showing first, then his shoulders, a little more of him visible with every weary step. When he finally topped the staircase he sank to his knees.

He wore rough-woven clothes from some South End market stall. Sweat had plastered his dark curls against his scalp. When he stood up, he gawped at the carriages that were now alighting on the huge stone shelf. Messengers were street boys, always. No one else was hungry enough to accept a few coppers to climb the endless stairs.

I wondered who had hired this one and why. A desperate family wanting to cure a crippled child? Maybe a woman too old to climb the steps, but frantic to help a bedridden husband?

Another carriage alighted on the dark stone and the messenger boy's eyes went even wider. He stared as the bay mare's hooves touched the stone, her gait perfect, smooth. I saw him swallow hard. All the carriages were fancy; all the parents in fine clothing. This had to be more silk and silver than he had ever imagined in his life. I envied him. Once he had delivered his message, he could go back down the steps. He could leave.

I heard my father's voice and turned. "Hahp? Are you deaf?" he said quietly, frowning. I tried to meet his eyes but found myself staring past him at the gigantic iron doors. Whatever was beyond them was invisible in the dark interior.

My mother came to stand beside me, and suddenly she had me walking, her hand on my arm as though *I* was supporting *her*, leading her along. My father stayed a half step ahead of us, square-shouldered and stiff.

I wrenched around to look back at Gabardino. He was waiting as he always did—at parties, at parades, at school, at wedding feasts, waiting in the wind, in the rain, in the summer sun. But this time, he would leave without me.

I felt a shadow fall over my face, and I lifted my head sharply as we passed into the shade of the overhanging cliffs. The monstrous doors were very close now, maybe twenty steps away.

"Good morning," my father said as we came closer. None of the wizards answered. I saw trickles of sweat coming from beneath my father's iron gray hair. I hesitated, and my mother slowed with me, her hand still perched lightly on my forearm. My father lengthened his stride. My mother could not keep up, but she kept me moving. I closed my eyes as we passed from daylight into darkness.

Sadima lay awake. Sometimes she could not keep
to her bed. It felt like slender, tender hands were guiding
her as she slid from beneath her blanket and dressed,
then went over the windowsill and dropped into the
yard, the grass cool on her bare feet. When she was little,
she had just run down the road, then across the meadow
on the hill, then back, using a fruit crate she had hidden
to get back over the sill. But as her legs got longer, she ran
farther—and she didn't need the crate anymore.

Sometimes she just danced in the cool night air, imagining the world beyond the goat meadows. There was a city
far to the west, by the sea. Limòri. Papa said it was a
wicked place, that he never wanted her to ask about it
again. But Sadima had pestered Micah until he had told

her all the stories he'd heard about it and everything he had overheard, too. Half the world was water, Micah said. Sadima wanted to see an ocean. To taste it.

On this full-moon night, to celebrate her tenth birthday, she slipped outside and ran, silent, happy, across the yard and down the path that led to the River Road. She knew if she followed it far enough, she would come to the village. She had seen Ferne twice in her life. Only twice. Papa said she didn't need to go places, that she needed to cook, to care for the goats and her mother's flower beds.

The slow melody of a purple-tail call led her off the path. She followed both the sound and the shivery sensation of the night breeze ruffling feathers. When she spotted the bird, silhouetted against the face of the big yellow moon, she stopped, listening to it, her eyes closed to hear better. The bird was proud, looking out over the land from a treetop.

The time slid past Sadima like creek water. It was the gray lightening of the sky that finally made her realize it. She pulled herself back, lowered her eyes, and stretched. And it was only then that she saw the wolf cub. It was sitting at the entrance to a den, a low arch of rock visible through the ferns behind it.

Sadima smiled at the pup. She took a single step toward it. It dropped low in front and left its little tail high, wagging. Sadima got on her knees and the pup ran toward her. Sadima wrestled with it. She tumbled the pup carefully, lying on her back, answering the soft grunts and squeaks it made. She worked her fingers though the soft fuzz of its baby coat and felt its thoughts. It had no siblings. There had been one. Meat was scarce. *Lonely, lonely, hungry.* Sadima pulled a stick along the ground. The pup stalked it, leaping like a born hunter. After a long time playing, the pup's thoughts changed. *Happy, tired, sleepy.*

Sadima had set the wolf-child back inside the den entrance and was walking away when she heard the low growl. She turned to face the pup's mother. The wolf circled her, inhaling the scent of her baby on Sadima's clothes. Then she lowered her ears and tail and walked past, weary from the night's hunting, ready to doze, to let her single pup nurse.

Sadima ran home as the sun cleared the horizon, half expecting to find her father or Micah running up the road looking for her, but she did not. She ran across the pasture and straight to the barn. She was milking when Micah came in.

He smiled at her, then yawned. "Up early?"

"Yes," Sadima said. It was not quite a lie. She wanted to tell him about the wolf. But she knew he wouldn't believe her, and he might tell Papa she was lying again.

— 8 —

The dim cavern smelled like stone and dust. Cold-fire torches set high on the walls cast wide half circles of light. My father turned toward some benches at the other end of the massive room, and my mother followed him. I shuffled along beside her. There were families ahead of us and behind us. Everyone was silent. I saw a tall boy who reminded me of my brother for an instant. Had my father told Aben? Did he know I was being sent here?

"Hahp." My mother tightened her hand on my arm. She had arched her back, lifting her breasts and her chin and dropping her shoulders to make her neck look longer and more graceful. "Hahp," she repeated in a low voice. "No pranks, no jokes. Your father can't settle things here."

I nodded, staring at the torches on the far wall. She

laughed merrily, startling me, then tilted her head prettily and leaned close. "Hahp, people are watching. I see Teller Abercrome." She laughed quietly a second time, shaking one finger at me as though I had made some clever remark.

I saw the ferocity in her eyes and tried to smile. This was like a ballroom to her—and ballrooms were her battlefields. The Abercromes had produced several wizards. I knew this because my father had told me, his voice bitter. They were known for their massive wealth but were several generations past the ones who had actually earned it. It was old money and very respectable. My father hated them.

My mother laughed again and I tried to force a smile, to play her game. The opinions of the women watching us mattered desperately to my mother, because they mattered to my father. His family had never produced a wizard—nor had they tried to. I was the first Malck to be brought here. No doubt everyone in the room knew that.

My mother nudged me, smiling wider. I bared my teeth and hoped it looked like a smile. I had missed my chance to jump from the carriage and hadn't had the courage to leap off the cliff. I was slow-witted and a coward, as my father had pointed out a hundred times. Would the wizards send me home an imbecile? Or sell me off to a slaver to clean stables in the south? All my life I had heard stories—everyone had. My father said it was all nonsense. But the wizards weren't bound by the old Kings' Laws, nor the Eridians' Divine Laws, nor any others.

My mother led me to the right and I saw ten stone benches in two rows of five, each one a sculpture, carved from the living rock. The stone was smooth as glass and cold through the cloth of my trousers as I sat down. My mother kept one hand on my forearm. My father sat beside her, his posture rigid.

There was a lectern of stone too, carved out of the floor. I stared at it. Everyone did, even my father. This was a *school*. Of course there would be a welcome program for the parents. Would there be a Welcome Day speech and tamarind tea and biscuits?

The wizards were lined up along the wall behind the lectern now, their hands tucked back into their black sleeves, hoods up, barely discernible. The silence went on so long that there was an uneasy rustling of cloth, tiny coughs, whispers. I looked over my shoulder and counted. Ten. Was this all? The class would be ten boys? I recognized one—Levin Garrett—he was my age. I had known him at Tolisan Academy, my second boarding school, and I hadn't seen him since. He tipped his head slightly to acknowledge me, then lowered his eyes. I faced front, staring at the empty lectern again.

"We have opened the Great Doors," a grating voice said. "Soon we will close them again."

I blinked. There was a wizard at the podium. He was glaring at us as though we had all somehow offended him. Was this the headmaster? I swallowed hard. His pale eyes flickered over the benches, and he cleared his throat but did not speak again. My heart was flailing like a bird trapped in a box. I saw my mother staring.

"The course of study is difficult," the man finally said

in a thick, strained voice, as though each word pained him. "One of your sons will emerge from the Great Doors a wizard—or none will. Some stay . . ." He fell silent, then went on. "Most who fail stay within our walls and remain with us, becoming part of the school." He paused again. "Parents will be informed."

I heard whispering rise, then fall when the wizard lifted his head and cleared his throat once more—but then he only stared upward, over all our heads. What was the matter with him? A slick nausea-sweat rose on my skin and I shivered.

The wizard seemed to focus on us. Then he waved one hand vaguely. "The parents will leave now." An audible feminine gasp went through the little group and he tilted his head as though it puzzled him, then gestured again, more emphatically. My father got to his feet. My mother hesitated, then stood, leaving her hand on my shoulder I could feel her trembling. She leaned down to kiss my cheek and whispered something I couldn't hear over the thunder of my own pulse. Then my father took her hand and led her away. He did not look back at me, and he kept my mother from giving me so much as a glance of farewell. She tried to turn, I saw her, but his arm was around her shoulders and he held her to his side. I watched them until they were back out in the sunlight, then gone.

— 9 —

Sadima walked the herd home slowly, playing her woodsflute, keeping the melody staid, measured. The goats were all pregnant, their hips swaying like fat women carrying laundry baskets. They weren't thinking about much: grass and cold creek water, their babies, kicking at them from inside. And they shared a drowsy hope that there would be corn in the trough when they got back to the goat yard.

Sadima smiled. Her chores were mostly done at home. She had the clabbered curds wrapped and dripping in the spring house, and the older cheeses had all been dipped in melted beeswax. Micah had told her a tale of a vast city somewhere in another kingdom far away where Gypsies danced and a princess lived in a tower higher than the clouds. She could see it in her mind, and she wanted to paint it.

But she would have to wait for an evening when her father went to sleep early. She had to hide her paints from him. He hated seeing her awake and not working at something. He was the same with Micah. His own hands were almost never idle—unless he was in the grip of his sadness.

As Sadima came around the last bend, she saw her brother running toward her, his eyes bright. "Hurry! I talked Papa into letting you come buy a horse with me. Don't give him time to think better of it."

Grinning at her brother, Sadima nudged the hindmost does along, begging them to go faster. They did, to please her. "How did you get Papa to—," she began, and Micah interrupted.

"He sees how good you are with the horses. I told him I wanted your help deciding. Now hurry!"

"Thank you, Micah," Sadima said, still smiling, clapping her hands to get the does trotting. It was a rare thing, her getting to go anywhere, much less to Market Square. Very rare. It scared her—but she wanted to go.

"Be quick," Micah said as they got to the gate.

Sadima kept the goats trotting, straight through the farmyard and into their pen. Then she shut them in and sprinted to the barn. She filled two buckets with corn and ran to the long wooden feed troughs. Micah was already back in the house when she finished and hurried up the path. She banged the door open, then saw her father sitting on the wooden bench before the hearth. She dropped to a walk, keeping her face composed as she went down the hall.

Once she had closed her bedchamber door, she danced to the basin to wash her face. She stripped off her faded workaday shift and pulled on her only good dress. It hit her midcalf now, but it wasn't too tight. Micah said she was growing like a willow shoot—straight up.

Sadima combed her hair, reaching behind her back to loosen the tangles near the ends, then working her way up, pulling too hard, jittering, impatient. She made sure her brushes and paints were all hidden and safe beneath the loosened floor plank—she was nearly certain Papa sometimes went through her things.

Micah was waiting when she came out. He arched his brows and tilted his head toward the door. *Hurry.*

"Get your shawl," her father said. Micah's shoulders dropped. This was an old argument and one that could easily explode. Papa was convinced that getting chilled would kill her. He was convinced that *everything* could kill her.

"But it's so warm—," Sadima began, closing her mouth when her father's eyes went dark and empty. One more word and he would be angry. Two more words and he would rise from his chair to slap her. That would make Micah furious and Papa would glare at him, daring him to say a word. Then, worse than anything, Papa would lapse into one of his silences.

Sadima went back down the narrow hall. Her shawl was old and ugly and made of heavy gray wool. She put it around her shoulders and followed Micah out the door, murmuring a good-bye even though she knew her father would not answer. Once they were out of sight of the house, she pulled the shawl off and hid it in the gooseberry thicket beside the goat path that led to the high meadow.

Micah watched her, smiling. She smiled back, then stopped to pull a thorn from her heel. When she looked up again, Micah was staring at clouds along the horizon. In the past year, he had grown a soft beard and had gotten even more handsome. Would he be like Papa when he got older?

Micah lowered his eyes. "What are you thinking about, Sadima?"

"Papa," she said, telling as much truth as she dared.

"He's barely sleeping again," Micah said. "Almost every morning when I rise he's just sitting, staring at the fire or the door—or the wall. When I speak to him he doesn't answer."

Sadima saw the worry in her brother's eyes. "I hate him when he's like that."

Micah looked stricken. "Don't, Sadima. He can't help it. He wasn't like this before."

Sadima looked aside. *Before.* She knew what had changed her father. Even though neither of them had ever talked to her about it very much, she knew that her birthday had been her mother's death day. Mattie Han had been the only one who would answer her questions, the only one who had told her about Micah running until he could barely stand; about the old magician; and how Micah had kept her warm and safe that first terrible night. Sadima could not imagine anyone cruel enough to lay a newborn baby on a cold floor. The oldest of the goats remembered that night, the barn door opening, the smell of her birth-blood. She shivered.

"Are you chilly?" Micah asked.

Sadima shook her head, then smiled at him. "I'll race you," she said. She peered up the road to pick a finish line. "To the oak by Nick Kulik's gate." She jammed the words into one rush of breath as she took off.

The dust was soft, deep, and warm, and Sadima flew over the ground, jumping the cart ruts. She heard Micah behind her as he caught up, then slowed. He stayed a few steps behind her until the tree was close, then sprinted, pretending to gasp and strain, still losing by half a stride. They stumbled to a stop, laughing. When the laughter settled back into silence, Sadima glanced at him. Her brother. She loved him more than she would ever love anyone. He was her best friend—her only friend. Papa didn't even allow her to visit Mattie's daughters.

Sadima walked closer to Micah as they passed the farms and the jumbled circles of stones that had been on the land forever. She asked him for the story and he told it as he always did, slowly. There was only a little to tell. The people who had lived within the ancient circular walls had talked to the trees and the rivers. They had not left footprints, walking or running. They had been able to fly as high as birds, and they had been gone so long that the rain had rounded the stones they had cut from the earth and squared so they could build their walls.

"Do you think it's true?" she asked when he was finished. "How would anyone ever learn to fly?"

He shrugged. "Who knows? Someone made the stone circles a long time ago. But the rest is just a story, Sadima. Like the ones about magic or the North Wind talking to the wolves."

Sadima pressed her lips together. If she was ever close to wolves again, she would listen carefully. Maybe they knew the North Wind story. She glanced up and saw Micah looking at her. She longed to tell him about the animals, how she could hear their thoughts sometimes. But she didn't dare.

Sadima was quiet until they had crossed the Westward Road, both wider and smoother than the one they were on. She looked down it, hoping, but as far as she could see, there were no wagons or riders today, no strangers to watch. On the last downhill, she could smell the square, the vegetables and the early berries, the keen iron-smoke from the blacksmith's fire, and least familiar, the musky stink of people. She was uneasy, scared as well as excited. It was always hard at first—all the smells, all the scraps of thoughts and feelings from the animals, all the voices and colors and noises.

As they joined the crowd, skirting the vendors' tents, Micah noticed when she shivered, and he put his arm around her. She caught a glimpse of a black-robed woman telling fortunes behind the shoemakers' tents. She stared and Micah tightened his arm, pushing her along a little faster.

"Papa will never let me bring you again if you tell him we walked this close to them," he said.

She nodded. "I won't tell." She knew better. No one hated the magicians more than her father did.

"Sadima? Is that you?"

She turned, recognizing the voice. Mattie Han was coming toward them, her uneven gait as familiar as her crooked grin. She hugged Sadima, then straightened, balancing her weight against her thick oak cane. "I spotted that red hair," Mattie said. "Prettier every time I see you." She looked up at Micah. "Which is rare as a blue moon."

"She came to help me buy a horse," Micah said.

"A pony for her?" Mattie asked happily. "Sadima, you'll be able to come visit me and my girls. It's not far at all and—"

"We are here for a plow horse," Micah interrupted quickly. "Tiny is getting too old to work."

Mattie nodded, disappointment clear on her face. "Tiny. I remember that nice old bay. I guess a lot of us are getting old."

The Caller's shout made Micah look toward the barns. "We'd better hurry. I want to get a look at the horses first."

"Come with us," Sadima said, but Mattie shook her head.

"I have to mind the store. Laran and Tessie stayed home today." Mattie cupped Sadima's chin in her hand. "If you ever lack anything, you know where to come." She lifted her eyes to include Micah. "I am your mother if you ever need one."

Micah nodded. "Tell Laran hello for us?"

"I will," Mattie said. "She will be sorry she missed you."

Once Mattie went on, Micah took Sadima's hand and pulled her through the crowds, nodding at people who greeted him. The crowd was thicker than Sadima remembered from the last time Papa had let her come, and she felt almost dizzy with the sounds and smells. Overlaying the scents of human sweat, unguents, and garlic, there was a heavy smell of overripe fruit in the air. All this was mixed with the bitter smell of the paperbark trees—they were budding, the new leaves were sticky with sour sap.

"Let's go this way," Micah said, veering off. "It's a short-cut."

Sadima followed him closely downhill, then across the log bridge that spanned the creek. They climbed up the steep bank on the other side to come out behind the barns. Sadima could see the corrals, and she felt the raw edge of fear before she saw the horse.

It was a tall, heavy-boned, gray gelding, surrounded by a circle of angry men, a few carrying leather whips. Sadima could see long streaks of blood in his coat, the shadow of a dozen bloody welts across his back. A crowd had gathered. "Make them stop," Sadima whispered to Micah when he caught up. "Make them stop hitting him."

He took her arm. "I can't. They won't listen to me."

Sadima walked forward, pulling him with her.

"Get that animal out of my barns," the Caller shouted. "I don't want anyone hurt."

"Sell him for whatever you can get," one of the men said. He was holding a halter, the rope trailing in the dirt. He spat in the dust, then lifted his head. "I don't care if he goes for dog meat. Sell him cheap."

Sadima stared. The gray was terrified of them all, but

mostly of that man—the one who owned him. She saw the beatings for an instant, felt the cut of the whip. She wrenched her arm free from Micah's grip and slipped between the rails. Two of the men reached out as she passed, but they were too startled to catch her as she ran toward the horse.

"How cheap?" Sadima demanded, stopping just outside the circle.

The men laughed at her. One reached down to nudge her away and she swatted at his hand.

"How cheap?" she asked again. "Three coppers?" She glanced at Micah. He was climbing through the fence.

"Three coppers?" the Caller repeated, looking at the man with the halter. He nodded. "Three," the Caller said again. He raised his right hand and looked at Sadima, then past her—and she knew he was waiting for Micah to make the decision.

"We'll buy the horse," Sadima said, her shoulders squared and her jaw set.

"Are you sure?" Micah asked from behind her. Sadima turned to meet his eyes and nodded. All she wanted was to get the gelding away from these men, away from the whips. He was so scared, so angry. He wanted to kill them. Micah was fishing in his pockets for the coins, ignoring the head-shaking and quiet laughter of the men in the circle.

Sadima walked a few steps, then stood where the gray could see her. He lifted his head. She met his eyes and asked him to come with her. He switched his tail and shook his mane, afraid to believe her. She walked closer and stopped, her hands loose at her sides, letting him see her heart. He lowered his muzzle to inhale her scent, and she held very still as he walked toward her. She closed her eyes when she felt his warm breath in her hair, then along her cheek.

It was only then that she heard the ringing silence that had fallen among the men and beyond them, to the people watching on the far side of the corral and beyond. They were all staring at her. She moved a little to one side.

"Throw the halter, please, sir," she said softly, and the man tossed it toward her. She wouldn't need it, but she didn't want to draw any more attention. She slipped the halter over the gray's muzzle, then back over his ears. Then she stood still, pressing her hands against his neck for a moment before she took the lead rope in her hand. She could hear him. He was hoping she meant to take him with her. Sadima took a step and he moved with her, his head low, his ears forward. The circle of men parted. Then, once she had lowered the slide bars, the crowd outside the fence stepped back to let her through.

The gray followed her closely, and she could feel his body warmth on the back of her neck. Sadima kept to the road—it was too much to ask him to wade an icy creek. "Everything will be set right," she told him. "You will have hard work to do, but my brother and father will never hit you, and I will bring you corn and oats and sweet hay every day." She touched his neck, to comfort him. She felt his sore heart warming, easing.

"The pasture is big enough to gallop and there are two other horses for friendship—Tiny and Ginger. Tiny is old but Ginger plays on a cool morning, still."

The gray heaved out a long sigh. It tickled her skin, lifting her dress collar, pushing her hair aside. "I know you're shy," Sadima said. "But you can stand off by yourself when you like—it's a big pasture. My goats are silly, but kind," she added. "They have their own yard. So do the chickens. Our rooster is arrogant, but his wives are mostly pleasant."

The gray exhaled again and shook his mane.

Sadima walked him slowly, thinking about all the cruel things people did to animals. If everyone could hear what she heard, feel what she felt, they wouldn't think animals were very different from themselves—and maybe they would be kinder.

"Wait for me!" Micah called, and Sadima stopped. The gray stopped with her, his muzzle resting on her shoulder as she turned to look. Behind Micah, Sadima saw the crowd; they were still staring.

"That was stupid," Micah scolded her. "If you ever do anything like that again, I won't ask Papa to let you come again. Ever." When she didn't answer, he grabbed her arm. "That was dangerous, Sadima."

Sadima nodded, knowing he couldn't understand. There had not been a single instant when she was in danger. She was *not* stupid. And she knew she couldn't explain. She had tried, and she had learned: Neither Micah nor Papa would ever believe her. It scared her to think it, but she knew it was true: No one would ever believe her. She wasn't like anyone else.

~ 10 ~

"Pairs!"

I jerked around. A wizard with close-cropped hair was gesturing broadly, the sleeve of his robe swinging with the movement.

"Line up in pairs!"

He sounded angry. I was sure he had said it several times before I heard him. Were we choosing roommates? Levin was already standing with the tall, dark-haired boy. I glanced past him. Crap. There were four pairs already formed—I was the only one without a partner. I got into line alone, then spotted a boy standing off to one side, his arms folded across his chest. I recognized him. It was the messenger boy from the ledge. He stepped into line beside me without saying a word.

I wrinkled my nose and heard whispers in the line ahead of us. I knew what they were saying without being able to hear. How could a messenger boy be here? Had one of the others brought a servant? Could we do that? I wanted to ask, but I was afraid to. Whoever he belonged to, he stank of sweat and fish.

"Follow," the wizard said, turning, then walked away. We all marched after him, passing out of the huge chamber, away from the sunlight. Away from everything. It was like being swallowed by the earth, by darkness. Not one of us dared to whisper again. There was only the sound of our footsteps as we tried to keep up with the wizard.

The boy beside me kept his shoulders squared and his head high, but his eyes were wide and he stumbled once, over nothing but his own feet. He really did stink, and twice, as we went around corners, I tried to ease forward, to mix up the order. I didn't want to end up his roommate if that's what the pairs meant. I did my best, but it was impossible. The wizard walked too fast—we were all strung out behind him, everyone just trying not to fall behind.

When I heard the fish boy whispering to himself, it scared me. Was he crazy as well as smelly? If he was a servant, surely he would share a room with his master, not with me. I walked to one side to keep away from him. I couldn't see his face clearly. I couldn't see anything clearly. The torches were getting farther apart as we went.

The wizard took a sharp turn and the fish boy veered back toward me to follow the line. "Left," I heard him whisper distinctly—then, more faintly, "Right, left, right . . ." and then I lost track of it, but I understood instantly what he was doing. So. He wasn't crazy, he was smart. But I still didn't want to live with him.

I walked faster, trying to talk sense to myself. This initial line could not be for roommates. We would eventually end up in a food hall with a nice steaming lunch awaiting us, and someone would explain how roommates were selected. If I could, I would pick Levin.

The wizard stopped so abruptly that we all bumped into each other. "You two," I heard him say to the first pair in line. "Here."

Then he started walking again and we all scrambled to get around the two boys who stood uncertainly in front of a narrow doorway. Seconds later we turned up another tunnel, then turned again. Fishboy was whispering the sequence as we went, but I was sure he was already confused. No one could remember that many turns.

"Two here," the wizard said at the next stop. We were all wary, and no one stepped on anyone's heels this time. And then we went on again, half running. I saw doors that we didn't stop for and felt a deep uneasiness swelling in my gut as we went on, making more turns. Were these our rooms? Who lived in the ones we were passing?

The next two boys were left in front of a door without the wizard really stopping at all; he just pointed at it and kept walking. How could he walk so fast? We were all running. Next, Levin and his partner stood aside, and it was only me and Fishboy behind the wizard, sprinting to catch up every few strides. He went on so long I wasn't ready when he stopped. I blundered into his shoulder and he shoved me off, then pointed at the door. Then he strode away without looking back, disappearing into the darkness beyond the next torch.

The bloody birth-water had long since soaked into the grass, and Sadima was getting scared. The doe goat lifted her head, then stretched out again, panting. Rebecca had given birth easily every year for as long as Sadima could remember. But this time she was heavier and wider than she had ever been—and she was no longer young. She had been straining for hours and she was getting weak.

Sadima stroked the doe's face and neck with both hands, feeling weariness and thirst through her skin and something cold that lay beneath it. Fear? "I'll get water, Rebecca," she told the doe, then rocked back on her heels and stood up, reaching for the little tin pail she had carried along that morning to pick dewberries. It lay beside a length of flax cloth she had brought in case she needed to make a sling to carry Rebecca's newborns home—she had left her carry-sack, her paints and paper hidden at home.

Running downhill to the creek, Sadima tried to decide. She could leave the goats alone and run home for the cart. Her father and Micah were using Ginger and Shy to harrow the barley field, but old Tiny could pull the cart well enough with no more than a doe's weight in it—*if* she could even get Rebecca into the cart. But the decision was thornier than that. Sadima knew that if she left and wolves smelled the birth-blood, the whole flock could be scattered, killed. Without their milk and cheese—and without the money from selling the extra milk—they would face a hungry winter. And Sadima knew her father would let them all die before he asked anyone for help. That would be Micah's job. Or hers.

The sensible thing was to take the rest of the herd with her and come back for Rebecca. But the old doe would be terrified at being left behind. She might kill herself trying to follow, or wolves might find her.

Sadima dredged the pail through the clear current and lifted it, cold water spattering her legs, then started back uphill. She kicked at a rock and welcomed the scraping pain in her toes. She deserved it. She should have been mindful. It would have made sense to leave Rebecca home in the goat yard where she would be safe from wolves at least. And Rebecca was a friend, a goat-sister almost. Surrounded by unhappy thoughts, crying, Sadima trudged back up the hill. She was almost at the top of the rise when she heard someone shout her name.

She spun around and saw a young man staring at her from the far side of the creek. He was wearing a long black robe. As she watched, he jumped the stream, then started toward her. "Are you Sadima Killip?"

She bent to pick up a fist-size rock.

"Please," he said, "I have come a long way to talk to you."

Sadima wiped at her tears, then hefted the stone. "I do not talk to magicians." She took one step backward. Then another. Her heart was unsteady in her breast. She turned and ran up the hill, the pail bruising her thigh, half the water sloshing out. The goats were all watching her as she set the bucket down beside Rebecca. Sadima tried to calm herself; she knew she was scaring them. She set the rock down, too.

Rebecca did not open her eyes at the smell of water. Sadima bit her lip and glanced back. The man was more than halfway up the slope. "Go away, magician!" Sadima shouted. "My father and brother will kill you if they see you here."

"My name is Franklin," the young man said clearly, coming on as if he hadn't heard her. "Is that goat sick?"

Sadima shook her head, furious. "She's birthing. I must tend to her now."

The magician nodded as he stopped about a wagon's length from her. "How can I help?"

Sadima lifted the rock again, then dropped it. "You can't." Her eyes flooded with tears. "*I* can't. She's getting weak."

Rebecca groaned. It was a small, defeated sound. Sadima rubbed the old doe's neck, trying to comfort her, trying to understand what was wrong.

"Perhaps you could lend her some of your strength," the magician said quietly.

Sadima blinked, stunned. She had never thought of it that way, but she understood him instantly. There was an odd feeling of something flowing *into* her from the animals. She had felt it all her life. "If I could reverse—"

"Yes," Franklin said. "Exactly."

Sadima placed her hands on Rebecca's face again. There was the usual flood of images and feelings coming from the doe. Sadima closed her eyes, fighting the current to a stop, then pushing it backward, sending all the strength and courage she could find within herself into her old friend.

For a long moment, nothing happened. Then Rebecca stirred and opened her eyes. Slowly, she rolled onto her belly. Sadima sat back on her heels, then grinned up at Franklin. He was smiling. Rebecca shook as though she was waking from a nap.

The doe pushed with the next contraction, then the next—and Sadima saw a tiny hoof emerge, then recede. "She loves you," Franklin said. "We think that makes it easier."

Sadima barely heard him. Three contractions later, two tiny hooves emerged from the doe's body. Minutes later, Sadima pulling gently to ease the passage, the first kid was born. She waited until the placenta came, then tied off the umbilical cord with a strand of wire-grass. The second kid came easier. Then a third one was born soon after, smaller than the others, then a *fourth*, a big-boned doe, an odd dun color Sadima had never had in her herd before.

Sadima rubbed them all dry with wads of sedge grass.

Without speaking, the magician helped, watching her carefully, then imitating her. Sadima used a clean corner of the linen to mop her own face. "Thank you," she said, looking up. "Had you not come, she would be dead." She shook her head. *"Four!"*

"Is a doe with four kids rare?" Franklin asked.

Sadima looked at him. "Where do you live that you don't know how many kids a doe has?" she asked.

"Limòri." Franklin smiled at her and Sadima found herself blushing. She wanted to ask if the stories her brother had heard were true, if there were people there with green skin and boats bigger than houses. Instead she lifted the smallest kid and cradled him close to keep him warm. The others were all lying against their mother, sleeping. Rebecca was licking the dun.

"I am not really a magician," Franklin said. "Somiss says no one is, not yet."

Sadima looked at him. "Who is Somiss?"

Franklin glanced up at the sky, then back down to meet her eyes. "My master. I have been in his service since we were very young children. He is the most brilliant man alive. Do you have magicians in your marketplace? Do you know the old stories?"

Sadima nodded and felt gooseflesh rise on her arms. "If you mean the winter-hearth tales of wars and wizards and ships on the sea, my brother has told me a few."

Franklin smiled. "Somiss says they are at least partly true. Perhaps entirely." He tipped his head. "When did you first understand an animal's thoughts?"

Sadima hesitated, looking into his dark eyes. She had never been able to tell anyone. Her father had punished her for lying when she had tried, years before. Micah was certain the rat that had touched her face had been diseased, its instincts dulled. He had told their father that her small-ness and foolish lack of fear had calmed Shy.

Franklin sighed. "I know you have kept it secret to keep from being called a liar. I also know it is true."

Sadima looked past him at the sky. How could he know something about her that her father and brother did not? She lowered her eyes. Franklin was waiting, his face kind and calm and handsome.

"Always, I think," she said quietly.

Franklin waited again, just looking at her.

Sadima lowered her eyes to stare at the ground, and she repeated what Micah had told her about the rat. "He says I was just past a year old then. And he says the rat was sick," she said. "My father says he once saw a rooster in my lap, staring up at me—that I was clutching it so tightly I had half strangled it. But I remember it, a little, and I wasn't holding him tight . . . the rooster and I were talking. In an odd way." She looked up. "It isn't thoughts exactly, not words, but I understand them. I have never feared an animal."

"Not even snakes or wolves?"

She shook her head. "I found a wolf's nursery den once—the mother was gone. I played with the pup and when the mother came back, she understood that I meant no harm. She was tired and had been gone longer than she meant to." Franklin was leaning toward her, listening to every word. Sadima exhaled, smoothing her tattered, dirty dress. "Why did you come here? To me, I mean?"

Franklin smiled again. "We heard a story about you taming a vicious horse."

Sadima explained what had happened and told him what Micah insisted was the truth.

"Somiss says there is no point in arguing about music with a deaf man," Franklin said. "Do you hear words in your mind?"

Sadima blinked. "From the animals? Never."

"I meant from people," Franklin said.

Sadima shook her head. "Have *you*?"

His face lit like a candle in a dark room. "Maybe. Almost. And I think it is possible with practice. We spoke with a man who remembered a fireside tale with what he called silent speaking in it. In the tale, the wizards could talk without speaking. Imagine it. If people could really understand each other, cruelty would end, war would be impossible. . . ."

"I have thought that," Sadima said. "About animals."

Abruptly, Rebecca struggled upright and stood unsteadily, then lowered her head to drink from the berry pail.

Sadima smiled at Franklin. "Thank you so much," she began, about to ask him if he would be in Ferne for a while. Then she caught herself. "I should start home," she said. She glanced at the newborn kids.

"I will be glad to help you carry them. If your parents do not mind, I would appreciate a bed in your barn for the night. It is a long journey back to Limòri. And we could talk again, perhaps?"

Sadima shook her head. Franklin waited politely for her to speak. "My mother died birthing me," she said, unsure why she was telling him. "The magician who came to help her only robbed us and let my mother die. My father and brother hate—"

"Of course they do," Franklin said. He looked stricken. "That is exactly what Somiss wants to end, forever. The liars, the fakes. He hates them too." He glanced at the sun, then back at her. "The day is nearly done. Let me help carry the kids at least part of the way."

Grateful, Sadima made a back sling of the flax cloth and put one of the smaller kids in it. Then she hoisted the big-boned dun into her arms. Franklin carried the other two, one beneath each arm. They walked slowly down the hill, then followed the narrow, rutted road toward the farm. Rebecca was unsteady on her legs, but her head was high and she kept nosing Franklin to remind him to be careful with her children. The rest of the flock followed. When the does shied at a fallen log, Franklin asked Sadima why.

She made an effort to understand their minds, then turned to Franklin and explained that they were remembering a time when a log much like this one had hidden a snake.

He looked like she had handed him a gift. "You are living proof that silent-speech between people is possible," he said. "I wish you could meet Somiss. I am trying hard to convince him to study it." Franklin leaned close to kiss her on the forehead. "I am so glad you did not throw the rock. Thank you, Sadima." His lips and his voice were so warm that Sadima blushed again, then smiled at his jest.

At the last turn in the road, they stopped. "If Somiss is right, if magic can be resurrected," Franklin said, "there is no reason for anyone to be poor, or hungry, or to die young, or suffer too much with age. And if I am right about silent-speech, war and fighting, even murder, would disappear if men truly understood one another's hearts."

His eyes were lit from within. Sadima smiled. "If people understood animals' hearts," she said, "they would be kinder. Animals are so—" She broke off, searching for a word. "Honest," she said finally.

Franklin touched her cheek, and she felt like he had touched her heart. "Come to Limòri if ever you can," he said. "Maybe you could help us gather up the magic."

Sadima nodded without speaking, her throat tight with an emotion she could not name. Franklin helped her find a way to arrange the three small kids in the linen sling. He placed the bigger dun in her arms. It was very awkward, but she had only a little ways to go. He held her hand for a moment, then turned to go. Sadima watched him walk away.

That evening the sitting room felt small and close, and her father's silence pounded at the walls. Micah noticed her restlessness and she had to lie to him, pretending that Rebecca's difficult birthing had upset her.

But that night, unable to sleep, she slipped outside and stood in the darkness looking westward, imagining herself living in a shining city where no one would tease her or call her a liar for understanding what animals felt. She wanted to live in a place where her father's sadness wouldn't weigh on her heart every moment of every day and she would be able to go anywhere she wanted, have friends who knew the truth about her and loved her for it. Maybe she could learn silent-speech with people. At least she would have her own life, and Franklin might one day give her a real kiss.

Then her shoulders dropped and she felt tears rising in her eyes. Papa would die of worry if she left, and Micah would never forgive her. This *was* her life.

— 12 —

Fishboy watched the wizard go, then glanced back at me. Before I could say anything, he put his hand on the silver door latch. It was shaped like a swordfish leaping, every scale perfect, the tiny fin-ribs visible. Had every door had a handle like this? I hadn't noticed. Or was this one a joke because of my roommate's perfume?

Fishboy opened the door. He went in, then stopped, leaving it wide open behind him.

"Is it our room?" I asked quietly—and even that seemed too loud.

He didn't answer. I leaned to see past his tall, bony frame. There were no torches in the room—no light at all except the dim half rectangle of torchlight shaped by the doorframe.

I took a step inside. "Can you see a lamp and a striker? Are there beds?"

No answer.

I took another half step and stumbled forward. The door slammed shut behind me.

"What are you doing?" Fishboy demanded in the sudden, complete darkness. "Open the door."

"I didn't close it," I told him, searching for the handle behind me. I couldn't find it for a moment, and when I did, it wouldn't move. "It won't work."

"Then this is some kind of test," Fishboy said. He sounded matter-of-fact.

I squinted, trying to see him. "What are you talking about?"

"They'll find out who gets scared, which ones lose their wits or—"

"Fine," I cut him off, trying to sound as calm as he did. "If it's a test to see who can feel around in the dark until they find lamps or candles, you move to the left and I'll—"

"No," he said sharply. "There could be snakes or—"

"There are no snakes," I said, just to make him shut up. He was crazy and he stank, and I didn't want him for a roommate. I would go back out and sit in the tunnel until someone came back. I reached behind myself to try the door handle again. After a moment, I turned and extended both arms. Nothing. I turned in a circle, my arms out. "Where are you?"

He didn't answer, but I could hear him breathing—so his calmness was an act. Somehow that made me feel better.

The darkness was pressing against my skin and I imagined the mountain of stone overhead. "I can't find the door," I said. "But there have to be cots, a table, something with a lamp on it."

He still didn't answer.

That did it. "Don't be an ass. Say something so I know where you are."

There was only silence.

"I'm going to find the lamp," I said with my teeth clenched, trying to stay angry so I wouldn't feel scared. I took a step forward, then another, reaching out, waving my arms high, then low, expecting to bump into him.

I didn't. Maybe I had veered to one side?

I took a small step, then a longer one. The darkness was so complete it almost made me feel off balance. "Have you found anything?" I asked, without really meaning to.

"No," Fishboy said. I stopped, glad he had answered, but amazed that he was behind me now. So I *had* turned at an angle from the door and gone right around him. I moved away from his voice, stopping to run my fingers through empty air after each step.

"I am going to make a sharp turn to my right and try to find a wall," I said aloud, hoping he would answer me. He didn't. "I must be walking right down the middle of the room," I said. "I haven't touched a bed, a desk, or anything else. Have you?"

"No," he said so quietly I almost missed it.

I made a quarter turn and took a step.

"Go slow," he said. "There could be pits with scorpions. Anything."

"Shut up," I said, trying to control the hammering of my own heart. Wizards. Why would they do this to us, scare us like this?

"I think you should come back," Fishboy said, from somewhere in front of me.

I stopped. "Did you find the lamp and you're just trying to scare me?" He made a sound, but didn't speak. "You win," I said loudly. "I am scared *pissless*. Just light the lamp and—"

"I don't have it," he said from behind me. *Behind me*. "How many steps have you taken?"

I shook my head, trying to think. "Ten? Fifteen?"

"Stand still," he said from somewhere off to my right. My *right*.

"I am," I said, turning to face his voice. "You're the one moving around, changing sides."

"I'm not," he said quietly. "I am four small steps inside the door."

I shook my head. "You crapping liar."

He was quiet. I could hear him moving, then he stopped. "I am not lying. And I can't find the door now."

The air felt too thick, too still. My heartbeat was so loud I wondered if he could hear it.

"Turn toward my voice," he said, "then take a single step and stop. Be careful, slide your feet—and count each step aloud."

I nodded. It made sense and I did it, my legs stiff and wooden. "One step," I said, "straight toward you, I think."

"Good," he said. "Now I will take one toward you. There. One step."

"Two," I said aloud, heading toward his voice.

"Two," he repeated, only a little to the left of where I had thought he was.

"Three," I said, and I slid my feet over the stone. Sweat had coated my face.

"Three," he said. "And I am veering a little to my right toward your voice."

We had counted thirty steps apiece when the door swung inward, hitting me in the back. The wizard was carrying a torch. He leaned in, lighting the room.

I stared at the walls, at the cots placed against them, separated by a narrow aisle. The room was, perhaps, six paces long and four wide.

"Come with me," the wizard said, and turned back into the corridor, walking fast. Fishboy followed him, and I ran to catch up.

— 13 —

On her seventeenth birthday, Sadima's father died.
The funeral songs seemed thin and frail, but the silence
between Micah and Sadima was heavy, which would have
suited Papa. The spring mist that hung between the morning
sun and the meadow felt right too. Only eleven people had
come—all close neighbors. Most of them were Mattie Han's
children. One of her girls, dark-haired Laran, stood so close
to Micah all day that Sadima finally realized what she had
somehow missed over the past three years. She had been
so caught up in her painting, her goats, her own longings,
that she had not seen it. Her brother was in love.

It felt odd to have guests. Walking back to the house,
Sadima realized two things: With their sad and silent father
finally lying beneath the soil next to their mother, she

could stop hiding the inks and paints Micah had bought for her over the years. There was nothing now to stop her from painting on the front porch instead of in the high meadows with only the goats to see. And there was nothing to stop Micah from marrying.

It took less than a week for him to say it. She had just finished carrying in the day's water and was still tired from the back-and-forth treks to the well in the yard when she sat down beside him to eat boiled barley and curds for breakfast.

"I want to marry Laran," he said, then fell silent, waiting for her to say something. She could only nod, fighting a strange mixture of joy and fear as she ate.

"Laran will never make you feel unwelcome here," Micah added, standing up from the table to wash his bowl.

Sadima nodded, staring at the bare, clean little farmhouse kitchen where she had begun every day of her life. "I know," she told her brother. "Laran is as kind and good-hearted as Mattie."

Micah looked startled. Had he been expecting her to argue against his marriage? He set the bowl down and poured a mug of tea, then pulled his chair out again. "So, then, if you don't think it too soon after Father . . ." He trailed off and met Sadima's eyes. "I'm sorry, Sadima, if this has caught you by surprise. Laran and I were afraid to upset Father, and we have waited a long time. But—"

"Stop, Micah." Sadima waved one hand to brush away his awkwardness. "There is nothing to apologize for. Knowing Laran will be here makes it easier for me to leave." Sadima wondered if she meant it. She had day-dreamed about leaving for three years. She exhaled, watching her brother's brows arch, then settle in an expression of puzzlement.

"Leave?" He said it as though he wasn't sure what the word meant.

Sadima nodded. All her life she had wanted to be like everyone else, a girl with a mother, with a father who spoke and smiled and let her have friends, a girl who had no secrets to keep. Now she only wanted to go where someone understood her. Micah was happy here, he could fall in love here. She couldn't.

"Sadima," Micah said, shaking his head, "don't go. Shopgirls in Ferne barely make enough to eat. I can't let you—"

"I have decided," she said quietly. And she saw worry in her brother's eyes, and beneath it, something else. Relief? Probably. This little house would barely hold a family—and Laran would want to make it her own.

"I am going to Limòri," she said, and Micah's eyes went wide, then narrowed.

"I will not let you. Father always said—"

"Our father hated himself and everything in this world." Sadima covered her mouth with one hand, shocked by the anger in her voice. She met her brother's eyes. "You say he wasn't always like that, but for me he was, Micah. He always hated *everything*." Sadima straightened her spine and lifted her eyes and told him about Franklin. He listened without interrupting, but she saw his fists tightening. "Talking to him made me feel like I belong somewhere," she said slowly, watching her brother's face. "Things happen to me. I am not the same as everyone else, Micah. I—"

"Mattie Han has a way with animals too," he interrupted. "It's a kind heart, no more than that."

"No," Sadima said, determined to make him understand, make him forgive her. "I can feel what they are feeling. I understand them. And talking to Franklin changed me forever, Micah. He understood *me*, and I—"

Micah threw his mug across the room, smashing it on the hearth. "A man who says he believes *magic* is real?" he shouted. "Is he in Limòri? Is he the reason you want to go?"

Sadima nodded, frightened.

"How long have you been planning this?" The fury on his face was like a blow. Sadima could only shake her head as she fought back tears.

"I am just glad Papa died," Micah said tightly. "His heart was broken the day you were born. This would have gutted him. After what that magician did to Mama . . ." He paused, and Sadima couldn't find words to answer the agony in his eyes. He went out the door and slammed it so hard the windows shook.

Trembling, she went to her room—the room where she had been born, where her mother had died. She used her oldest shawl to make a bundle of her things. She put her brushes and paints into a wooden box that had belonged to her mother—but not all of them. Micah had brought the little clay caskets to her, one by one, in secret, bought with pennies he earned, pennies he stole from the milk money.

Perhaps he would have a child one day who would use the ones she left.

Sadima did her work slowly, her whole body wooden, heavy. Evening finally came. She went to sit in the front room, sure that Micah would come back to talk, would give her another chance to explain.

He didn't.

She slept where she sat, in an empty house.

The next morning she fed the stock, said tearful good-byes to the horses and the goats, then left for Limòri.

— 14 —

The wizard was carrying a torch and walking so fast we could barely keep up. After a hundred paces, there was no flickering cold-fire on the walls and the passage was dark as ink. Falling back even a step or two meant being out of the moving globe of the wizard's torchlight altogether. He turned abruptly and Fishboy nearly stumbled as we veered into another passage. When I glanced at him, his lips were moving. That jarred me out of my fear enough to pay attention this time. We had turned right. I began the list in my mind. *Right.*

The tunnel felt colder than it had, and there was a twitchy weakness in my knees. I felt half-sick. The wizard didn't look back, not once. What if I had to throw up? Would he stop? There was darkness ahead of us and behind us now. The wizard turned left and we followed. *Right. Left.* I ran a few steps to catch up and realized that there was a slight downward slant to the passageway. We were going deeper into the rock.

The wizard bore slightly left where the tunnel branched, then, almost immediately, he made a hard left turn where a passage crossed the one we were in at right angles. *Right, left, bear left, hard left.* Had we gone in a circle, then? I recited the sequence in time with my steps and began to calm down a little, but then we turned right, then left, then passed one tunnel without turning either way, then turned left again. The next three turns came just as fast, and I felt the sequence in my mind snap and scatter. I tried to start at the beginning, to gather up the turns in my memory, but I was only four turns into reconstructing it when the wizard turned again. I was lost. My stomach tightened and I glanced at Fishboy.

His lips were still moving.

I felt my eyes ache. I could not cry. I *would* not cry. This crap couldn't last more than a few days. The wizards just wanted to scare the piss out of us to start with, to make sure we were afraid of them, that we wouldn't cause trouble. I exhaled and felt a little better. That had to be right. What other reason could there be?

The wizard stopped so suddenly I bumped into him. He looked at me the way a man looks at horse manure stuck to his boot sole. He gestured toward a wide, arched doorway, then said, "Be quiet and wait," and walked away.

Fishboy went first, of course. I followed. The chamber

was big, with cold-fire torches set high, but the light still didn't reach the ceiling. There were four boys standing in the center, among them Levin and the boy who reminded me a little of my brother. They were whispering. There was one tall boy with blond hair who seemed to be trying to talk the others into something. Levin and the other two were listening intently.

The other group of four stood along the wall. One of them was thin and narrow shouldered, his hair wispy brown. He was talking to a boy who was shorter than any of us. He looked up and saw me staring, and I looked away.

In that instant a rasping voice cut through the whispers. "Who among you is child enough to misunderstand the word *quiet*?"

There was sudden silence. This was the wizard who had spoken from the lectern. I stared at him. He looked young, but his voice belonged to a man near death.

"Take all your clothing off."

A little round of whispers rose, then stopped without him saying a word. No one moved—we all glanced at one another, then at the wizard. Then I saw Fishboy start to undo the tie at the top of his tunic. The others were fidgeting. When Fishboy shrugged his rag-cloth shirt off and stood bare-chested, the wizard nodded approval and pointed at the floor. Fishboy obediently dropped his tunic in front of him and then stepped back to pull off his thin-soled shoes, then his trousers. Some of the other boys moved apart, turning their backs to one another, unbuttoning their shirts.

I reached up to touch my shirt front. It was pounded linen,

soft as doves' wings. My mother would be upset if she knew I was about to drop it on a gritty stone floor. The buttons felt unfamiliar and clumsy beneath my fingers, but I finally got it off, then my shoes and trousers. The stone was cold beneath my bare feet. I glanced around. We had all moved apart, each one of us undressing, then standing naked, by himself.

When the heap of clothes was complete and we all stood shivering before him, the wizard pointed at the pile—and a trickle of smoke spiraled upward from the cloth. "You were chosen from thousands, but only one of you will become a wizard," he said slowly. "Or, more likely, none." The fire spread, painting our faces with rust and gold, the smoke rising straight up. The wizard let the silence draw out, then cleared his throat. "Do not help each other."

I stared at him. No school allowed cheating. Was that what he meant? Or was it forbidden to study together? If that was what they wanted, why hadn't they given us separate rooms?

The flames took a sudden leap, and we all stepped back to stay out of the amber light that revealed our nakedness— all but Fishboy. He stepped forward, spreading his fingers across the wall of heat to warm his hands. Then he turned to warm his backside. The wizard laughed aloud, his hoarse voice scraping at my ears. Then he vanished.

I mean that. He didn't walk away, or slide into the shadows. He disappeared. He was there one instant, then gone the next. I was watching him, hating him, and he just faded into nothing. I could see straight through the space where he had been standing.

The moment passed, then another, then whispers began. Soon there were voices. We all stood awkwardly; everyone was talking without really looking at anyone.

In Levin's group, the tall blond boy said he thought he could remember the turns back to their room. The other three looked relieved. "Were you anywhere near us, Hahp?" Levin asked when I glanced his way.

I shrugged. "Probably not. Are you all in one room?"

Levin nodded, gesturing at the boy who knew the way back. "We were paired. But when we went through the door, it was a long passage that led to another room with four cots in it—"

"We found a hole in the stone behind our door, nothing more," a brown-haired boy said. "We went through it and found ourselves in the room with them." He gestured at Levin and the boy standing near him.

I listened, hoping, but no one said anything about being lost in the dark.

The first group of four had moved off—I could barely hear what they were saying, but it was clear that they were arguing about something. Maybe none of them knew the way back. Fishboy hadn't said a word, and I glanced at him. "Do you know the way? I tried to keep track, but I—"

"Didn't you hear him?"

I stared. "He didn't mean—"

"Yes," Fishboy cut me off. "He did. One out of ten. Or none if no one merits it."

He turned on his heel and went out the arched doorway. After a few heartbeats, I went after him. The torches in the tunnels were lit now, and I saw him break into a run. I sprinted, trying to catch up, fighting a strange, vague fear that came with being naked. The stone was cold and rough and hurt my feet with every stride, but I didn't slow down. Fishboy eased up just a little before each turn, so I managed to keep him in sight. I was pretty sure he meant to let me follow him, because once he hit that last straightaway, he ran faster, his long-legged strides making it impossible for me to keep up.

He left the room door standing open. I stumbled to stop, so glad not to be lost in the endless maze of tunnels. But then I hesitated there, reluctant to go back in. Whatever they had done to make the room seem huge—was it going to be like that again?

"They brought us lamps," Fishboy called from inside.

I leaned in. He had lit his and stood before it, facing me, apparently as comfortable naked as he was dressed. My lamp stood unlit on the desk facing the opposite wall. I moved toward it, using the darkness on my side of the room to hide myself. There were two enormous books stacked on each desk. And on the cots, I realized, there were robes—smaller, uglier versions of what the wizards themselves wore. These were a dusky, muddied ochre the color of shit. Fishboy put his on.

I turned my back to him and slid mine over my head, grateful just to cover myself. Then I began to itch. The cloth was rough as feed sacks. I sat down on the edge of my cot and stared at my bleeding feet. Fishboy was sitting at his little planked desk, facing the wall. He opened one of the thick books to the first page. He was *reading*. I stared at the title: *Songs of the Elders*.

I bent to touch the bottom of my feet. The blood was already sticky, drying. The cuts weren't deep—running on the stone had just scraped off skin. I glanced at him once more, then lay down, staring at the darkness that hid the arched stone ceiling high overhead. Of course, Fishboy could read or he wouldn't be here. But where had he learned? There were no schools in the South End slums of Limòri. There were no schools in the farm villages, either. Most people never learned to read. All the boys I had gone to school with had fathers who could pay the tuition. They owned ships and warehouses like mine did, or had old royal grants to import herbs or teas, or endless flax fields and brakes up north where slaves could still be bought and sold, or steaming vanilla plantations somewhere in the wild south. Was Fishboy a prince from the orchid coasts? Why would he be dressed as a beggar?

I shifted on the bed, the stiff robe scraping against my skin. Maybe he was the runaway son of some rich Eridian priest who had forbidden him to take the entrance exams here? Eridians had little use for magic. I exhaled. That made more sense than anything else. Fishboy might have been hiding in South End so his father couldn't stop him from coming here.

He kept reading. I started thinking. What were the wizards going to do to us next? I wouldn't be the one to graduate, of course, so what was going to happen to me? I shivered, every inch of my skin prickly from the touch of rough cloth. I was so scared. My thoughts got louder, until it felt like they were screaming inside my skull.

"It will be all right," I murmured, closing my eyes. Then I went on, saying everything my mother had said when I was little and having a nightmare. I told her how scared I was, how strange it was here, about Fishboy and the wizard and what he had done to us. I told her about the shirt. And, as stupid as it sounds, I felt better, barely whispering the words into the empty darkness. My thoughts quieted, then jumbled, and then I must have fallen asleep.

— 15 —

Sadima had started out following the little wagon-rut road the outlying farmers traveled to get to Ferne on market day. That had led to the wider road that veered west. She had stopped at the crossroads for a long time, looking back. She had never in her life been this far from home by herself, this far from her brother. She felt wary, like she was walking onto earth too thin and brittle to hold her weight, but she went on.

The westward road eventually ran across a wider one, a real road with wagons and carriages coming past her three or even four times a day. She walked six days on it, getting used to the weight of the bundle that held everything she owned. She paused at every crossroads, choosing the widest and most traveled road if she could not find a friendly soul to ask the way.

She ate berries and the bread she had brought from home at first. Then she stopped for half a day and painted two studies of wildflowers, which she traded to an astonished farmer's wife for a quarter wheel of cheese. At night she slept among the trees along the road, changing to a clean dress now and then—she had three if you counted the one with stains and holes that she had always worn to paint. When she found a creek on a warm day, she did her laundry as well as she could, hung the two wet dresses on bushes, and wore the tattered one until they dried.

After the sixth day, she needed no help finding her way. There was a wagon or a carriage in sight most of the time, and on market day the road was full of carts heaped with bright green squash, fat turnips, bundles of sheepskins, cloth, and every other thing she could imagine. So she just kept walking. Limòri. The very name was wondrous to her. It sounded like no other word she had ever known. All things amazing would be there, she was sure. It lay next to the sea. Her mother's candlesticks had come from across the ocean to Limòri, brought in a kind of great boat called a ship. The idea of a sea—of any body of water too big to see across, gave her shivers.

As she traveled, the countryside changed, flattened, and the soil darkened. The farms were lush and prosperous. Asparagus and wild blackberries lined the creeks and she ate both almost every day. Bay laurel trees grew in the pastures, and out of habit she cut sprigs, stripping off the leaves for drying. She gathered field dill and marjoram, too, and dug wild garlic as she went. She ate creek-washed sorrel and purslane where she found them, and everywhere there was shade and a little water, there was mint. It scented the air, especially on foggy mornings. She picked and dried as much as she could, weaving loose wiregrass bags in the evenings to carry the herbs.

On the fifteenth day, mixed into the persistent perfume of the mint, she could smell a smoke-salt-fish-mystery scent she thought must be the sea. One night, as she slipped off the road and into the trees to lay out her blanket and sleep, she noticed a glow on the horizon. Two nights later she knew it by its color—firelight. Torches?

The morning after that, a woman in a lovely blue dress had her carriage driver stop, the tall wheels creaking as the horses slowed. "Where are you walking from?" she called to Sadima.

"From Ferne, up in the hills," she called back. "I'm on my way to Limòri." Then she stared at the carriage. It was painted in beautiful scrolls of auburn and gold, and there were bright brass cleats on the wheel brakes.

When Sadima glanced up, the woman was smiling, her eyes wide. "It must have taken you most of a fortnight to walk this far. Have you come alone?"

Sadima nodded. "But I know someone in the city. His name is Franklin. He asked me to come join him." She saw a look of pity cross the woman's face and knew how feeble it sounded, how much worse it would sound if the woman knew that she had met Franklin only once, three years before.

"Is this Franklin an Eridian?" the woman asked tersely.

Sadima shook her head uncertainly. She had never heard the word before.

"Are you sure?" the woman pressed her. "They are wicked. My husband says they are bringing country girls into the city, forcing them to marry."

"No," Sadima said emphatically. "He's not Eridian."

The woman snapped her fingers. The footman got down while the coachman steadied the restless and beautiful chestnuts. "Come," the woman said. "You can rest your feet."

Sadima was dumbstruck. It was one thing to see a carriage from a princess story before her eyes, but to be asked to ride in it? The seats were deep green velvet, tufted, soft. And the horses! They were finer than any she had ever seen—they were sleek and groomed and they held their heads high. She turned toward them and felt their pride and strength. They had not wanted to stop and were eager to go on. They were afraid of nothing.

Blushing and ashamed of her soiled cotton dress, Sadima let the footman help her up the carriage step. She sat awkwardly on the bench facing the woman, hugging her stained shawl-bundle. The woman gestured and the driver loosed the reins. The horses burst back into a snapping trot and the carriage lurched. Sadima wrenched around to look over her shoulder.

"Sit beside me if you like," the woman said. "I hate to go along backward, facing the wrong way. It makes my stomach unwell."

Sadima rose and switched sides. The bench was wide, and she sat as far away from the woman as possible. A strong scent of roses surrounded her. Sadima clamped her arms against her sides, hoping her own unwashed smell wasn't tainting the soft morning air. She tried to think of something to say and could not. The woman broke the silence by asking her age.

"I am seventeen," Sadima said politely. It was hard not to stare. The woman's dress was embroidered with thread so fine and stitches so small it looked impossible. Who could do work that fine? Her shoes were made of some soft leather that shone like stream-pebbles in the sun. Sadima looked out at the countryside to keep from gawping. So they rolled along in silence for a time, until the woman asked her name and if her parents knew where she was.

Sadima told the woman her name, then hesitated. "I don't have parents," she said, and then couldn't say another word for a long, painful moment. "My father passed on not long ago," she managed to add. "But my mother died when . . ." Sadima trailed off again, unable to talk about her home, her family. Tears rose in her eyes.

"You poor little orphan," the woman said in a voice so full of pity that Sadima turned away, pretending to look at the little crossroads town they were passing through. *Orphan.*

The woman didn't speak again until they were climbing a ridge that looked down on Limòri. There were huge cliffs that rose above one end of the city and Sadima could see a sliver of open water through the trees that rimmed the ridge. The sea?

"Have you ever been to the city?" the woman asked. "Any city?"

Sadima shook her head as the carriage started downhill. She wanted to be polite, to chat with this kind woman, but she could not seem to do it. And silence allowed her to watch, to see everything that they passed.

At first there were smaller farms, then tiny ones, then houses. Then, with every stride of the sorrel horses, the houses seemed more huddled together. Before long, the proud horses were forced back to a walk. Hundreds of carts rolled along the road ahead of them.

Sadima was beyond astonishment. There were buildings that rose into the air as high as three or four houses piled one on another, made of blocks of dark stone. Had the ancestors of those living here now been among the ancient people around Ferne who had built the stone circle?

Sadima could not stop staring. There were shops and markets everywhere she looked, and the women all wore fine, bright-colored dresses. She turned. "I am to ask after Franklin in the market square. Do you know where that is?"

The woman nodded, then called out instructions to the driver. The proud horses arched their necks when he popped the whip above their backs and eased the outside rein to turn them at the next corner. The streets narrowed and were jammed with wagons loaded with fruits Sadima had never seen, cloth of so many colors that it made her wonder what could possibly be the basis of all the dyes. And there were things she had no name for. Many things.

The horses slowed to a start-and-stop walk in the tangle of carts, shaking their manes. Sadima felt tiny. There were more people in the square than she had ever seen in her life. Who would she ask? Then she caught a glimpse of a black robe and half stood. The woman lifted her brows. "Here?"

Sadima nodded. "Please. And I thank you so much for your kindness."

"My name is Kary Blae," the woman said. "I live on Ferrin Hill. You can ask anyone where that is. If you need anything, just tell the guard that I asked you to call on me—then give him your name." She lifted her head. "Stop here, driver."

"Thank you," Sadima repeated as the team halted, stamping their forehooves and switching their tails. She gathered up her bundle and jumped to the ground before the footman could help her.

— 16 —

The wizard pounded on the door.

I wrenched upright, my heart thudding. Was it morning? Maybe. I was hungry. I rubbed my face with my hands, blinking in the darkness. My neck was stiff—the cots had no pillows. I could hear Fishboy fumbling with his lamp. I had never lit mine. How long had he sat reading, studying the book before he went to bed?

The wizard pounded again. I shouted that we were coming as fast as we could.

The instant light filled the room, I swung my legs to the floor and felt the pain in my scabbed feet. The robe chafed the back of my neck as I stood. It was unnerving to be completely naked beneath the rough cloth. My thighs brushed as I walked. The robe rubbed across my bare penis when I raised my arms to stretch. I tripped on the hem. How long would this crap last?

I heard Fishboy urinating and saw a chamber pot I hadn't noticed the night before. Then he squatted over it, stinking up the room. When he was finished, I used it, fighting an impulse to gag. When I turned, he was standing in front of a basin set into the wall. It had a silver spigot, a little plainer than the ones we used at home.

The wizard pounded the door once more.

I leaned to whisper. "Hurry up!"

"Where's the water?" Fishboy whispered back, looking at me over his shoulder.

I hesitated, not understanding him for a moment. What son of any important family, anywhere in the wide world, could not work a simple water faucet? I remembered my father saying that some of the Eridians hated anything wizard-made. So maybe that was it? Fishboy was an Eridian, here to learn about everything his father hated? I reached past him and slapped the silver spigot. Clear water spilled into the basin and ran down the drain.

He stared, then bent over to wash his face and bumped his forehead on the spigot. The water turned off, which seemed to surprise him. He slapped the spigot as I had and turned it back on—then off again. Before he stepped aside, he touched the faucet twice more, the last time with a single finger, quickly, like a baby playing. There were nubby, rough washrags on wall hooks. No soap. He dried his face with one as I turned the water on. It was cold as ice.

I washed fast, wondering why they would use chamber

pots and cold water like South End slum dwellers. I straightened and was drying my face when I heard Fishboy opening the door. I turned to see a wizard holding a torch high over his head. He didn't say a word as he started up the corridor, my eager roommate at his heels.

I had to run to catch up, and it hurt. But I wasn't thinking about my feet. It was too strange to be naked under loose cloth, everything jangling as I ran. Fishboy was striding along, and I stared at the side of his face as I caught up. He was smiling. *Smiling?* At what? Being cold and hungry and scared? That startled me into stumbling on my robe hem again, and I came down on one knee. I got up fast, feeling the prickling sting of a bad scrape. Perfect. My feet were already sore. Now my knee would ache for a couple of days. Fishboy and the wizard never slowed, never looked back. Neither one of them bothered to glance at me when I caught up again either.

I tried hard to think clearly, tried to see ahead in the darkness. I was desperate to memorize the turns. But this time the wizard didn't turn for a long time—we went straight down the corridor.

At first the light from the wizard's torch slid along the walls on either side of us, the only relief in the darkness. Then, wonder of wonders, we turned right into a wider tunnel that had torches mounted on the walls. The light lifted my courage a little and I waited for more turns, but that was it. One right turn. The wizard stopped abruptly before an opening in the stone. He pointed at it, then walked away.

I felt weak with relief. Maybe the stupid, confusing route had just been first-day hazing. Maybe Fishboy was right and . . . I realized he had turned to stare at me. The smile was gone. "Hahp Malek," he said, very quietly, "my name is Gerrard da Masi. Not Fishboy. Remember that, if you live to remember anything."

He turned away, and I stared at his back as he went through the passage and disappeared into the shadows. It took me a few seconds to regain my wits. It wasn't hard to imagine how he knew my name. He had seen me standing beside the carriage. No one but my father had the white ponies, and the Malek name was famous for that and a dozen other things. And Levin had called me by name. But . . . had I been so scared the night before that I had whispered *Fishboy* loud enough for him to hear? What else had he heard? Me pretending to talk to my mother?

My cheeks flushed and I felt sick to my stomach as I stepped into the passageway, then stopped, midstride, startled by a wall of stone. I stood in front of it, cursing myself for not paying attention. Then, without warning, the stone opened.

That sounds impossible, I know, but that is what happened. It didn't slide one way or the other like the heavy ironwood doors at home. The rock just sparkled in a widening circle, then a hole appeared, the edges smooth and glassy as though it had melted, though I felt no heat. My father didn't know about this, I was sure. He would have bought it.

Stepping through, I saw that everyone else was already there. They were sitting in a ragged half circle before a wizard. He looked at me intently. His hair was milk white, cropped short, and his eyes were a deep, sad brown. His legs were crossed in an odd way that made me wonder if he was a cripple. His knees seemed twisted—the soles of his bare feet were visible. He stared into my eyes until I sat on the cold stone floor at the back of the group, my legs doubled uncomfortably against the hard stone. I looked at him, afraid. Then he lifted his head and spoke.

"Today you will begin to master your thoughts." He tilted his head. "Of course, that means giving up all hope of mastery." He waited for us to shift on the cold, gritty floor, to exchange looks. Then he smiled, a thin, cautious smile. "My name," he said quietly, "is Franklin. Welcome. It is time to flirt with paradox."

Sadima wandered through the square, clutching her shawl-bundle, too afraid to ask anyone anything. The people all seemed to shout, to laugh too loud, to get angry over nothing. She picked a direction and started walking, desperate to get back to the edge of the square, out of the masses of people and away from the din of their voices.

Coming around a big canopied tent, she was startled to see a man painting. A woman in blue-green ruffles sat before him, her chin lifted, her posture stiff. Sadima could see the likeness on the paper. It was good, flattering, but he had the hair color a little wrong. She looked past him. There were five or six painters working, and she watched them intently, learning new brushstrokes, marveling at the perfect images of buildings and at the pure quality of their pigments. And she envied the clever wooden stands that held the paper at an angle as they worked. Then, off to the side, Sadima noticed a woman in a black robe, walking fast, and she ran to follow.

The magician was a loud-voiced woman with her lips and fingernails painted black—and a stack of intricately inked fortune cards in her embroidered bag. Once she understood that Sadima didn't want her fortune told, that she was looking for two young men named Franklin and Somiss, she put the cards away. She introduced herself as Maude Truthteller, then just kept talking.

"They live close by," she said, then started off. "Somiss is the handsome one," she added over her shoulder, leading Sadima from beneath the enormous fig trees that shaded Market Square and back into the sunny street. "The girls try to catch his eye, but he never notices. He used to joke with Franklin, a lot—they were like boys when I first met them. But now he is too serious." She turned and smiled. "Love would do him good." Sadima nodded to show she had heard, but didn't answer. She had no idea what to say.

Maude was beautiful, beneath the odd face paint. The women on the boardwalks were all so well dressed, so pretty, so—*clean*. Their fingernails and their hair and their clothing. Didn't any of them do any fieldwork? The thought came too swiftly for Sadima to stop it, but she instantly felt foolish. What fields?

Sadima walked uneasily on the hard cobblestone street, following Maude, glancing back at Market Square. Every living soul in Ferne would not fill even a tenth portion of it.

"You're a pretty girl," Maude said. "Wink at Somiss and see what happens, will you?" She looked Sadima up and down, then arched her brows. "Perhaps wait until you've had a bath. Or two."

Sadima flushed, embarrassed. She ran her hands over her dress, then hitched her bundle higher on her shoulder and stared at the crowded street. She had pictured houses like the one she had grown up in, just crowded closer together. She had imagined dust and dirt streets like Ferne's, only wider. It felt strange to walk with stone underfoot. Her already journey-worn shoes wouldn't last long here.

"Just over there," Maude said, stopping to point. "The whitewashed one on the corner of da Masi and Market. They're on the third floor. See that little balcony?"

Sadima nodded, staring upward. How could houses be built so tall? What kept them from falling over?

"That's it," Maude said. "The stairs are inside. It's got a bright green door. Franklin painted it to cheer Somiss in the dark days of winter. They are almost like brothers, in some ways." She smiled, then leaned closer. "The old woman on the first floor owns the place and she's sour as fourth-day milk."

Sadima thanked her and Maude turned, her black robes swirling as she started back to Market Square. Sadima walked on, feeling almost faint. She was *here*. She had really done it. Was the old woman Franklin's mother? An auntie? What if Franklin didn't remember asking her to come? What if he didn't remember her at all? A swarm of dirty-faced children ran past her, and she felt one of them tug at her shawl-bundle. She held it closer, startled.

Legs stiff with fear, Sadima stood before the street gate for a long moment before she dared touch it. It was planked high enough that she couldn't see inside until she found the courage to nudge it. Then it swung inward—not into a room, but a wide hallway. Sadima went in, ready to call out to the lady of the house, when she noticed a door to her right, closed tight—and a staircase at the end of the hall. She tiptoed past the door.

The staircase was beautiful. The railing was iron, worked to look like roses on a trellis. The narrow steps wound in an upward spiral. As Sadima started up, she rested one hand on the railing, uneasy. On the second floor, she hesitated, looking down. She had climbed taller trees, but only a few times, and she had been able to clutch at strong branches for balance. It was unnerving to be so far from the ground indoors. When she started up again, her footsteps echoed off the plastered walls. On the third floor she walked away from the stair landing, happy to be able to stop looking down.

The green door was easy to spot. It was the only one on this floor. She stood trembling before it for so long that she found herself wondering what pigments had been ground to make the paint so bright. She lifted her hand, then lowered it. She raised her hand a second time and knocked, hard, before her courage failed. Then she stepped back and smoothed her dirty dress as best she could.

She heard voices inside, then the door opened a little.

"Yes?" It was Franklin's voice, and her heart pounded as he opened the door wider to look out at her. "Yes?" he repeated. There was no recognition in his dark brown eyes. She opened her mouth, but nothing came out. He smiled at her. "We have a man from Lord Albano Ferrin's employ coming soon, so you must hurry. What did you bring us?"

Sadima tried to speak again and found she could not. He was not wearing the black robe—he had on a tunic and trousers like anyone else.

"There is nothing to be afraid of," Franklin said kindly. "Who sent you to us?"

"You did," Sadima whispered. She swallowed. "You came to Ferne and my goat had trouble birthing and—"

"Sadima?" He stepped back and his eyes widened. "I have thought of you often. You have . . . changed." He smiled wider. "I am glad your father and brother allowed—"

"They didn't," she said, waving one hand to stop him. Her eyes stung and she looked at the floor, then back up at him. He apologized, and she could only shake her head. The truth was that she didn't want to tell him or anyone else about her father—or Micah. This was her new life, her real life.

Franklin's smile had faded. He stepped back. "Come in, Sadima."

She hesitated, then walked through the door into a cluttered room with a smoke-stained hearth, a battered table, and four mismatched chairs. There were squared leather boxes stacked on one corner of the table and she could see a grease-stained cookstove through a wide, plastered arch.

There was a basket of kindling and a stack of stovewood beside it.

As she came forward, she saw a narrow hall leading off the main room and glimpsed two closed doors. Before she could look away, one of them opened. A young man with blond hair strode toward her. His eyes were an odd, too light blue, his expression intense—and he was looking at Franklin as though she were not there at all. "This isn't the scheduled appointment." His voice was clipped, precise.

"No, Somiss," Franklin said. "This is Sadima Killip. I told you about her two years ago when I came back from Ferne and Drabock. The goat birthing?"

"Three years," Sadima corrected him, and he smiled.

Somiss glanced at her, through her, past her, then made a vague gesture with one hand. "Clear the books off and call me when Ferrin's man arrives."

Franklin nodded. "I will." He watched Somiss go back down the hall, then gathered up the squarish leather boxes and opened a cupboard to set them inside. Sadima stared. *Books?*

Franklin turned toward her, his eyes moving from her face to the bundle she was holding, then back. "Are you hungry?"

She nodded. "But I came to help. Like you said." She stopped breathing until he smiled.

"It will take time to convince Somiss," he said, "but we do need help. I don't know where you will sleep, but we—"

"In the kitchen on a pallet," Sadima said quickly.

Franklin pulled out a chair and asked her to sit down.

He took her bundle and set it in the kitchen. Then he crossed the room in three long-legged strides and reopened the cupboard. "Look."

Sadima watched him turn, holding out sheets made of paper that was as white as lilies. He looked excited, like a child carrying a Winterfeast pie, and it made Sadima smile. Maude was wrong. Franklin was the handsome one. His good heart was a beacon in his dark eyes. She reached out and took a single sheet of the paper carefully between her fingers. It was astonishingly smooth—and thin. How could such a thing be made? The paper the merchants in Ferne used to packet herbs and wrap lantern-glasses was heavier— and it was brown. She stared at the tiny squiggling marks that covered the impossibly fragile surface.

"It's strange, isn't it?" Franklin asked. "To think that Somiss's words are trapped there."

Words? Sadima stared at the tangle of lines, then looked up into Franklin's eyes.

He glanced down the hall, then leaned close to whisper. "Do you know what writing is?"

She nodded, feeling foolish that she hadn't guessed what the little marks on the papers were. She had heard of writing, of course, there was always some prince writing letters in the tales Micah had told her—or some king writing an edict to be read to his people.

Franklin leaned close. "Somiss taught me when we were boys. He wanted me to read the same books he was reading. I tried." He straightened and pointed at the paper. "This is his writing. It is very nearly perfect."

Sadima met Franklin's eyes when he glanced up at her. She had never met anyone who could read or write. She meant to say that, but when she opened her lips, this came out: "I was so afraid you wouldn't remember me."

He looked into her eyes. "I have hoped, all this time, that you would come." He made an awkward gesture toward the door. "You don't look the same, Sadima. You've grown up."

She smiled and hoped she wasn't blushing. "I am just glad you don't mind. I wasn't sure if—" A knock on the door startled them both. Franklin whirled and ran to the cabinet. He put the papers away, then turned just as Somiss shouted down the hall.

"Franklin?"

"I'll let him in," Franklin called back. Then he took Sadima's hand and pulled her to her feet. "It's the man from the Ferrins," he whispered, leading her toward the kitchen. "Somiss pays him for news of the king and of his own royal family. Stay out of sight and don't make a sound." He squeezed her hand, then ran to answer the door.

Sadima stood to one side of the arch, her heart fluttery. Somiss was royal? No wonder Maude was taken with him. Sadima had heard of royalty in campfire tales, but in the stories they were almost always wicked. She heard Franklin say something, then there was the sound of a chair being pulled back. She looked around, trying to calm herself with familiar things—the woodstove, the basin. The little kitchen was filthy. She pushed up her sleeves. There were rags hung on wall pegs above the washbasin. It would make no sound at all to wipe the table.

– 18 –

It was impossible to know when the sun rose.

Or when it set.

When we woke to door pounding, the slops bucket was always clean. We washed and shivered and used the bucket, then tried keep up with a wizard we had never seen before and who showed no interest in us at all. I asked once when they would give us something to eat, and the short, balding man who led us along seemed not to hear me. I asked him how long we had been here. He didn't even at glance at me.

I was so hungry. It was hard to sleep without a pillow, and I hated the feed sack I had to wear. The chafing became painful and bloody. And my feet were so sore and swollen that the first ten or twelve steps after I woke were pure torture.

Franklin's next two classes were idiotic—and it felt to me as though they were just a few hours apart. I was tired when I lay down and even more tired when the pounding on the door woke us. Franklin wanted us to quiet our minds in class. It seemed the dead opposite of what any other teacher had ever tried to get me to do.

At the end of the second class, he told us to start reading one of the two books in our rooms—*The History and Purpose of the Limòri Academy*. Good thing it was that one—the other was in a language I had never seen before. Gerrard must know what it was. I dreaded learning it. I had spent my first seven years speaking Yama until noon, Thereisti until supper, and our own Ferrinides until bed. A man who could speak those three, my father had said, could trade anywhere in the wide world, all the way out to the islands beyond the colonies. Little good any of it would do me now. Maybe Gerrard's father wasn't an Eridian. Maybe his father had planned on sending him here and had bothered to actually prepare him.

After Franklin's second class, I read the first page of the book, then my eyes closed. I am not sure how long I slept, but it felt like half an hour. Or less. The wizard who woke us for the third class pounded on the door, then took us on what felt like a completely different route. I memorized the first six turns out of eleven and could only hope that Gerrard-the-mighty would let me follow him for the first five coming back. He had let me so far, and I was grateful. He rarely spoke, and when he did, it was three or four words. It was like having a chair for a roommate. Worse. You can sit on a chair.

The third class was just as odd. Franklin seemed to have forgotten about the assignment. There was no discussion, no writing to be done, no mention of dates or facts or royal lineages to memorize. Nothing.

Franklin just stared at a point in midair and told us to quiet our minds. My thoughts refused to stop—most of them were about how empty my belly was and how much the stinking feed-sack robe had bloodied my skin. And I thought about my father. I thought about him in a way I am embarrassed to admit—but it was something I had done all my life. I imagined myself shoving him backward so hard that he fell—and was still.

My father.

Wherever he was at that very instant, if he snapped his fingers, servants would run in, intent on finding out what he wanted. He might be sitting down to a meal, I thought, staring at Franklin's closed eyes but seeing the kitchen at home. He might very well be eating Celia's excellent cooking at that very instant. And if my mother looked teary or worried about me, he would scold her, or worse. What had he told Aben? Anything? My brother would come home for Winterfeast. Would he be upset, finding out? He liked me, but he had never understood me. How could he? We were as different as night and day.

I heard Franklin say it again: *Empty your mind.*

Startled, I tried to look empty-minded, but not only was it stupid, it was impossible. I was scared and angry. And hungry. So hungry. My mind was *crawling* with thoughts.

When Franklin finally stood and told us to go back to

our rooms, I got up fast, ready to chase Gerrard down the long tunnels. He let me follow him, the same way he had been, slowing just enough so I could see which way he went. Once we were back inside our room, he positioned himself on his bed, sitting cross-legged, his face to the wall.

I went to the basin and drank cold water to quiet my empty belly, then sat on the edge of my bed. I wanted to go outside. I hated not seeing the sky. I stared at my scabby feet, adding to the list. I hated the twisting tunnels and I hated the wizards. And my father. Thinking *that* made me stop thinking, and I found myself staring at the back of Gerrard's head for a few seconds. I shifted a little, and the sound of my robe against the blanket seemed loud. I cleared my throat and it was like a shout.

I was sick of the constant quiet. No one ever talked before class, Gerrard rarely spoke, and the stone prevented any whisper of sound from the outside getting in. I missed hearing voices. I missed the sound of the wind in the salt pines at home.

I felt my eyes sting, and I stood up. There was no way out, no food, no one who gave a crap about what happened to any of us. I just wanted to go home.

No.

Not home, just somewhere else.

I pulled out the chair and sat at my desk, then stood up again. I picked up the history book, then lay down on my cot, feeling a slick stickiness in one armpit. I sat up again and looked. The rough material of the robe had rubbed my skin bloody so many times that the scabs were seeping a clear, yellowish fluid. I propped my back against the wall, tugging at the crapping robe until I had pulled the cloth away from the sorest places. Then I started reading, from the beginning, forcing myself to concentrate on the words.

The first chapter of the book recounted what every schoolchild already knows. The first Age of Magic had been long ago, so long ago that by the time the academy had been founded, no one knew anything about it, and few people believed the stories that had been passed down as children's tales.

It was the second chapter that said something I had never heard before. The first Age of Magic, it claimed, was ended by an alliance of power-mad kings and a general uprising of common people who had been duped by the kings into thinking the wizards were evil. Thousands of wizards had been killed in primitive, ugly ways—by ax, by fire, by quartering, by drowning. Their books had been burned, even their great city of stone had been cleansed of all life in what the book called the Kings' War.

I stopped reading and looked up. A stone city? Where? Here in the cliffs? I wouldn't call tunnels and caverns a city, but perhaps that was what it meant. The last paragraph explained that the kings had fought among themselves as well; that the whole of humanity was plagued with war for generations. I turned the page, expecting some explanation of why no one had passed down stories of the wars along with the stories of magic and wizards, but it wasn't there.

The third chapter of the book had a list of the kingdoms that no longer existed because of that war. It took up twenty pages because half the space went to maps, showing where the historic kingdoms had been. There were lists, too, like in any history book, of the succession of the royal lines of those nations. I only hoped we didn't have to memorize them. I wasn't any good at it and the lists were long.

I tried to begin the fourth chapter, but my eyes were too heavy. Listening to my stomach rumble, I let them sag shut. Had Levin read this? He had helped me memorize succession lists in third form, when we were both seven years old. He had helped me put a toad in the headmaster's coat pocket too. The old man had never caught us. We had both kept the secret.

I yawned and opened my eyes. "I wonder when they're going to feed us," I said quietly, aiming it at Gerrard's straight back. He didn't respond. It pissed me off. "Aren't you hungry?"

He turned, and I saw enough of the side of his face to see that he was irritated, maybe even angry. Without thinking about it, I swung my feet to the floor and stood up.

"You don't know what hunger is," he said quietly, looking at the wall again. He raised one fist. "Shut up, Hahp."

I stood staring at his back, half wishing he would say something more so I could answer with something that would set him off. I wasn't all that good at fighting, in spite of the tutors my father had hired when he got tired of me coming home with bruises and scrapes. But if we argued, then fought—what would the wizards do about it? Would they consider sending me home? The idea of walking back out onto the stone terrace made me quiver with hope. Was it possible they would expel me? I started to step forward, intending to tap Gerrard on the shoulder.

"Don't," he said quietly, when I leaned toward him, about to lift my hand. "If I have to beat you senseless so I can study, I will." His voice was flat, matter-of-fact.

I stood back. Then I sank onto my cot and pushed the book to one side. I felt . . . heavy. I lay down and went to sleep without really meaning to.

When the next unfamiliar wizard pounded on the door, I woke, splashed my face, pissed, then followed him and Gerrard down the corridor. The raw places on my skin were so sore it was hard to move. Had I slept a whole night? Or a few minutes?

We followed a different path again—it took half as long to reach the arched opening of the classroom chamber this time. It was thirteen turns. I could remember five. Franklin was cross-legged on the floor as usual, staring at nothing. Gerrard and I sat down and waited while the other boys came in. I rubbed my eyes, looking at the walls, the ceiling, anywhere but Franklin's blank-eyed face. Was it morning? Everyone looked uncomfortable, weary. How long had it been since our parents had left? A day? Three days? Six? Had anyone eaten anything?

"I want you to breathe with me," Franklin said once everyone was sitting in the leg-break position. I felt a ripple of nervous laughter rise in my throat and swallowed to stop it. Franklin's eyes flickered across the group and stopped on mine. My laughter evaporated; I saw pity on his face. *Pity?*

I looked away.

"Follow your breath with your thoughts," Franklin said in a reasonable voice, as though it made sense. Then he inhaled and we all sucked in air with him. I closed my eyes and imagined being the one to graduate. I pictured my father, nervous and diffident around me—which made me let the breath out in a whoosh. The air had had barely enough time to still itself inside my lungs before it'd had to turn around and rush out.

"Yes, Hahp," Franklin said quietly, as though I had said something aloud. My eyes jerked back to his face. He had not called anyone by name before this. Not once. Every boy in the room was staring. At me.

"Yes," Franklin said to everyone. "Breathing is circular."

He fell back into inhaling and exhaling, his eyes flickering from one face to another. I held very still, not wanting his attention to rest on me again. The air rolled into my lungs, turned, and rolled out, over and over. For a time I closed my eyes, but it was eerie, almost like the shushing sound of everyone exhaling in unison pulled at me, made me sway like a tree in the wind.

When I opened my eyes again, I saw a blur of dark robes behind Franklin, just a quick movement in the light of the torches, then it was gone. Another wizard? Levin's eyes caught mine, and he lifted his chin slightly toward the wall behind Franklin; then he nodded, the tiniest of movements. Before I could react, he closed his eyes, and I saw his shoulders rise and fall again.

~ 19 ~

Sadima slipped her shoes off to silence her footsteps, then wiped at the sticky tabletop, trying to listen, but it was impossible—Somiss and the man who had come to see him were almost whispering. They talked for so long that she had very nearly cleaned the whole kitchen, tiptoeing and moving things with care, by the time the man left. Once he had gone, Somiss went back to his room and Franklin followed. She could hear them talking. About her?

Uneasy, she opened the balcony doors. The sun had gone down. She carried the kitchen slops basin out and flung the dirty wash water in a wide arc, hearing it spatter on the cobblestones in the dark. She refilled it from the kitchen barrel, then warmed it with hot water from the steaming tin tub on the woodstove. The water barrel was half empty. She would have to ask where the well was.

Armed with fresh warm water, she wiped the table again, this time truly cleaning it. She went over the sideboard again too, then tiptoed into the sitting room. She stood still, poised to run back to the kitchen. But the muffled voices continued. She thought she could hear urgency, or maybe anger.

Pivoting on one bare heel, she wrung out the rag and set to work again. By the time Franklin came back into the sitting room, she had finished as much as she could manage without lye soap and scrubbing sand. He smiled at her from behind an armload of blankets. He looked tired.

"Somiss wants you to go," he said slowly.

Sadima pressed her lips together and gestured at the clean, orderly kitchen.

Franklin nodded. "I know. And I want you to stay. Somiss will too, after a time. I think that if you are willing to begin with cleaning and cooking—"

"I am," Sadima said quickly, wondering what he meant by *begin with*. If she could just be near him, if she could talk about her whole self, her real thoughts, instead of pretending to be like everyone else, she would be happy.

Franklin touched her cheek, then made a pallet with the blankets, keeping one to the side for her to cover herself. "Do you need anything else?" he asked as he straightened up.

Sadima fought an impulse to kiss him on the cheek, as she had often kissed Micah good night. The thought made her blush.

"Sadima? Do you need anything else?"

When she shook her head, he bade her good night and left. She heard his door close and the sound of his footsteps as he went to his room. She lay down, careful not to rumple the blankets beneath her. It was hardly a bed, but it was better than the uneven ground she had been sleeping on. Lying still, she noticed the strange smells that came in the balcony doors with the breeze and listened to the yowling of mating cats and the sound of distant shouts. Finally she closed her eyes and felt the weariness of the journey in her bones.

Sadima woke before daylight, as she had all her life. But there was no sound of roosters, or goats bleating, no sleepy owl's homeward cry, and it took her a moment to realize where she was. When she did, she sat up and smoothed her dress. Then she stood, refolded the blankets, and found a place for them and her shawl-bundle on the lowest shelf in the cupboard.

By the time Franklin and Somiss came out of their rooms, she had washed her face, made mint tea, boiled eggs, and fried thin slices of potato in oil and garlic. Without a word, she set the plates on the beat-up—but newly washed—table in the sitting room. Somiss glared at her, stared at the steaming food—then sat down and began to eat.

Franklin half turned so that Somiss couldn't see him wink at her. Sadima smiled a tiny smile. Back in the kitchen, she lifted the skillet and placed it on the cool side of the stove, then put another stick of wood in the firebox to keep the tin tub of hot water steaming. She glanced over her shoulder and met Somiss's eyes. He was watching her.

Startled, blushing, she turned back to her work. While Franklin was eating a second helping of potatoes, Somiss got up. Without a word, leaving his dishes on the table, he walked down the hall and disappeared into his room.

"Does he spend most of his time in there?" Sadima asked quietly.

Franklin paused in his chewing. "Almost every moment. I worry about him." He gestured at the food, the clean kitchen. "You are as clever and kind as I hoped. He'll get used to you, to the hot food. Just don't talk too much for a while."

Sadima nodded.

"He can sometimes get angry about small things," Franklin said. "If he does, just stay out of his way."

Sadima nodded again.

"I am glad you came," Franklin said. "Very glad. I hope you will stay."

"I want to," Sadima told him. "Why aren't you wearing the black . . ." She trailed off, making a gesture to indicate a long robe.

Franklin shrugged. "Somiss decided that it was wrong to look like the people we hope to displace. The fakers. The cheats."

Sadima nodded. It made sense. "Have you talked him into studying the silent-speech?"

Franklin put one finger to his lips and whispered the answer. "No. And I may never. He has found some old story that says it was the downfall of the wizards."

Sadima sighed. "But you and I could—"

"Maybe one day," he said, and smiled at her as though she had said something that had made him happy in a way that no one else could. Before he set about his own work organizing Somiss's notes, Franklin gave her a few coppers for supplies. She walked to Market Square, feeling timid and small and too shy to ask directions of anyone. But after half the morning had passed, she had learned the sections of the market. She saw Maude, from a distance; she was reading someone's fortune, her eyes intent on her customer's face. Sadima walked closer. Maude spotted her and waved, smiling, then went back to her work. Sadima waved back, amazed at how happy she felt.

That evening Franklin was delighted with the chicken and rosemary dumplings she made. He pretended to eat like a starving man for the first few bites, making her laugh. Then he thanked her again for staying.

When Somiss finally came into the sitting room, he was silent, lost in his own thoughts. He said nothing at all until he asked Sadima for more salt, speaking so quietly that she had to lean toward him to hear. When he was finished, he pushed back the chair and stood without a word. Passing, he touched Sadima's cheek. The coolness of his fingertips startled her and she flinched, but he was already past her and didn't notice. She turned to see Franklin watching her closely. "I think he liked the food," she said.

Franklin nodded. "He did. I told him I could do twice the copying work I have been because you are doing so much. He likes that. And he seems to like *you*."

And you? Sadima wanted to ask. Do you like me too?

But she carried the plates to the kitchen and began to clean up instead.

As she spread the blankets on the floor that night, doubling them over twice to make a thicker pad, she was smiling. Cooking and cleaning were as familiar as old friends. And staying out of Somiss's way would be just like staying out of her father's way. Franklin was good and kind and she would get to go to the market often. And Maude had waved at her like a friend. Sadima fell asleep, still smiling.

— 20 —

It was the fifth class—or the sixth—and Franklin was
not there waiting for us. We all stood silent and stupid
with hunger. Gerrard kept close to the arch, standing apart
from the rest of us. Levin sidled so close to me that I could
smell his sweat. We all stank. It was impossible to take a
real bath without soap, leaning over the little basins, and
our robes had not been washed.

"Have you eaten anything?" Levin whispered, his parted
lips not moving at all. I shook my head—minimizing the
gesture as he had done, as we were all learning to do.
I heard whispering behind me, but it stopped abruptly
just as I caught a hint of movement in the shadows.
Levin instantly moved away. I put my back to him and

stared at nothing. No one made a sound. We were all scared. What were they watching for?

A cold sweat rose on my forehead. I tried to still my thoughts, breathing like Franklin had taught us. It didn't work. I hooked one finger in the neck of my robe to pull the rough cloth away from my skin and had to take a step backward to keep my balance—I was that light-headed from hunger. Squaring my shoulders, I thought I saw another movement in the shadows. I blinked, then rubbed my eyes and stared. Three or four others turned too. The rest noticed us and turned. The torches were set high in this room and the shadows were deep. But as we watched, the shadows shifted and became—a wizard. Then he disappeared.

"Follow me," he rasped from behind us.

There was perfect silence, then scuffling as everyone turned. I heard one of Levin's roommates curse an instant before the pale-eyed wizard stepped forward into the light, his white skin and icy eyes a stark contrast to his black robes. He walked a crooked path through us, like we were shrubs in a garden that he had to make his way past, then he kept walking, straight out of the chamber.

Gerrard pivoted and went after him. The rest of us ran until we caught up, then slowed, most of the boys sorting themselves out by habit, falling in beside roommates.

"Jordan?" I heard Levin whisper, and I saw him reaching out to steady a tall, thin boy with dark eyes and straight brown hair who had stumbled. *Jordan.* A name. I had learned someone's name.

We turned right, then left, then right again, then we

made a few quick turns and I lost track of all but the first four. At the end we went straight on for so long that my legs began to feel shaky. Finally the wizard stopped. Sneering, he made a grand gesture, like a house page welcoming guests for a formal dinner, ushering us into a huge chamber with low stone tables flanked by backless benches. I could smell *food*. My mouth flooded with saliva and my eyes clouded with tears.

The wizard gestured impatiently at the benches, and we all sat down. Then he walked to the front of the room and lifted one hand. The stone wall parted—which no longer shocked me. The thing that made me blink was the jewel it revealed. It was faceted—each facet no more than an eye-lash-length across—and it was as big as one of my father's cargo ships. Twenty men could have stood on its top without falling. It rested on a flat black pedestal of stone. Like the tables and benches, the pedestal looked like it had been carved from the solid rock.

"Somiss?" It was Franklin's voice. We all wrenched around to see him walking toward us. My heart lifted.

The pale-eyed wizard turned too, irritation plain on his face. "Yes?"

"Would you like me to—"

"No," Somiss cut him off. "I would not. Please go."

Franklin looked sad, disappointed. For a few seconds they just stared at each other. Then Franklin simply walked away. No disappearing, no opening in the rock wall, no magic. He left the way we had come in.

There was a shushing sound as we all exhaled. Franklin

taught us ridiculous things, but I don't think anyone was afraid of him. I wasn't. The pale-eyed Somiss was terrifying. And he was staring at us, waiting for us to turn back from watching Franklin leave.

"Watch closely," he growled. Then he faced the impossible gem and touched it, his palm flat against its surface. There was a sound like distant thunder, then something high, like faint screams, then a barely perceptible flicker of bluish light in the room. Then a tray as big as any my father's house servants had ever labored to carry appeared on the flat stone pedestal in front of the massive gem. It was piled with fruit and cheeses, with loaves of bread, dark and light, braided and plain. I had to cover my mouth not to cry out.

"You will learn to use this stone as I have," Somiss said quietly in his grating voice. "Or you will die."

And then he wasn't there.

— 21 —

Sadima moved about the kitchen quietly, so she could hear the interview.

"Repeat it," Somiss said, and there was impatience in his voice.

Sadima glanced into the sitting room. The old man wrinkled his brow as he started over. The words he uttered were strange—like all the old rhymes. Sadima was realizing that many people knew several, and some knew a dozen or more. She didn't know even one. Had her mother?

The people who came up the stairs to talk to Somiss were all different. Some were old, and most were women, but there had been a young man the day before who had surprised Somiss by insisting that there was a tune that had to be sung just after the rhyme had been said to make it "proper."

Sadima stirred the soup, then stood with her back against the wall just inside the arch, still listening.

"Again," Somiss said. Sadima heard the old man sigh. She could hear Somiss tapping his pen against the table. "Again," he repeated.

The old man started over once more. When he was finished, Somiss was silent.

"Is that all you need me for?" the old man asked.

"Do you know any more rhymes or sayings in the nonsense words?" Somiss asked.

"I do not," the man answered.

"Then leave, please."

Sadima heard the door open and close and knew without looking that Somiss had not risen from his chair to see the old man out. Nothing about the people seemed to interest him except the rhymes he was working so hard to record. He never even asked them when they were taught to recite the rhymes. He should. It might help him learn what they meant.

Sadima stirred the soup once more, then slid the iron pot across the stovetop, away from the firebox. It could simmer for hours on its own now. She opened the balcony door and slipped out, looking for Franklin. She could see a long way down Market Street, but she couldn't spot him. Not yet. It wouldn't be long. He had only walked down to Market Square to buy more paper.

Tiptoeing, she crossed the kitchen to peek through the

wide arch. Somiss was gone, back in his room. He had left his notes from the interview scattered on the table, as he usually did. Sadima went in and picked them up, tapping the sheets of paper into a neat stack. Franklin was convinced that Somiss was a great scholar. He certainly wasn't a neat one. If it wasn't for her and Franklin keeping things ordered and organized, Somiss would have a pile of paper that no one could ever make sense out of.

"What do you think you're doing?" Somiss demanded from behind her.

Sadima was startled out of her thoughts. She turned, her heart thudding.

"I asked you a simple question," he said.

"I have been stacking the papers for Franklin," she said carefully, "since I came. He seems to appreciate it."

Somiss took a step toward her, then shook his head and stopped. Without saying anything else, he went back up the hall and into his room, slamming the door so hard that she flinched.

Sadima went back into the kitchen. She washed her face and combed her hair, then smoothed her dress. She found small things to do, going to look out the balcony doors every few minutes. She finally saw Franklin, walking back up the long hill, a big parcel beneath his arm. She ran downstairs and made her way through the crowd, veering into the street to avoid a group of beggar children. They broke her heart, but Franklin had warned her. They would steal her shawl if they could pull it from her shoulders.

"Is everything all right?" Franklin asked once she had fallen into step beside him. "Is it Somiss?"

She nodded. "Yes. He was irritated with me for stacking the interview notes."

Franklin looked at her. "Did he shout at you? Hit you?"

She shook her head. "But he slammed his door hard enough to shake the world."

Franklin exhaled. "It should be all right, then. Anything can make him slam a door. And I found a bargain on the paper. That will cheer him up." He put his arm around Sadima and pulled her close, their strides matching. "I will try not to leave you alone with him again. What will we have for supper?"

Sadima smiled up at him. "Roast pork with baked apples." His eyes widened and she laughed aloud.

Then he sighed. "But Somiss likes fowl better. We could buy a chicken there?" He pointed at a butcher's kiosk.

"He liked the rosemary," Sadima said, remembering. "I can make that again." She felt Franklin's arm tighten around her shoulders.

"Thank you, Sadima," he said. "You have made everything better, *everything*. I have never been so happy." He held her closer for a few seconds. And then he let her go.

— 22 —

The big chamber was silent and still for a few seconds.
Then one of Levin's roommates, the tall blond boy, took a
step toward the food. "We should take turns," he yelled.
But then he moved forward another step. In an instant, we
all had, then one more. We ended up in a broken circle
around the pedestal, all of us pushing forward, then
wrestling each other back.

I couldn't take my eyes off the food.

"We should take turns," the blond boy shouted again.

For a moment I saw nods, and then I heard someone yell
in agreement. But then Gerrard stepped forward and bent
over the tray, his robes hanging like a curtain between the
food and the rest of us. A second round of shouts slammed
into the stone walls; there was anger in the voices now, and

desperation. Shouts bounced off the stone, everyone demanding that he wait until an order was decided.

Gerrard ignored them, and the blond boy stepped up and swung at him, a big clumsy uppercut. Gerrard's whole body was jolted when the punch landed against his ribs. He straightened and spun around, holding his robe up out of the way with his left hand. His right foot hit quick, hard and low. The blond boy doubled, collapsing. The shouting increased, and I glanced around at the faces. They wanted to kill him. But Gerrard bent back over the tray.

The blond boy was in a ball on the floor. Others were stepping over him to get at Gerrard. But before anyone could, he suddenly backed away. Jordan tried to hit him and missed when Gerrard dodged to the side. Jordan fell, carried to the floor by his own angry fist. I was thrown to one side, and another fistfight started so close to me that blood speckled my face and robe. I ducked, backing away.

Bent over to protect my face, I saw a plum rolling toward me on the floor. As I reached for it, it sparkled and then it was gone. "Don't drop anything!" I shouted, straightening up. "Don't let any of it fall!" But the fighting had spread and no one heard me.

Frantic, I shoved between the fights and shouldered two boys aside. In the few seconds I had before I was dragged backward, I managed to grab a piece of cheese the size of my fist, a loaf of bread that I tucked under one arm, and two oranges. Someone elbowed me in the stomach. I fell, hanging on to the food, rolling onto my back so that it didn't touch the floor.

Shaking, I managed to crawl backward, away from the fights—and I saw Gerrard beside the door. His eyes caught mine; then he turned. I staggered up and meant to follow him. A scream of agony made me come to an ungainly halt, glancing back. Someone had pulled the tray onto the floor and it was sparkling, the food seeming to glow for an instant. Then it all disappeared. I ran into the corridor.

Gerrard was not quite running, but he was walking fast. I followed, staying as close as I could. His stride was slower than usual and wide-legged, and I got close enough to see why. He had gathered the front of his robe into a makeshift sack. I blinked. Why hadn't I thought of that?

Once we were back down the long straightaway, he turned, and I followed him. Then he turned again, without an instant's hesitation. The small boy from the group I didn't know at all shouted from behind us. I stopped. Gerrard didn't.

"They're all still fighting," the boy said as he got close enough to talk. He matched his pace to mine for a stride or two, then sprinted to grab Gerrard's sleeve. "You got more than anyone else. I couldn't get anything!"

Gerrard jerked free and kept walking. The boy started crying, his face flushed. He was smaller than the rest of us. Was he younger? I gave him one of my oranges and he wiped his eyes, thanking me over and over. Then he looked at me and said this: "I don't want to die."

"Somiss can't mean that," I told him. "Our parents would never allow it."

I glanced after Gerrard. He was still walking. I heard him laugh.

"Hey! Tally! Wait!" the boy shouted at someone coming toward us down the dim passageway. "Give me a little of your food? Anything? Please?"

Gerrard was getting too far ahead and I turned to follow him, but I could hear the voices behind me.

"Please, Tally? You know me. We went to Argents together. We were friends. You know—"

"Shut up, Will."

Three more names, I heard myself think as I hurried to catch up with Gerrard. Jordan, Tally, and Will. It was a comfort, somehow, to know the names, even though I couldn't see Tally very well in the dusk between the torches. I was pretty sure he was one of Levin's roommates, the one who looked a little like Aben.

And Somiss, I thought. Now I even had a name for the wizard who scared me the most.

"Look! There he is! The one who took so much," someone yelled from behind us.

I heard Gerrard make an odd sound. Was he laughing again? He was gathering his robe, hoisting it almost to his waist. Then he ran, the backs of his pale legs showing as he sprinted away from me.

I ran to keep up, ashamed that I had to depend on Gerrard to find the way back, but sure I would never find the room again without him. Behind me, I could hear someone else shouting at Will to shut up, to stop begging. I could hear footfalls, too. At least a few of them were chasing Gerrard. He knew it—he was running hard. I could only struggle to keep him in sight.

Gerrard turned left down a narrow corridor. He turned twice more, then a third time. I followed and couldn't hear the voices anymore. And then we were there, back at our room, more or less safe, and we had food. Food!

I tore off a piece of the bread and shoved it in my mouth. It was sweet, made with honey, and it was so good I nearly wept. I laid the rest on my desk: A beat-up loaf of brown bread, an orange, and a ball of hard cheese. Gerrard had to lean over his desk to spill the contents of his robe-front. I couldn't help but stare, and he turned to meet my eyes. "Don't touch it. Ever."

I sat heavily on my bed. Gerrard had four loaves of bread, half a cheese wheel, five or six oranges, a melon, and four apples. He also had a swollen eye, blood oozing from just above his cheekbone, and split knuckles on his right hand.

I had been among the first, I had been standing right in front of the tray. Why hadn't I thought to use my robe? I knew why. Because I hadn't been thinking at all. I had been desperate to get away from the fights, scared that I would get hurt. I had proved it again. I was a coward.

Without thinking, I went out into the corridor, walking blindly until I came to the first branching tunnel. I walked down it a ways, then stopped, my back against the cold stone. Then I cried until I couldn't cry anymore. Gerrard didn't even look up when I came in and crawled onto my bed. He was studying.

"Not in there," Franklin said quietly.

Sadima turned, her hand on the door to Somiss's room. "I thought, since he will be gone until noontime, that . . ." She stopped because Franklin was shaking his head.

"No. Never go in there. Never."

Sadima smiled. "It can't be that dirty, and if it is—"

"Sadima," Franklin said slowly, "Somiss doesn't allow it. No one goes in his room."

Sadima stepped back from the door. "Not even you?"

Franklin exhaled. "Not even me, not since we left his father's house."

Sadima shrugged. "Then I'll go get water. The barrel is nearly empty. Seven blocks west, then five north, Somiss told me."

Franklin shook his head. "He has never carried water in his life. There is another well, much closer. I'll show you."

"You should go back to your copying," she said, making a shooing motion with her hand, hoping he would insist. And he did.

On their way out, the landlady accosted them in the hallway. Franklin walked faster, pulling Sadima with him, telling Mrs. Terret that Somiss would have the rent soon. They half ran into the street, and Franklin turned east, still walking fast. After a half block, Sadima tipped her head and raised her eyebrows. "Is Somiss always late with the rent money?"

He laughed. "When you are puzzled, your nose crinkles."

Sadima felt her cheeks get warm. "You could say the same for any barnyard dog!"

Franklin handed her one of the empty buckets, then put his free arm around her. The length of their steps matched. "You look absolutely nothing like a barnyard dog," he said, and when she looked up, she saw that *he* was blushing.

She leaned against him and they walked close, without speaking at all, until they came to an alleyway. Franklin guided her down it, then across a narrow street, then between two buildings. Coming out of the narrow passageway, Sadima saw a line of people across the street, all with buckets in their hands.

"See? Much closer."

"And my question?" she reminded him. "In the stories, the royals are always rich."

He nodded as they walked across the cobbled lane. "His family is very wealthy. His father has turned a small fortune into a big one. But it is his mother who is giving him money to do this work. She inherited much of her mother's estate. Money isn't the problem. It's Somiss finding ways to meet with her to get it. And they both fear his father finding out. He would be furious."

Sadima slowed to step up on the boardwalk. "Why?"

Franklin looked irritated. "Because *he* would fear the king finding out what his son is doing."

Sadima started to ask why any king would care if Somiss was writing down nonsense rhymes in a language no one understood. Then she started thinking about the old stories Micah and Mattie Han had told her. The stories with wizards in them didn't have kings. And the reverse. She asked Franklin what it meant.

"That's it, Sadima, exactly that. There are stories about kings who ruled everything, then there are stories of powerful wizards. Somiss isn't exactly sure what it means, or which stories are oldest or which, if any, are true. But it is easy to see why kings wouldn't want wizards in the world if you give it a little thought."

Sadima nodded. It made sense. And it made her uneasy.

"I don't want you doing this alone," Franklin said as they took their place at the end of the line. "The buckets are heavy when they are full."

Sadima smiled at him. "I am much stronger than you think I am. I have lived all my life on a farm, Franklin."

"I remember being astounded that you could carry all four goat kids," he said over his shoulder, moving up when the line did. "You were so small then, slender as a grass stem."

"Will Somiss take advice?" she asked. He turned and listened intently as she described the way Somiss barely spoke to the people who came, how he never asked anything at all about when they used the rhymes, what they thought the songs meant.

He nodded. "You're right. I will tell him."

When it was their turn, Franklin insisted on lowering the buckets. Sadima stepped out of his way and nodded at a somber young woman who was behind them. She didn't respond. She was dressed head to toe in rust red robes embroidered with many colors, and she wasn't carrying buckets. She had two waterskins slung across her back. Her hands were tattooed in swirling patterns—and she was looking intently at Franklin.

Sadima tried not to stare. It was early, and the tall buildings were casting shadows at an angle across the stone-paved square around the well. Still, the silver bangles in the woman's ears shone against her honey-colored skin. Sadima smiled and tried again. "May I ask where you are from?"

The woman frowned. "From long ago and all too near." She drew the words out, almost singing them.

Sadima smiled politely at the strange answer, then stood quietly until Franklin turned around, moving slowly so that the water didn't slosh. "I'll carry them," he said when she reached out to take one of the buckets. "And I am going to keep this chore. Somiss studies so late that he is rarely awake early. He won't even notice if I do it first thing in the morning."

Once they were across the street and on the narrow path

worn between the two buildings, Franklin glanced back. "Did the Gypsy woman talk to you?"

"That was a Gypsy?" Sadima asked. "Micah told me they only wear blue."

"Different clans wear different colors," Franklin explained.

Sadima told him what the woman had said.

"They usually refuse to speak to people outside their clans," he told her. "Somiss thinks their language is close to the original one, from the time magic began. He thinks all the old rhymes are in that language—though the words are certainly blurred by now."

Sadima looked up at him. "Why hasn't he just learned it then?"

Franklin shook his head. "They won't teach us anything. We tried. I was beaten up a few nights after we visited their camp to ask if they would help. Somiss got away, but I couldn't."

Sadima was stunned. "He left you? Were you hurt?"

Franklin looked at her, then glanced away. "Not beyond what could heal in a fortnight. And they might have killed him, Sadima. I told him to run."

They rounded the corner and had to stop to let a horse cart go past. Sadima felt the weariness of the mare in the harness but forced her attention back to Franklin. "The language is sacred to them, every word," he was saying. "That reinforces Somiss's theories. He is trying to figure out a way to get their help. It could save him a lifetime of study, if they have a written form, and even if they don't, it would put him years ahead of where he is now. We asked; they wouldn't answer."

Sadima hurried around him and opened the street gate, then followed him up the stairs. Standing before the green door, he set the buckets down carefully, then put one finger to his lips. "I think I hear him," he whispered. "He's come back early, checking on us. You go first and take the water. I'll be up in a few minutes."

Sadima nodded, and waited until he had gone back down the stairs. Then she opened the door and carried the buckets into the kitchen. Somiss was standing by the table, one of the chairs pushed back. He watched as she poured the clean water into the kitchen barrel.

"This morning I found myself wondering what was for supper," he said quietly.

Unnerved by his stare, Sadima smiled. "I hadn't thought about it yet. Do you have a preference?"

He shook his head. "It has all been much better than Franklin and I were doing for ourselves. Have you seen him? I expected him to be here working on the copies I need."

Sadima walked around him with the empty buckets and set them out on the balcony. "They'll dry best out here," she said, then turned to scan the crowd in the street. She felt a stone lift from her heart when she saw Franklin, walking away. She stepped to the railing and cupped her hands around her mouth. "Franklin," she called. "Somiss was just asking if I had seen you!"

He spun to face her. "I'll be right up," he shouted back.

Sadima turned and nearly walked into Somiss. He stood in her way and she looked at him, waiting, her pulse rising. After a long moment, he stepped aside.

~ 24 ~

I finished my food the next day. All of it.

I had promised myself I would eat only a little of the cheese and just enough bread to dull the ache in my gut, but I couldn't make myself stop. Later, when Gerrard had his back to me, studying, I moved to the foot of my bed so that I could see his food. I was pretty sure he hadn't touched it. I counted the apples and oranges, my mouth filling with saliva. My father often imported oranges from Levern. Celia used them fresh in salads and compotes. She made tart jams that my father loved.

I lay down and made myself read the history book. After the kingdoms and successions, there was a chapter on the beginnings of the academy itself. The Founder had begun his work on recovering the old language when he was very young and had slaved at it, barely taking time to eat or sleep. Limòri had been a smaller city then, and much less safe. There were beggar children in the streets, many of them orphans from families shattered by the king's endless wars. They were hungry enough to kill for food. There were Gypsies, who came into the town and often robbed people or attacked women and sometimes kidnapped babies to raise as slaves.

The king then had done nothing to stop these things, nothing to feed the poor orphans. The Founder was of royal descent. He could have been the next king, but he gave it up to begin the academy. His royal family had thought him deluded, and they had tried to kill him several times.

I closed my eyes, the book open on my chest, wondering if the Founder had hated his father too. I lay awake a long time wishing I had been born to a poor family in South End. If I had, I would be more like Gerrard, and I either wouldn't be here at all, or, if by chance I was, I would at least stand some small chance of surviving. Learn or die, Somiss had said. *Die.* Had my father known all this?

The following morning Gerrard ate an apple and a piece of cheese. He ate sitting in his desk chair, with his back to me. I tried not to watch; I even tried to read, but I couldn't. I could *smell* the apples. I had never felt hunger in my life, not for more than a few minutes. At home, if I wanted something to eat, I had asked Celia. If she hadn't already made whatever I was asking for, she would set about preparing it. At every school I had attended, full meals came thrice each day, and fruit and simple foods were put out in baskets and trays in the food hall for anyone studying late. Or in my case, for those who crawled up on the roof to stare at the stars and talk to friends. I had shown half my class the way up to the school roof. Their fathers had been kinder than mine, apparently—they had never needed an escape. I looked up at the stone ceiling. How long before I could sit on a roof again? Would I ever?

I must have slept, because I woke when a wizard pounded on the door. It was a tall, thin man this time, with a high voice. I wondered why it was a different wizard every time. There had to be a reason. Maybe they all drew straws and the losers had to guide the students?

Franklin gave us another ridiculous class, making us learn another pattern, telling us to feel the air moving in and out. No one could concentrate, I don't think. I couldn't. It was torture for me, knowing that food was as close as my own stinking room, but I couldn't have it. Gerrard seemed to have no trouble concentrating. He seemed calm, steady. Why not? He knew he could eat when he wanted to.

At the end of class, Will raised his hand, the way anyone would in any usual classroom. Franklin gestured. "Yes?"

"I'm hungry." Will's voice was cramped by desperation.

Franklin nodded. "I know. You all are." He hesitated, then stood, his long legs unfolding. "Did Somiss explain how to make food?"

We all shook our heads, and Franklin stood perfectly still. His face stayed smooth and calm, but I thought I saw anger in his eyes. "After our next class," he said, breaking the long silence, "I will show you."

My heart was rabbit-quick inside my chest. I couldn't wait to have him walk us to the food hall, make more food, let us eat without fighting, then patiently watch us practice until we could all feed ourselves. I glanced around the chamber at the others. Their faces reflected what I was feeling—betrayed and scared. Why did we have to wait? Franklin, who had seemed kinder than Somiss, didn't seem to care whether or not most of our bellies were caving in.

Back in the room, Gerrard ate a little, then turned and looked at me. "You should study," he said flatly. "The more you think about your belly, the worse it hurts." Then he picked up his history book and sank down on his bed.

I stared at him, then looked at the food on his desk. He had eaten sparingly—most of it was still there—but he had eaten. "I don't need your advice," I said, feeling anger spreading inside my chest. "You aren't the one starving. You took more than your share and now you're just—"

Gerrard leaped at me like an animal, his eyes narrowed, his face suddenly an inch from mine. "You don't know anything about me, you spoiled little shit." He lifted his right fist and I thought he was going to hit me, but he didn't. He lowered it slowly, an odd expression on his face. "Can't you understand anything? The wizards don't piss around. They mean it. They will let us die. And they are hoping we will fight."

I glared at him. "Then they are all crazy," I said quietly.

Gerrard shook his head. "No, they aren't. Everything

terrible they do to us is for a reason. Everything. That first day when we got lost in here," he gestured at the small room. "Keeping us hungry like this, the classes—"

"Breathing classes?" I interrupted. "*Breathing?*"

His eyes narrowed. "Of course. It's like crawling before we . . ." Then he shook his head and turned his back on me. He didn't say another word, and my starving, unfocused mind finally figured it out a few moments later. He had realized, midsentence, that he might be helping me.

— 25 —

Sadima woke to a gentle touch on her shoulder.
Franklin was bending over her pallet. "Somiss will be gone
for half the day," he said. "He has to talk his mother into
helping us, and his father is gone this morning."

Sadima pushed her hair back from her face. She had
been hoping they would both leave long enough for her to
bathe and wash her dress.

"I want to show you something," Franklin said. "Hurry."

Sadima rolled up her blankets and washed. Maybe he
was going to take her to the sea? She glanced through the
arch as she dried her face and felt her hopes sink. Not the
sea, not today. Franklin was sitting at the table waiting for
her. There was a stack of Somiss's fine white paper beside

him, and he had two quill pens and an ink pot. Two quills. Sadima felt a shiver tickle the back of her neck.

"See if you can copy this," he said when she sat down. He made three quick strokes on the paper.

Sadima picked up the quill. It felt odd and awkward in her hand—but familiar, too. It was about the same size as the paintbrushes Micah had brought her, one by one, hidden in his pockets. A little ache ran through her body. She missed painting—and she missed her brother. She thought about the artists in Market Square. She had meant to go back, to talk to them, but there was always a shirt to wash, a meal to cook.

"Sadima? Just try it."

She glanced at the figure Franklin had drawn and replicated it.

He looked astonished. "That's perfect. Try this one. It's an *s*—the first letter of your name."

Sadima copied what he had drawn, and he told her the names of two more letters. She repeated them. Then, without prompting, she drew both a second time, hoping to make him smile.

Franklin pulled her to her feet and kissed her forehead, then let her sit down again. "Try this." He wrote quickly this time, his fingers guiding the quill in tiny curves and arches. Sadima glanced back and forth from his paper to hers, copying the characters almost as quickly as he had written them.

Franklin grinned. "You could begin making fair copies of

everything he is doing now, today, whether or not you could read what you had written. It's amazing. I have never known anyone who wrote so precisely the first time they tried it." He wrote her name and she copied it perfectly. Then she copied his name. "How can you do it so well?" he asked.

"I paint," Sadima said, warmed by his approval. "I used to, I mean. Just flowers and the woods and sky," she added, not wanting to exaggerate. "And portraits of my goats."

He took the practice sheet and laid a clean piece of paper in front of her. Then he went to the cupboard and brought back a page of Somiss's notes. She copied it, careful to leave a little space after the odd little dot marking, just as Somiss had.

Franklin was nodding, smiling. "This will convince Somiss once and for all to let you stay," he said. "He hates making copies, and he isn't satisfied with mine. You sit down while I cook. You have earned breakfast service, m'lady." Sadima laughed. While he went to fetch water, she stared at the practice sheet for a moment before she tucked it into the box that held her paints. Her name and Franklin's, side by side. She traced the letters, saying his name slowly, then her own again. The second letter and the last one were the same in her name. She said her name slowly again, looking at the letters. Was there one letter for each sound?

They had just begun to eat when the door banged open. Somiss's face was contorted with emotion, but he did not speak.

Sadima stood up, meaning to go into the kitchen. But Franklin stood at the same time and they bumped shoulders. She sat back down as Somiss paced the little room like a bull in a cramped paddock. Finally he began to speak.

"My father suspects something. So my mother told him I had gone off, maybe to Yamark or Thereistine, she wasn't sure. I can only hope he believed her." Somiss covered his mouth and chin with one hand. His eyes were flitting from the ceiling to Franklin's face, then back. "She says she can't risk helping me anymore, not after today. He will have a dozen people watching her." He exhaled and his shoulders dropped. "We were just beginning," he said, his words muffled. Then he looked up. "She had only a few coins in her chamber. I have paid the rent. There is not a copper left for food or anything else."

"I can work," Franklin said.

"Where?" Somiss demanded, as though hope offended him. "And then who will keep up with the copying? If I do it all, I won't have time for anything else."

Sadima looked at Franklin. He met her eyes, and the question was plain enough. She nodded. "I want to show you something," he said to Somiss.

Somiss watched, incredulous, as Franklin wrote a string of letters and handed Sadima the inked quill. She copied them, then looked up at Somiss, hoping he would be as pleased with her efforts as Franklin had been. He didn't look happy, he looked stunned.

"She reads?" he asked, as though Sadima wasn't sitting

at the table at all. "It's against the ancient decree, Franklin, unless she has some lineage you haven't bothered to tell me about."

Franklin shook his head. "She can't read. But look at how well she copies. This is her first try, Somiss, today, this very morning. I just wanted to see if she could do it, to take the burden of copying from you—and from me."

Somiss stared at him. "And she has no idea what she has written?"

Franklin shook his head. "I could teach her and—"

"No," Somiss interrupted him. "You will not. Why break King's Law if she can copy this well without meaning?" He turned to Sadima. "I spend half my time making copies to compare, to mark up, and to save, so the work won't be lost. So does Franklin." His face darkened. "That costs a few coins each month too, Franklin, the paper and the cost of the safe-box at the money changer's."

Sadima stared, watching them. Somiss sounded like a worried child. Franklin reached out and gripped his shoulder. He was murmuring reassurances that were almost fatherly, telling Somiss how intelligent he was, how capable. Something stirred in her heart.

"With practice, I will be able to do most of the copying, I think," she said softly.

They both turned to look at her. Somiss met her eyes. "But you must pretend to be our maidservant, no more. Always. It is against King's Law for any commoner to read or write. I cannot imagine convincing a magistrate that someone who writes so well cannot understand what she has written."

Sadima nodded. "I give you my word," she said. "I will never tell anyone."

"You will still have to cook and clean," he added. She nodded again.

"I will help with her other chores," Franklin said, and the warmth in his eyes made Sadima blush. She went to the kitchen to make a third plate of food. While she fried the potatoes, Somiss sat at the head of the table, talking to Franklin in a low voice. When she brought his food, he glanced up at her, then caught her wrist and looked into her eyes.

"You will stay with us. But whatever you learn, whatever we discover, you have to keep secret. Not just the writing, *everything*. Not a word to anyone, ever. To your grave. You must vow it."

Sadima glanced at Franklin. He smiled joyously, then quickly lowered his eyes. In that instant Sadima understood something wonderful. He had been afraid that Somiss might make her leave. He wanted desperately for her to stay.

"I vow it," Sadima said, turning to look at Somiss again. "Never a word to anyone."

He reached out to touch her cheek. "On your life," he said.

"On my life," Sadima repeated without hesitation, and she saw Franklin smile again.

Somiss stood and went down the hall to his room. Once

he was gone, Franklin embraced her, picked her up, and swung her around. "We are going to change the world," he whispered in her ear as he set her down. His face was bright with hope and belief. "The poor will eat," he said. "The sick will heal. No woman will ever have to die as your mother did." His face was lit from within. "No more fakes, Sadima! The magic will be *real*."

Then Sadima tipped her head back, and he kissed her.

— 26 —

"Come closer," Franklin said, and we all walked
toward him. I could smell food—roasted meat, fruit, pastry—
the chamber smelled like Celia's kitchen on Winterfeast
morning. I was almost dizzy again; my battered feet felt
light and strange on the stone. I had to keep swallowing
a weird, bitter saliva that rose in my mouth. There had been
a shoving match to work out the order of the line, all of
us staggering a little, off balance, weak—all but Gerrard.

I stood wide-legged near the end of the uneven line, trying to steady myself, to clear my head. I had to learn to
make food—*had* to. I believed Gerrard—and my own eyes.
Somiss had meant exactly what he had said, and Franklin
could not or would not help us. Tears flooded my eyes, and
I turned to hide my face from the others.

When I turned back, I saw that Levin was to my right and a little behind me, with his roommates. The tall blond boy was standing straight and stiff, tears running down his cheeks, too.

I watched Levin lean close to him. "Are you all right, Luke?" The boy nodded. Levin's eyes brushed across my face, then he looked aside. I bit at my lip and faced front again just as Franklin lifted his hand and gestured vaguely at the torches set high on the walls. They flared, and it was suddenly as bright as day.

I blinked, lifting my hand to shade my eyes. Nothing looked real. Franklin looked older than time itself. The gem sparkled as the flickering light coursed over its facets—and the ceiling was much higher than I had thought. And from there, my thoughts scattered like dry leaves in wind. After being so long in dim light, bright light was almost unbearable.

I rubbed my eyes and squinted at the boys around me. They were standing in loose groups, lined up in an uneven curve before the gem. They all looked sick and scared, swaying on their feet, licking their lips. Involuntarily I touched my own tangled hair. We were filthy; our eyes were rimmed in red. Will and his three roommates were staring stupidly at the monstrous gem, their eyes only half-open in the glare. Levin, Jordan, Luke, and the boy I thought was Tally stood closer together. Gerrard was at the far end of the line, keeping a little apart as usual. His face was rigid and his arms were folded. He did not look scared and desperate, and I hated him for it.

Franklin was silent, like he was waiting for something.

What? For us to fall over dead? I rubbed my eyes again. The light *hurt*.

"Begin," Franklin said.

And we all fell into the pattern he had drilled into us, inhaling slowly in unison. Then we opened a tiny passageway in our closed lips and allowed ourselves to exhale, slowly, steadily, the circular path the air took almost unbroken. I closed my eyes, comforted by the sound we had all gotten so used to, the rhythm of breath laid over the silence of the stone like a quilt on a bed. Franklin's class was the only place I hadn't been terrified.

I felt my muscles loosen. Then, for no reason, I pictured my mother, outside my father's study, the heavy door closed and barred, her ear against the wood, silently weeping at whatever she was hearing. I saw myself going down the long curving staircase. I was only four or five, but I knew it was time to hide. My father hated it when my mother cried. Celia was not at the baking table or in the cavernous pantry. She didn't come into the kitchen until much later, her hair undone and her cheeks flushed. I could see her as though I was still five, still standing in the same room. I opened my eyes to make the images stop, then shut them again to keep out the glaring light. Without meaning to, for the first time in my life I understood how cruel my father really was and why my mother hated Celia.

"Hahp?" I heard Franklin say. "Quiet your thoughts."

My eyes flew open again, but he wasn't looking at me—he was facing the other direction, his back to all of us. I blinked, then struggled to catch up, to rejoin the pattern. It was the only thing that seemed to make sense, the only thing that might save me.

"Close your eyes," Franklin said aloud, without turning.

I obeyed, and the dusk beneath my lids was a comfort. In my mind, I turned over and over the new thing I had realized about my mother's anger and sadness, about Celia. Had there been others? Why not? There were always serving girls in the house, many of them pretty.

Carefully, I parted my eyelids just enough to see Franklin at the other end of the line now, his hands on Luke's wide shoulders. He was leaning close, and I was pretty sure he was whispering something. Luke nodded and stepped back. Franklin stood a moment, looking at him. I shifted my weight and felt the off-balance tug of weakness. Franklin moved to the next boy, then the next. When he came to me he said only two words: "You can."

"Open your eyes," he said once he had spoken to each of us—probably saying the same two words of encouragement. He was looking at each of us now, his eyes moving from one face to the next. "What you must do," he said, "is imagine the food completely, in every detail, then touch the Patyàv Stone." He faced the huge gem, stood very still for a few heartbeats, then turned sideways so that we could see as he pressed both palms against the faceted surface. There was a little flash of blue-white light and the strange faint wailing sound, like metal scraped on stone.

I cried out without meaning to, and I heard other voices besides my own. We all leaned forward to stare at a tray of food even more varied and wonderful than the one that

Somiss had called into being. Without meaning to, I took a step toward it.

"You must make your own food," Franklin said in a flat, weary voice. And as he said it, he pushed the tray from the black stone pedestal and threw it sideways. Apples, chunks of cake, cheese, and roasted meat scattered across the floor, flickering with sparks as it touched the stone. And an instant later it was all gone—vanished.

"No," I heard Levin whisper.

Then there was only painful silence in the chamber. Franklin looked sad, every line on his face deepened. But his shoulders were squared, and when he spoke again, his voice was even.

"You can learn to do this. Close your eyes. All of you. Keep them closed."

I obeyed. I think everyone did. My belly ached, and I listened with my ears, my heart, my whole body.

"Imagine a toy that you loved when you were small," Franklin said. "Choose something that you played with for hours, looked at for hours."

I swayed on my feet and felt my shoulder bump someone else's, but I didn't open my eyes. A toy? The darkness behind my own eyelids felt vast, vacant. Then I remembered the blue horse. My father had brought it home from one of his journeys. I couldn't remember where it was from or why he had given it to me. I remembered most clearly how it had felt in my hands. The stone it had been carved from was heavy and cool, even in the summertime. The horse was rearing, and the sculptor had carved its cascading tail in a way that formed a tripod with its hind legs. It could stand in dirt, on floors and deep carpets, pawing its little blue hooves at the sky. I had often pretended that it was galloping, racing through the pine trees. I remembered a little chip in the stone, caused by my dropping the horse on our hearth one evening. I had cried and my father had slapped me until I quieted.

Abruptly, I realized that Franklin had not uttered a word in a long time. I tried to open my eyes—and found I could not. It scared me, but I could hear the solid, steady rhythm of the others breathing around me. My fear subsided.

I had played with the horse endlessly. I remembered whinnying in a high, enraged squeal, imagining that the horse could save my mother when my father got angry with her, that it would prance between them and fix him with a cold blue stare and he would not dare touch her.

"Hahp?"

It was Franklin's voice. An instant later I felt his hands on my shoulders, and I opened my eyes. "Do you remember a toy?"

I nodded.

"Vividly?" he asked, and I nodded again.

He led me closer to the gem and maneuvered my leaden body until I was standing within reach of it. Close up, I could see that every tiny facet was, in itself, faceted. How? I knew how diamonds were cut—I had seen my mother's jeweler at work. But who could have done this?

"Hahp?" Franklin said, and my thoughts scattered like startled birds. "Imagine the toy," he whispered. "When you see it clearly, when you can hear it and smell it and feel it and taste it *completely*, touch the stone."

Weirdly buoyant with hunger, I drifted back in time far enough to be playing with the horse, holding it in my hands, pressing it against my nose and mouth. I heard the smooth shushing sound of my silk tunic, the crackle of the pine needles breaking as I galloped the toy horse along the ground. I remembered tasting an odd wet-rock flavor when I had licked it, curious to see if it tasted like blueberries because of the color.

Only then did I reach out blindly and press my hands against the surface of the enormous gem. It was ice-cold. There was a flash of light, the odd sounds, then the little horse was there before me on the platform of dark stone. I stared at it, my mouth open, hearing a sound that I finally recognized.

The others were cheering.

I turned to look at Franklin.

He was no longer there.

Sadima had spent most of the morning walking the
crowded boardwalks in the north end of Limòn. She had
learned a hard fact: There were so many hungry children in
the streets that shopkeepers often traded a morning of
sweeping or carrying for a small meal. Many of the children
begged as she passed, holding out their dirty hands, singing,
"Please lady, please lady, please lady."

Sadima sighed, wishing she had money to give them.
She wished she had money to buy food for herself,
Franklin, and Somiss, too. They had barely eaten for the
last eight days, mostly gluey puddings and thin soups.
She had to find some sort of employment. But why
would a shopkeeper hire her when there were hundreds
of children who would work for less—and whose plight

was so touching? Franklin hadn't found anything either.

Somiss was angry all the time. It was as if he couldn't understand what not having money actually meant. Franklin had explained it to her. Somiss had never been hungry for longer than a quarter hour in his life.

Weary, her empty stomach churning, Sadima wondered how much farther she should walk. She turned a corner—and stopped. People behind her veered to pass. She heard a man's voice, low and irritated, but she did not respond. The street ended twenty paces in front of her—at the sea. The endless blue water began at the planked docks and extended all the way to the horizon. The moored ships were beautiful, bigger than the house she'd been born in, the dark wood of their hulls battered, a hundred shades of earthy brown. Far beyond them, rolling humps of water tumbled over, foaming white at the crest. Waves. There had been sea waves in one of the stories Micah had told her. And now, here she was, staring at the sea.

A second bump on her shoulder reminded Sadima that she had stopped in the middle of a busy boardwalk. She started forward again. Only with conscious effort did she finally drag her eyes away from the water and back to the storefronts. She scanned the signs, remembering what Franklin had explained.

Six or seven on this block only had lettering. That meant they catered to royals and the wealthy merchants who were often their friends. Most had lettering as well as paintings that showed what was inside. A few had only the paintings—which meant they sold cheaper goods, darker, rougher bread, tough, stringy meats, straw-stained eggs.

Sadima noticed a cheese vendor's sign and headed toward it. The shop door was heavy, and silver bells jingled as she opened it, her empty stomach reacting to the smell of fresh cheese. The woman inside wore a close-fitting cap, embroidered with flowers and vines. Wisps of graying hair had escaped around her ears. "May I sweep or do some other work for you?" Sadima asked her.

She shook her head. "I hire the orphans for that." There was an odd rhythm to her speech. She looked Sadima up and down, then tilted her head. "A farm girl? Do you know how to make cheese?"

Sadima smiled, hope swelling inside her. "I do." Then she shifted uncomfortably when the woman looked her up and down a second time. Sadima knew her dress was tattered and roughly made. She had worn her best one to ask for work, but her best was worse than any dress she had seen on any woman here, aside from the Market Square beggars.

"Tell me," the woman began, taking off her apron. "Tell me what you know about cheese making."

Sadima nodded. "Goat's milk or cow's milk? With rennet or without?"

The woman smiled a little. "Both," she said. "My family has a farm outside the city. My father brings the clabbered milk twice a week. We work with rennet, usually. Hard cheese brings a better price." She crossed her arms, arched her brows, and waited.

Sadima began quietly, but by the time she was past the

curds and pressing, she saw the woman nodding in agreement at most of what she said, and looking interested and puzzled by other things. "Why would you heat the curds twice?" she asked when Sadima finished.

"My father learned from my mother and he taught me. I never tried it with only one, but surely it would make a softer cheese."

The woman nodded again. "My youngest sister is heavy with child—she lost her last one and none of us wants her working now, so we are in need of help. If you can come in every day midmorning and work late one or two nights out of seven—?"

Sadima nodded quickly.

"We are Eridians," the woman went on. "Bound by oath to honesty and sacred labor. We work hard, and I will expect you to work hard."

Sadima nodded again, not caring what the woman's family believed or what oaths they took. "What can you pay me?"

The woman laughed at her bluntness. "Three coppers a week until we see how you work."

Sadima nodded and told the woman her name.

She smiled. "I am Rinka."

They sealed the bargain with a handclasp. Then Sadima left, walking slowly, memorizing the way.

Franklin was coming down the stairs as she came in the street gate. "I managed to borrow two of these from Maude," he said, pulling a shiny yellow apple from his pocket. He handed it to her and watched as she took a bite.

"Did you find anything?"

Sadima explained. "So I will still have most nights and all of the mornings to copy for Somiss."

Franklin brushed her hair back over her shoulders. "You will save us," he whispered. She felt his lips brush her ear, and she raised her chin, hoping he would kiss her, but he released her and stepped back. "Thank you so much, Sadima." Then he dropped his voice to a whisper. "I am going to work tomorrow too."

Sadima waited for him to say more. When he didn't, she tilted her head. "What sort of work?"

"I am not going to tell you," he said. "Somiss will not approve if he finds out, and I don't want him angry at anyone but me." He bent close again. "Somiss is happy today. He found an old Gypsy woman who claims to know a dozen of the nonsense songs."

Sadima nodded, then looked up at him. He was smiling. "What is it, Franklin?"

He touched her cheek. "Somiss is better. His rages have abated. We eat better, the place is not filthy and jumbled, even your soft singing as you work soothes him, though I don't think he would admit it." He pulled her tight to his chest for an instant. "I am so glad you came." Sadima felt herself fit perfectly against him, as though they had been cut apart long ago and had finally been rejoined. She lifted her chin, again expecting him to kiss her. But he released her, and she stepped back. There was an odd look in his eyes as he turned away.

Late that night Sadima tied her hair back and bent over

the water barrel with a candle to look at herself. Her cheeks were less round than she remembered, and her neck seemed longer. Was she pretty? Micah and Mattie Han had always said so, but was she? Pretty enough to make Franklin think about her more often than he thought about Somiss?

When she heard footsteps in the hall she blew out the candle and crept to her pallet. She pretended to be asleep as Somiss came in, carrying his own candle. She opened one eye and watched him through her lashes. He was fully dressed. She could hear him whispering to himself. He sounded upset, but she couldn't understand what he was saying.

He dipped a cup in the bucket and drank, then went back to his bedroom. Sadima heard his door close. She waited, listening, but the only sounds came from the street below—someone shouting in the distance, crickets. Was Somiss still working? Every morning he handed her a dozen or more papers to copy. Lately it seemed like in addition to barely eating, he barely slept. She knew Franklin would want to know that Somiss was up late, but she decided not to tell him.

— 28 —

The instant everyone realized Franklin had left us, Luke came at me and shoved me away from the stone. I almost fell, and I dropped the horse when I flailed my arms to keep my balance. It bounced, sliding across the slick stone, and then, like the food that Franklin had used to taunt us or encourage us or whatever he had meant to do, the blue horse sparked like iron rubbed across flint and disappeared. I felt tears rise in my eyes again. That toy horse was one of my best memories.

And now it was gone.

I heard a noise and turned to see Luke pushing at another boy who had stepped forward—it was Jordan, one of Levin's roommates, the tall, skinny one with straight, dark brown hair and dark eyes that stood out again his fair skin.

"I'm first," Luke said. "Just get back."

"You have to be first at everything," Jordan said. "To wash, to piss, *everything*. I want to go first this time. I—"

Luke straight-armed him, his open hand flat against Jordan's chest. Jordan took one awkward step backward, then jumped to the side. Luke's own weight carried him past—he stumbled and fell to his knees.

"Make a line," Levin was shouting. "Anyone who wants to fight, take it somewhere else and let the rest of us try to eat."

There was a general murmuring of agreement and a line formed—with a little more shoving, but no fists. Gerrard was last. I went to stand behind him, still furious with Luke for making me drop the horse. I resented every second he stood motionless in front of the stone, too, trying to picture whatever it was asses like him played with when they were little. When he finally lifted his arms and put his hands on the gem, nothing happened. Nothing. "I almost got it," he said, waving one arm. "Just let me—"

"It's my turn," Jordan said from behind him.

Luke's hands were balled into fists. Jordan wasn't as big, but he was ready. You could see it in the way he stood, his chin jutted out, his weight up on the balls of his feet. Weak as he was, he wasn't afraid of a fight. "Go to the back of the line," he said in a tight, low voice. "And if I can't do it, I'll be right behind you. Then Tally, then Joseph, then everyone else."

I looked at the boy behind Jordan. Tally. I had been

right. But he didn't look so much like Aben now; his face was thinner and his hair was wild and dirty. Joseph had to be one of Will's roommates, then. He was almost as big as Luke, but he always stood with his shoulders rounded and his head down.

"Just go, Luke," Will pleaded. He was crying, not bothering to hide it. "Tally? Make him."

"Go!" Tally hissed. "Get out of the way—fighting like this is stupid."

"They're right," Levin said flatly. Several of the others echoed what he had said.

I watched Luke, seeing the utter desperation in his eyes. Had he eaten his pittance of food in one day like I had? Had he gotten anything at all before the tray had been knocked to the floor? He let out a sound like a low growl, but he moved off, shuffling toward the back of the line. Jordan stepped closer to the huge gem.

Jordan tried, but nothing happened, and he came back to stand behind Luke as Tally moved forward, then Joseph. I watched, hoping desperately that someone would manage to make food. Even if I didn't get to eat a crumb of it, I would at least know it was possible. I closed my eyes and tried to practice what I had done with the toy horse, but with food. I could see Celia's griddle cakes—I could smell them and taste them, and I could feel them in my mouth. I could hear the sound of the butter in the frying pan sizzling beneath the batter.

Every time I heard the line move, I opened my eyes, stepped forward, then closed them again, remembering everything I could about the griddle cakes: the silken, perfect-brown surface, the moist, bubble-riddled insides. I had to keep swallowing. I was drooling like a dog.

I glanced once at Gerrard. He stood to one side, a step out of line, his eyes on the massive gem. Then I looked back over my shoulder and saw that the others were watching me. They thought I could make food, or they hoped it. I certainly meant to try.

Then, abruptly, I realized what would happen if I made a plate of Celia's griddle cakes appear. There would be a fight. I would get hurt, almost certainly, and I wouldn't be the only one.

I stepped forward again when another one of Will's roommates failed and went to the back of the line. Two ahead of me now. I heard someone whisper, "Good fortune, Rob."

Rob. But I didn't open my eyes to fix the face to the name. I didn't care. I just wanted to eat. But I knew that if I tried and succeeded, someone would take the food away from me. Half the boys were bigger than I was. Luke stood a head taller, and so did Joseph. I shivered at the thought of going to sleep hungry again, beaten up.

I felt myself sweating, sharp, smelly fear-sweat. Piss on all the wizards, I hated them for turning us into animals. Would the one who graduated end up like the flying horses? Able to do strange, wonderful things, but with cold, dead eyes, changed forever into something else?

I had been in the orchard once when a wizard was working with the colts. I had hidden, eating apples from the stacked harvest crates, watching from a distance. I wasn't very old, maybe five or six. My father had forbidden me to go near the stables when the wizard was there—everyone had been warned. So I knew he would beat me if he found out.

I had stayed crouched down between the apple crates and stared, entranced, expecting to see magic. But the bay yearling had only walked in a circle around the wizard, shaking its head like flies were biting it, scuffing its hooves. It had looked sick, and I remembered being sad, pitying it.

I swayed on my feet under the weight of the memory. I was so light-headed that every thought seemed too vivid, too full of meaning. I could smell the apples, see the blue sky and the bay colt walking. Grass stubble had prickled through my trousers, but I had held perfectly still. I had so wanted to see the magic that made colts learn to fly.

I opened my eyes when I heard footsteps and a sound of disappointment. Now it was Gerrard's turn. He stood wide-legged in front of me and took longer than anyone else had to step forward and touch the gem. But nothing happened for him, either. His shoulders sank, and he turned and walked to the back of the line without looking at anyone.

Then it was my turn again.

"Come on, Hahp," I heard someone whisper behind me. Levin? I wasn't sure. But whoever it was, they weren't just asking me to hurry. They were pleading with me to succeed. I thought about what Franklin had said to me, and I felt myself sweating again. If I managed to make food, there would be fights. If I didn't, there might be fights anyway—if they were hoping hard enough, they might come at me for failing.

I moved up and closed my eyes, trying to think about griddle cakes. Then, without meaning to, I saw the crates of apples very clearly in the darkness behind my eyelids.

Apples.

Perfect.

It had been early on a chilly morning and there had been crows circling overhead. I could see the beads of dew on the thin gold and red apple skins. I noticed the perfect curve of the stems, and I remembered rubbing my thumb across the puckered texture of the blossom remnant in the hollow at the bottom of the fruit. I saw them, I smelled them, I could taste them, and I remembered, very clearly, the sound of biting into them. I had been afraid the wizard would hear it. I brought all these thoughts into my mind and held them. Then I stepped forward with my eyes closed.

The icy cold of the gem shocked me again as my out-stretched palms flattened against it. I saw the flicker through my eyelids, then opened my eyes, my whole body trembling.

A crate of apples sat on the pedestal.

There was a long moment of silence, then the whole line ran forward, whooping, laughing. There were enough apples to give us all a dozen or more, and I used the front of my robe to take my share, then turned to see Gerrard standing back, empty-handed. I opened my mouth to speak, to make sure he knew I wanted him to have apples too—but then I saw Somiss in the wide-arched entry to the chamber.

The laughter died.

"Fools!" Somiss rasped. "Do you think he means to help you? Or keep you weak?"

Then he looked straight at me.

Then he wasn't there.

29

"Are you all right?" Franklin asked Sadima as they went down the stairs together in the dawn-dusk, each of them carrying an empty water bucket. "I have never been so hungry," he said. "Half a potato for the whole day again?"

His stomach rumbled as he said it, and she smiled at him. "Farmers' children learn to live on snow and turnips in the winter."

He hesitated at the top of the stairs to let her go first. "I worry most about Somiss. And you are working very hard, both early and late."

Sadima didn't answer. She was rising before dawn to copy for an hour or two before she made breakfast, then cleaned up, then ran all the way to work. Her evenings were just as busy. "I will get paid in a few days," she said.

"And Somiss told me that maybe we won't need to work much longer."

"No. He is just wishing," Franklin said as he opened the street gate. Once they were away from the door, walking on the crowded boardwalk, he went on. "Somiss's father has hated him since we were boys. Even if he doesn't find out what we are doing, Somiss won't dare ask his mother for help again."

Sadima blinked. "How can a father hate his own son?"

Franklin slowed his step. "That is a very long tale that would only bore you. But it is true." He smiled, thin and wry. "His father hates many people."

Sadima shook her head as they stood aside to let a vendor push his cart past them. "That is very sad."

Franklin nodded. "It is." He looked at Sadima. "And it is more serious than that. Anything Somiss does that threatens the king could be considered treason—and his father would be suspected as well."

"But why wouldn't the king want to see his people fed and the sick among them healed?" Sadima asked him.

Franklin took her arm. "Because the people would follow anyone who could do that for them—then the king would no longer be king—and he knows it."

"Does Somiss want that?" Sadima asked. "Does he want to be a king?"

Franklin shook his head. "No. He wants people to admire him for his good works, nothing more than that."

Sadima slowed as they reached the first turn. "Are you sure?"

Franklin looked into her eyes as they rounded the corner. "Yes. I have known him since I was three and he was two and a half. He has always wanted to do something amazing, something that would make his father proud. He would give anything to make his father love him."

Sadima didn't answer. It made perfect sense to her. Before she came to Limòri, all she had ever wanted was for her father to love her for herself—even though she knew he never could. Now she wanted something much more complicated.

At the well, Franklin leaned close to her. "If Somiss's father finds out what we are doing—and if he takes it seriously—we are all in danger. If it comes to that, you must go home."

Startled, Sadima shook her head and spoke without thinking. "I belong here with you."

Franklin smiled and put his free arm around her shoulders. "We are both grateful for all that you are doing to help," he said. "But we don't want you hurt."

Sadima turned her head to hide her anger. *We?* Somiss wasn't grateful for anything, and he didn't spend a minute worrying about her—or Franklin. A cat darted out of an alley and brushed Sadima's leg as it ran past. She felt its urgency to find someplace to hide before the dogs woke up. It underscored her own fear. How long before Somiss put them in danger?

"Is he interviewing people every day?" she asked Franklin.

He shrugged. "The Gypsy woman comes tomorrow," he said. "He has been staying in his room most of the time."

"I will be able to buy food in a few days," Sadima said.

Franklin nodded. "Again, you save us."

Sadima smiled.

Franklin touched her cheek. "I will soon be bringing in enough to help. Somiss will keep working, though he will want to be more careful now because of his father."

"Is Maude still telling people that you want to learn songs and rhymes?" Sadima asked.

Franklin shook his head. "No. I've asked her to stop, at least for now. Others know us and what we have been doing, but not *why*."

"But won't Somiss's father figure it out?"

Franklin shook his head. "Not easily. He will think it is useless studying. Somiss has always had an interest in languages. He speaks six. He is a scholar born into a family of ruthless businessmen, which is part of the reason his father cannot love him."

Sadima led the way down the passageway between the buildings. "What is your new work? Is it such a secret?"

Franklin laughed. "From Somiss, yes. He would never forgive me." His stomach rumbled again. "It must be torture for you, making cheese when you are so hungry."

Sadima shook her head as they came out into the sunlight. "In bad years we would save half the barley for seed, no matter what. You can get used to hunger."

Franklin shook his head and filled the buckets, then picked them up so they could start back. "Your courage is remarkable."

Before they had taken twenty steps, Sadima shivered in the cool morning air, and Franklin set the buckets down to put his jacket around her shoulders.

"After we get the water in, do you want to come with me?" Franklin asked.

Sadima glanced at him and saw a flicker of something she didn't understand in his eyes. She nodded. "If you want me to."

"I do."

"I told Somiss what you said about asking when the songs were sung to help learn their meaning," he said as they walked back into the street. He pulled her closer as a six-horse hitch clattered past, the horses blowing plumes of steam in the cold air. "He thought it was brilliant."

"He did?" Sadima looked up at him.

Franklin nodded.

They hurried up the stairs, tiptoeing once they were inside, then leaving again, silently. "You must promise me that you will never tell Somiss what I am doing," Franklin said on the way back down the stairs. "Not now, not five years from now. Never."

Sadima nodded solemnly. "I vow it. I will never tell."

Franklin smiled at her, then walked faster.

When he led her to a cloth canopy painted with crescent moons and ellipses, she looked up at him. "No."

He nodded "Yes. I tell fortunes very well, Sadima. Come in, I will prove it."

Maude Truthteller was sitting in a draped chair, and she stood up and yawned. "Morning," she said to Franklin, then arched her painted brows at Sadima. "He swear you to secrecy too?"

Sadima nodded.

Maude grinned. "He forced me into an oath that would scald a teakettle."

"Somiss would never forgive me," Franklin said quietly. "He hates all this—the thought-guessing, the intuitive reading of people's eyes and hearts . . ." He waited for Maude to turn away, then looked at Sadima and lowered his voice to a whisper. "It is almost silent-speech."

Sadima nodded, trying to hide how uncomfortable she was, how torn. Maude was the kind of magician her father and Micah had both hated so much—someone who took money pretending to have magical skill.

"Over there," Franklin said. "Please sit." He pointed at the second table—a much smaller one, at the rear of the canopy. Was Maude charging him something to put it there? Probably. That was why he wasn't making much yet. He had to lure customers and keep them coming back. She noticed a hat with a wide brim hanging over the back of his chair. He followed her eyes.

"I wear it all day. No one ever gets a good look at me. Sit," he repeated. Sadima lowered herself into the chair where Franklin's customers would sit once the market crowds came. She shifted her weight, sliding forward until she was perched on the edge of the chair seat.

Franklin took her hand in his, and it startled her into blushing, but he turned it palm up and her blush faded. "What are you doing?"

"Maude reads the lines. She is teaching me."

Behind Sadima, Maude laughed. "I only read palms because people want me to read *something*."

"But what you told me yesterday bears out," Franklin said without looking up. "The old man with a break in his life line had an accident that nearly killed him as a boy."

Maude said something quietly, and Sadima glanced over her shoulder. A girl of ten or eleven in a fancy dress had stopped to talk to her. Customers came first. Sadima wondered for an instant what a fortune-teller in Ferne might have told her when she was a girl. That she needed friends? It wouldn't have mattered. Her father would never have let her go visiting anyway.

"Sadima?" Franklin said, pity in his voice. She looked back and found him staring at her. "I never understood how lonely you were when I first met you."

Sadima jerked her hand free.

Franklin smiled tentatively. Then he leaned close to whisper. "I can hear your thoughts sometimes. Never perfectly and not often, but I can hear them. "

Sadima stared at him. What else had Franklin heard her think? She had thoughts about him. . . .

"I should go back now," she said. "I have to get to work early today."

Franklin blinked. "I thought you wanted to learn about the silent-speech one day, to see if we could—"

"I don't anymore," she said, knowing how childish it sounded.

"Let me finish."

He reached for her hand, but she stood up and took a step back. He apologized and tried to talk her into staying, but she left, walking fast. Halfway to Rinka's shop, she wondered if Somiss was hiding thoughts too—if that was his real objection to silent-speech.

30

Three classes with Franklin came and went and I was the only one eating anything at all, I was almost certain. Then three more. Then I lost count. I had no idea if each class marked the passage of a day—in fact, I was almost positive the time intervals were never the same. But *days* had passed; I just wasn't sure how many. Everyone was getting thinner.

I could feel the others staring at me, wondering if I was making meals of roast duck and orange custard appear when no one was there to see. I wasn't. I was living on apples. I had tried real dinners, griddle cakes, bread, cheese—and I couldn't manage it, even though I had some idea what I needed to do. It was the tiny details. Unless I could hold them all in place perfectly, nothing happened when I touched the stone.

We all saw each other going back and forth to the chamber. Levin, Jordan, Tally, and Luke almost always walked together. So did Will and his roommates. Maybe some of them had the same problem I did: I still wasn't sure I could find my way without Gerrard. I could remember the turn sequences only so far, then I got mixed up.

When I got to the food hall, if anyone else was there, I waited for them to try—and leave—before I would approach the stone. They would glance back at me as they walked out, their feet dragging. No one talked now, not even a few words. I tried to go before Gerrard, though, because I was afraid he would walk out if I went last, and leave me to get lost in the tunnels.

Once I had my half-dozen apples, I would stand close to the entrance, waiting, while Gerrard tried and failed five or six times. It made no sense. He practiced constantly. He sat on his bed with his eyes closed most of the time, going through the breathing patterns. But when he faced the faceted stone and pressed his hands against it, nothing happened.

I never made a crate of apples again, of course. I usually made six at a time. Enough to carry back, hidden in the sleeves of my robe so no one would decide to beat me up for them—but I was always hungry. And eating nothing but apples, day after day, began to upset my gut. I shit water about half the time, and it was hard to sleep because of the cramps. I felt stiff and dull-witted. I was too weary to think.

Franklin taught his classes as though we were all fine, as though nothing was wrong. I hated him for it. More than once I realized he was watching me. Did he watch everyone that closely?

That really was the worst thing of all: Franklin acted like nothing was going on, like he had no idea that we were starving. "Now," he said in his soft voice, "use the third pattern. One in-slow-out-slow, then twice fast, then slow again. Begin."

It was idiotic. We were on our fourth pattern and most of the time I was so light-headed I couldn't remember any of them until he reminded us. I found myself just staring at him more and more, my thoughts spinning.

"Sir?" Will said one day when class was nearly over.

"Yes?" Franklin responded in his maddeningly calm voice.

Will cleared his throat. As thin as he had gotten, he looked like a six-year-old. "How long before we are given food?"

Franklin didn't answer.

Will cleared his throat again. Everyone was staring at him, except Franklin. His eyes were fastened high on the far wall, as though he hadn't heard.

"Will is wondering how long before we are fed," Joseph spoke up. "Somiss said we would die, but most of us are thinking that was . . . an exaggeration," he finished, his voice dropping.

"It isn't, Joseph," Franklin said, so quietly that I wasn't sure I had heard him correctly. But every face in the room went slack, so I knew I had. I glanced at Gerrard. He looked terrible. His eyes were hollowed out and his wide shoulders looked skeletal beneath his robe.

"If our fathers had known this," Joseph said, "they would never have allowed us to come here."

"They were told they would probably never see you again," Franklin answered. His voice was flat, emotionless. He stood up, and the torchlight caught the side of his face. He looked so old it was like looking at a stacked corpse in Beggar's Field except there were tears coursing down his cheeks. Then, before anyone else could say anything to him, he vanished.

We sat without moving, all ten of us, blinking, staring. I couldn't know what the others were thinking, but I was sunk in a bitter hatred for my father. It was almost a comfort.

31

As always, Sadima rinsed the curds carefully, then
wrapped them in the thinly woven cloth they used to keep
flies off. Rinka was humming quietly as they worked.
Rinse, wrap, press, hang. There were a hundred hooks
above the long copper trough. Sadima hung each batch of
finished curds one hook farther to her right. The last one of
the day would be tied with a strip of red cloth so Rinka
could see the age of the curds at a glance and keep track of
how much they did each day. They salted and wax-dipped
the oldest cheese first.

"At home we use herbs," Sadima said.

Rinka looked up. "I would love to, but we can't afford it."

"Why?" Sadima asked, setting the wrapped cheese
between the pressing boards and weighting the top one with

one of the flat stones that lay within reach. "Marjoram and rosemary don't have to cost anything. I know where we could find—"

"No," Rinka interrupted her. "There is a royal family that sells herbs in Limòri. The king forbids anyone else bringing them into the city at all."

Sadima turned to stare at her. "Why?"

Rinka glanced around the shop. There were no customers; the place was empty. Even so, she lowered her voice. "Simply to increase the wealth of the royal families."

Sadima was amazed. In Ferne people grew their own herbs, or picked them wild. She was very glad she had brought her own. She would have a hard time cooking without them. She told Rinka about the woven grass bags of herbs in her bundle.

Rinka shrugged and smiled. "The king is not likely to send archers and guards to search your little kitchen. It is a bad law. Eridians believe that the fruits of the earth and of the mind belong to all equally."

Sadima glanced up from the copper trough and the batch of curds she was rinsing.

Rinka smiled. "Erides was a wise woman."

"Is she dead?" Sadima asked.

Rinka nodded. "Yes, yes. She is gone three hundred years, killed in the long ago and all too near. But her words live, and her good heart."

Sadima had been keeping her hands moving, wrapping each bundle of curds tightly, then weighting a pressing board on it and going to the next. She had been about to ask Rinka if the woman in the carriage had been right, if the Eridians were bringing girls into the city to force them to marry—but now her thoughts were scattered.

"Long ago and all too near," she echoed. "A Gypsy woman at the well said those same words to me when I asked where she was from."

Rinka smiled. "A Gypsy Eridian? That is a rarity. And she must have liked you. Eridians give our prophet's wisdom only to the ones we know can hear it."

Sadima smiled but stayed silent, thinking. *Long ago and all too near.* Maybe it meant that bad things that happened once could easily happen again. The thought made her sad.

When Rinka fell back into her soft humming, Sadima was relieved to be distracted from her somber thoughts. This time it was a soothing, strange little melody that ran in circles in a clever way.

"Does that have words?" Sadima asked.

"Only nonsense sounds," Rinka said. She sang it through, her voice clear and true. "It's like all the silly old songs our mothers teach us," she said when she was finished. "My mother sang it to put me to sleep. It worked for my daughters. There is something about the tune—my mother swore by it. She was a Gypsy, very beautiful."

"Was she Eridian, too?"

Rinka laughed. "No, no, not her. Pure Gypsy, no loyalty to man nor god nor prophet, only to her clan."

"I would like to learn the song," Sadima said, knowing Franklin would be as glad to have something new to give Somiss as he would be to have a real supper.

"Do you know this one?" Rinka said, then began to sing another tune in her high, sweet voice.

Sadima nodded. "I have heard it," she lied. She did not want to explain to Rinka that she had grown up without a mother. "I like the old songs," she said carefully. "Would you teach them to me?"

"So long as it doesn't slow our work," Rinka said. "My mother said she had been taught a dozen or more—but she taught me only three. Here's the first."

It was a lovely tune, and Sadima hummed along with Rinka until she had it. Then she learned the strange words Rinka's mother had taught her. They sang it together a dozen times, then Sadima hummed it quietly to herself off and on until they were finished with the curds and were pouring milk into the clabbering pots to begin another batch. Then she asked to learn the second song. They worked until the sun went down and the moon rose—and then for a long while after that. When it was finally time to go, Rinka produced five copper coins. *Five.* Sadima thanked her, overjoyed. She had been expecting three.

"You are worth every bit," Rinka said. "Tell me if you need more before the next seven-day. I don't want you going hungry."

Sadima felt giddy as she left. Tired as she was, she nearly danced down the boardwalk. She found a man washing his shop floor and talked him into opening his door. She bought a whole chicken, plucked and ready to cook, three big, sweet yams, and a half round of white butter.

At home she built up the fire after she tiptoed in and

filled her biggest pot with water. Once it had boiled, she banked the fire carefully. By the time she woke the next morning, the chicken was done, tender, the meat falling from the bones—and the yams were cooked through, fragrant, ready for butter. Franklin came out of his room and Sadima watched, laughing aloud when his eyes went wide with surprise. "Rinka paid me even more than I thought."

Franklin came closer to smell the steam from the pot, then picked her up and swung her in a half circle. He kissed her, a quick touch of his lips on hers. "I have never been this hungry," he whispered in her ear. "Somiss took the coppers I brought home and spent them on paper and ink."

Sadima heard Somiss's door open, and Franklin set her down. He stepped away from her as they both turned. She glanced at him. He reached to push his hair off his brow, then wiped his lips on the back of his hand, and she realized how afraid he was of Somiss finding out that they cared for each other.

"Sadima has gotten us real food!" Franklin said as Somiss came into the sitting room. An odd look crossed Somiss's face and Sadima stared, startled by how thin he had gotten. How long had it been since she had seen him? Five days? Six? He had been thin then. Now his cheeks were angular, the skin tight. But his eyes were shining.

"Not eating seems to clarify my thoughts," he said. "The work feels effortless." He smiled at them both. "Maybe I will eat tomorrow," he added, and he sounded like a child, pleased with himself. "Or the next day." He filled a cup with water and smiled at them again before he went back to his room.

— 32 —

I dreamed about food every time I closed my eyes, then I woke up muddled and weak—and saw Gerrard, hollow-cheeked and pale, but sitting up straight reading the history book or practicing what Franklin was teaching us.

I had no idea how he could make himself concentrate. It was getting harder for me to talk, harder to think, and I couldn't eat more than two apples a day. Something had soured inside me—it was like drinking vinegar. My stomach cramped so painfully that I could barely stand it. At least I wasn't quite starving. Not yet. But it was easy to imagine getting too weak to walk.

Every day, if they *were* days, I sat through Franklin's class, my gut churning and my saliva tasting like ashes. Then I had to wait until Gerrard decided to go to the food hall, which meant staying awake so that he couldn't go without me. Why couldn't I just memorize the turns on my own?

One evening—if it was an evening—after we had been to Franklin's class, I watched Gerrard reading for what felt like eternity before he finally stood up and walked into the corridor. I got up and followed him as always. And as always, he acted like I wasn't there, twenty paces back, struggling to match his long stride.

Three boys were already there when we walked in. Tally was facing the stone, his shoulders hunched. Joseph and the boy whose name I still didn't know were sitting at the tables. Joseph had his head down on his arms and looked like he was asleep. Scared, I walked closer. I could see that his eyes were open. So I went past and found a place to lean against the wall.

I watched Tally concentrate, then step forward and touch the cold surface of the stone. Nothing happened. He pivoted on one foot and left, his face contorted with misery. Joseph got up and went to stand before the stone.

I sat down on the floor, leaning back against the wall. Apples. I had come to hate them even though I knew I was the lucky one, having anything at all. I squeezed my eyes shut, then opened them again. The other boy was whispering to Joseph. Gerrard was watching them, looking annoyed. I yawned and closed my eyes, thinking that once they were finished, I could get to the stone before Gerrard did—I was closer.

And that was the last thought I remembered having. I

am not sure how long it was before I finally woke up. I can only suppose that Gerrard and the other two took turns while I was sleeping, then decided, one by one, to leave. I do know this: When I woke up, I was alone.

It terrified me. "He has to come back," I heard myself say out loud. And I knew it was true. But when? We usually came not long after Franklin's class. What would happen to me if I missed the class altogether? No one ever had. What would Somiss do to me?

I cried. If anyone had been there with me, I might have been embarrassed enough to try not to, but I was alone, and I cried a long time. After that, I walked around a little, trying to stop sniffling. Gerrard would come back. He would. He had to. The bastard had to be hungry, unless he had finally managed to make food. I had left apples on my desk for days, hoping he would take one or two, but he hadn't. I paced to the arched entrance and looked down the corridor both ways. Between the pools of cold-fire light from the torches, it was dark as midnight. Was it? Was everyone asleep?

I finally made three apples and ate one. My stomach wrenched, but my head cleared a little and I could feel my thoughts like pond water must feel the fish swimming. I was helpless to stop them or even slow them down. Had anyone else eaten anything? Were we all going to die? Was it possible?

Muddled and shaky, I paced back to the gem and made four dozen apples appear. I spent a long time placing them along the passageway outside, just within the outer reach of the torches' light, where someone would notice them. Then I picked them all up again, one by one, and threw all but two onto the floor. The sparks glittered over them and they disappeared.

Crap.

Shit.

I was too much of a coward to help anyone else, and I couldn't help myself. I wanted desperately to eat something that filled me up, that would stop the grinding pain in my belly. What was different about the stone horse and the apples? Why could I imagine both of them clearly enough—but nothing else? I forced myself to think.

The toy horse had been almost magical to me. It had carried me on long rides in my imagination. Nothing, no feat of magic or heroics was beyond it. Every time I played with it, I dreamed up magical things.

I thought about the day I had hidden in the orchard. I had been afraid that the wizard would see me. I had been even more afraid that my father would. So why hadn't I gone back to the house? What was worth that risk? I exhaled. I had *expected* to see magic. Not just the light of the cold-fire lamps or the wind dying down so the fleet could come into the harbor or my mother's smile when her terrible headaches receded. I hadn't hidden just to see the result of the magic. I wanted to see the magic itself, and I had been so sure I would. . . .

I turned and walked toward the gem, a fragile idea forming itself in my thoughts. I imagined the orchard, tried to feel like I had that day, then I switched the image in my mind to a plate of griddle cakes, steaming, the odor of maple syrup and sweet butter and the sound of the batter on the hot skillet and the way the air began to leave the dough the moment they were laid on a plate, like a sigh. I stepped forward and touched the gem *believing* that I would see magic, not the griddle cakes—*magic*.

And the light flashed and I heard the sounds, and then the griddle cakes were there. Steaming. Buttered. Perfect. I glanced toward the arched doorway. I was alone. My vision blurred with tears, I bolted the food like a South End dog and ended up gagging, almost puking. The instant I was finished, I pushed everything—the tray, every crumb, the fork—onto the floor and wiped the table with my robe hem. Then I picked up my two apples and walked into the corridor and sat by the wall to wait for Gerrard.

My stomach churned at first, but then it settled and I slid back and forth between waking and something like sleep. When I heard the light shushing of bare feet on stone, I opened my eyes. It was Gerrard. And he was alone. When he came closer, I saw him lift his head like a hound. Could he still smell the food? "Has Franklin been here?" he asked me.

I shrugged and slumped against the wall. "Maybe. I fell asleep."

He nodded. Then he walked past me. I watched as he stood before the gem. When he put his hands on it, nothing happened. Then he turned and came back out, walking, as he always did, fast enough to stay ahead of me.

"Thank you for coming to get me," I whispered when we got close to our room. He didn't answer me. I wasn't sure he had heard me, but I couldn't make myself say it again. There was no reason to assume he meant to help me get back. He had probably just wanted to try the stone once more. I set the apples on my desk and hoped he would take one. He didn't.

Feeling better than I had in a long time, I opened the history book. Paging past all the kingdoms and maps, I came to a section about the Founder. It was six pages of fancy language, but this is what it said: The Founder was the only one who saw any value in magic, the only one brave enough to risk death to study it and turn it back into the astounding force for good that it had once been. He was the only one who had believed it was possible, and he had pursued it through hardships that would have stopped anyone else. He was brilliant and he was honorable and admirable. His family had tried to stop him—they had been too self-centered to see what he was doing, too selfish to appreciate him.

I closed the book thinking that there were thousands of people who admired my father the way the writer of the book admired the Founder. Few liked him. And no one had ever asked me or my mother, or Celia or Gabardino or any of the families of servants who lived in simple huts, summer and winter, and worked day and night just to eat. I wondered what the Founder's family and friends would say about him if they were still alive.

Once she had been paid again, Sadima bought another pair of shoes. It was a pleasure to have sound, stout leather between her feet and the cobbles. She scuffed them up so they wouldn't look new. If Franklin or Somiss noticed them, they must have assumed she had brought them with her. Neither of them said anything.

Walking to and from work she practiced the three songs that Rinka had taught her. She had asked when and why they were sung too, and the answers had been interesting. The evening she was sure she knew all the words, she sang them for Somiss while Franklin tended the soup she was making for dinner.

"That one soothes children to sleep," she said after the first one. He had her sing it again, more slowly, and he wrote down the words. Then she sang the second. "That one is to be sung to the corn and barley seeds before they are planted."

"Did your family do anything like that?" Somiss asked, his eyes flickering across her face, then to the ceiling, then the candle that stood between them, then back.

"No," Sadima said. "But these are Gypsy songs, and maybe they—"

"Gypsy?" He slid the candle aside and leaned across the table to grip her forearm.

Sadima nodded. "Yes. Rinka's mother was a Gypsy. That's one of the reasons I thought they would interest you." A flicker of motion caught her eye and she saw Franklin standing behind Somiss. He was shaking his head. She closed her mouth and felt stupid. Of course. Somiss would be angry if he knew Franklin had talked to her about the Gypsies' language. He so seldom exchanged more than three words with her that she had never thought about having to hide anything.

Somiss leaned forward. "Sing it again. Very slowly."

Sadima started and stopped, watching Somiss's quill scratch at the paper. When he finished he put it aside. "There is one more? Is it a Gypsy song too?"

Sadima nodded. "Rinka's mother taught it to her. She married Rinka's father against the wishes of the whole clan. No one ever came to visit, not even when—"

Somiss slapped the table, startling her into silence. "When was this one sung?"

Sadima bit her lip, angry until she saw the worry on

Franklin's face. Somiss was so thin, so tired. "When some-one died," she answered Somiss. "Rinka said it was to keep the spirit of the loved one close."

Somiss made an impatient gesture. "Sing."

Sadima sang the last song over and over until Somiss was satisfied that he had the words right.

"Thank you, Sadima," Franklin said when Somiss stood up and walked away without so much as glancing at her.

Sadima shook her head when she heard the door down the hall open and close. "He needs to eat."

Franklin shrugged. "He has, a little, I am almost sure, though he isn't admitting that. And he will soon tire of fast-ing. His interests are always very intense and—" Franklin paused, then didn't go on.

"But it's like he's drifting further and further away," Sadima said. "Half the time, he doesn't notice either one of us."

Franklin nodded. "His mind is racing faster and faster, he says. I wish I could *make* him eat. He's too thin."

"So are you," Sadima said. "Has he talked you into fasting?"

Franklin looked out the balcony door at the sky. "Ask Rinka if she can spare you one day soon. Maybe if we get him outside, walking in the woods like when we were boys, his appetite would win over his will."

Sadima nodded, looking at the side of his face in the light of the stout candle. "Tell me you are not starving yourself to please him, Franklin," she said in a low voice.

He turned toward the kitchen. "Somiss asked me to fast

for eight days, to see if it affected me as it has affected him."

Sadima stood up and followed, angry with him. "Has it? Or are you simply dizzy from not eating?"

"The interesting thing," he said, stirring the onions down into the broth, "is that after long enough, you simply forget you are hungry."

"How long has it been since you have eaten?" Sadima asked, keeping her voice low.

Franklin smiled. "Only four days. I am tempted to eat a cup of the soup," he added, gesturing at the steaming pot on the cookstove. "It is like Somiss said, though. My thoughts fly."

Sadima made him sit down. Then she ladled up two bowls of soup and buttered the bread. "Eat," she said when Franklin glanced up at her. "He won't come back out until we are both in bed. He never does."

Franklin stared at the bread, then picked up the spoon and lifted it to his lips to take a tiny sip of the broth.

Sadima bent over her food, hoping Franklin would eat more if she didn't stare at him. The room was quiet, and the small sounds of eating in the silence reminded her of her silent father, her too quiet home. She sighed. She missed Micah.

"Tell me about your brother," Franklin said.

Sadima looked up, startled.

He ducked his head, then whispered, "When I was younger it was all very vague. But the fortune-telling has made me practice. It is a word here and there, a feeling. Nothing more."

Sadima shook her head, "It makes me . . ." She searched for words to tell him how she felt. "I feel like you are peeking at me through a window, watching me when I don't know you are there."

He looked stricken. "I'm sorry. It probably isn't all that different from what you do with animals. Just now, it was a familiar feeling about silence, and his name. That's all."

Sadima nodded slowly, wishing he would lean across the table and kiss her to apologize. But he didn't, and she wondered if he ever would again. She touched his hand. "Try not to do it. Please."

He nodded, then looked down at his soup.

"I do miss Micah," she said. "But he wouldn't forgive me for this." She lifted her hands to gesture at the notes stacked on the far end of the table, Somiss studying in his room, all of it. "You can't imagine how much he hates magicians."

Franklin looked up. "My mother died when I was nine. I went to her funeral and watched all my relatives wail and cry. No magician robbed us, they just all refused to come."

Sadima stared at him. "Why?"

Franklin shrugged. "A family that lives in South End isn't likely to have the necessary fee, even if they sell their—" He stopped.

Sadima stared at him.

Franklin shook his head, then sipped at the broth in his spoon. Sadima moved the plate of bread closer to his hand, and he idly took a piece.

"*Franklin?*"

They both turned at the sound of Somiss's voice. Sadima set down her spoon and glanced at Franklin. His face had gone white.

"What are you doing?" Somiss demanded. "I said eight days, didn't I?"

Franklin stared at the bread, then let it drop as though he had mistakenly picked up dog shit. He pushed the bowl away from him. "I was eating just a little and—" he began.

Somiss came closer, his eyes on the crumb-strewn table. "A *little*?" He snatched the bowl and smashed it against the wall.

"Why should he starve himself just because you—" Sadima began, then stopped. It was not the rage on Somiss's face that halted her. It was the agony on Franklin's. She stood and went into the kitchen, leaving them alone. Sitting in the dark on her pallet of blankets, her arms around her own knees, she could hear Franklin talking. His voice was low and earnest, and Somiss's voice was cold as winter ice. They were still talking when she lay down and closed her eyes. It took a very long time for sleep to come.

– 34 –

I sat in Franklin's class with my eyes closed. His lessons had become mindless. I could do all the patterns without thought or will. But I was in agony again. I had finally figured out how to make something besides apples, and Gerrard hadn't gone back to the food hall for two days—if you counted Franklin's classes the way you would count a sunrise. He hadn't gone when I was awake, anyway. Was he trying to kill me? Shit. I had finally managed the magic, but I couldn't find my way to the food hall to do it.

"That's very good, Hahp," Franklin said. I jerked my eyes open. I didn't want to be the only one he called by name. I didn't want to be the only one eating, either. I glanced at Gerrard, sitting off to the side as always. His eyes were closed. So were Levin's. Maybe no one had heard

Franklin. Maybe no one cared at this point. They were all thinking about their aching bellies. I was. I forced my eyes closed and kept pace with everyone else. After a moment, I could feel the air turning in its long circles again.

Once we had worked our way through all of the six patterns Franklin had taught us, he stood up and disappeared. He had been leaving abruptly since the hunger began. I had stopped wondering whether he was kind and it hurt him to see us getting weaker or if he didn't give a shit. It didn't matter. Either way, he wasn't helping anyone, and I hated him for it.

No one got up for a long moment after Franklin was gone. I made sure that I was the fourth or fifth to rise, that I moved slowly. No one talked now. They just shuffled out in two groups of four. I followed Gerrard as always. Walking back, Gerrard and I passed Levin and his roommates—something that almost never happened. As we did, I heard Levin whispering a string of nonsense. "Late to ripen lentils and rotting rice don't make rich landowners rejoice."

I blinked, afraid he had lost his wits, or that I had. Passing from torchlight to darkness, then back, I followed Gerrard, listening to my own thoughts. They were too loud, beating against the inside of my skull. If everyone else starved to death, would I graduate and be a wizard? That seemed crazy. But so did everything else here. Why hadn't Franklin just reminded us how we felt about the toy when we were little—that simple, pure kind of expectation?

Gerrard turned right. It was hard for him to stay ahead of me now, I could tell, so I slowed my pace. Even he was getting weak with hunger. What would I do when he was too weak to move? Gerrard turned left and I followed. Was I the only one who couldn't learn the turns? Then I heard my thoughts reciting Levin's doggerel. *Late to ripen lentils and rotting rice . . . Left, right, left, right, right . . .* I stopped, understanding at last. Levin had figured out a way to remember.

"Gerrard?" I said quietly. He didn't turn, and I hurried to catch up.

Once we were inside our room, Gerrard went straight to his desk and sat down, pulling the heavy history book toward him. Then, abruptly, he stood up and went out the door. I followed.

The first few turns were easy. Right, left, right, then left again after a ways. So. Rustling limbs rub against the little house. . . . The next two were rights, so I added to the sentence. Rustling limbs rub against the little house and really ruin it. I repeated it to myself three or four times and felt my chest loosen, my fear easing. There were two lefts after that, close together. Rustling limbs rub against the little house and really ruin it at long last. I kept adding words until we were in the long straight corridor and almost there. I was still dizzy-headed and ravenously hungry—but the weight of my fear had lightened and my thoughts were flying.

And I realized this: If I wanted to hide the fact that I was eating, this was exactly the way to do it. I should follow Gerrard as I always had, and follow him back with a few apples in my hands, as before. Then I would find times to come alone and make sure the hall was empty before I ate a full meal—to avoid anyone knowing, and to avoid facing the torture of deciding whether to give food away and risk Somiss's wrath again. I did not love myself for that last thought, but it was true. I was scared shitless of him.

Gerrard went straight to the front and stood before the stone. I held back. If I didn't get a turn this time, I didn't care. I would just follow him back to the room and come later. I slouched against the wall as he stood, rigid as the stone we stood upon, then stepped forward and touched the gem. Nothing.

He made a low sound that frightened me, and I stood up straighter as he turned. His face was wet with tears. "Go ahead," he said. "Laugh."

I shook my head. "Never. You let me follow you."

Then he stared upward a long time before he faced the glittering gem again. "It isn't fair," he said in a voice so low that I had to move a few steps closer to hear him. "I didn't *have* a toy."

I didn't answer. I had no idea what to say.

"I found a bit of silver-threaded cloth once," he said, as though he was speaking to the stone, not to me. "The bigger boys stole it from me. I had it half a morning, no more than that."

"But can you remember it?" I asked, not knowing I was going to speak.

He shook his head without turning. "Barely."

"What did you love when you were little?"

His shoulders shook and I thought he was crying, but he was laughing—a limping, misshapen little laugh. "Food," he said. "Any scrap, anything anyone dropped or threw away because it was rotting. Have you ever been to South End?"

"Yes," I said quietly, knowing in my heart that he was not lying. But if he was a street child, not the son of some prominent Eridian, how had he gotten here?

He lifted his chin but still didn't turn. "I don't know who my mother was, much less my father." He exhaled and squared his shoulders. He tried touching the stone again and nothing happened. I saw his fists clench.

"What was the best meal you ever had?" I asked him quietly.

He was silent so long that I thought he wasn't going to answer me, but then he spoke. "A rich lady bought me a dish of fish stew once. From a vendor. She leaned down to put it in my hand and I could smell her perfume. I ran away from her, to hide before the bigger boys saw what I had. It was evening, and I found a place between stacks of wooden crates on the docks."

"Fish stew? In a broth?"

He nodded. "Thin, reddish broth. It was wonderful. Onions. Potatoes."

"Pretend you are there, between those crates, smelling the stew," I whispered, "just about to taste it." Then I shut my mouth and held very still.

Gerrard's fists slowly loosened.

"The stone is magic," I whispered. "Touch it. You will see the light flash and the food will appear. I promise."

After another long moment he stepped forward and put

his hands on the gem. An instant later there was a flash, and a tin bowl of fish stew was sitting on the black stone. He rushed toward it. Using his sleeves to pad his hands from the heat, he set it on a table and blew on it. When he finally tipped it up, I could tell it still burned his mouth, but he drank a mouthful anyway, then blew on it again.

I walked forward quickly, closing my eyes when I got close to the gem. I pictured the silver service my mother was so proud of, the graceful bend of the ornate spoons that had been her mother's grandmother's. She had a service for two hundred, and twice a month she had the house staff count the pieces to make sure none had been stolen. I had played with them since I had been able to toddle into the kitchen. Celia had let me stir the eggs and cream together for her dumplings. My mind clasped at the memories of the dumplings, but I forced it back to the spoon. When I could see it clearly, I reached out. There was a little flash.

I took the spoon to Gerrard and he thanked me, his eyes glassy as he stirred the soup, still blowing. I went back to the stone and tried to make a roasted chicken. It didn't work, but I managed soup of my own, steaming oxtail soup, the way Celia made it, of course. I took the bowl and a spoon for myself to the table and sat across from Gerrard. He ate the first bowl fast, then made another. I ate slower. I met his eyes when he finally looked up. "Thank you, Hahp," he whispered.

I nodded, then I looked past him, toward the entrance. Shit. Before I could warn him, Somiss was beside the table, glaring down at us. He tilted his head, staring at Gerrard's right hand. Then he made a sound of disgust and disappeared.

Gerrard held up the silver spoon, shaking it at me. "He knows I couldn't do anything like this. He *knows*."

"Are you ready?" Franklin whispered, coming down the hall. "I can hear him pacing around his room."

Sadima nodded. Somiss had eaten a little for breakfast, nine mornings in a row. Franklin was doing the same. It wasn't enough. They were both far too thin. Somiss was convinced he was working faster and better than he ever had, that hunger somehow improved his mind. It seemed crazy to her. If hunger made people smarter, why couldn't the street orphans find ways to live without having to beg and steal?

Sadima watched Franklin as he checked the parcels of food she had packed, arranging them in the carry-sack for the tenth time. "Bring your paints," he said. His face was eager, his eyes intense. He went to the cupboard and came back with four sheets of paper—not the kind they used to copy songs and rhymes. It was stiff, the surface textured like cloth. She looked up at him, astonished. He smiled. "I asked the artists in Market Square what kind to buy."

Sadima kissed him quickly, suddenly, on the mouth, giving him no time to move away or worry that Somiss would see. She got out the slender box of brushes and colors and twined four slim sticks of kindling into a square frame for her carry-bundle so she wouldn't bend the paper.

"Somiss?" Franklin called down the hall. There was a wordless shout in answer. Franklin paced to the little door that opened onto the balcony and opened it. Sadima saw a patch of very blue sky. They stood in silence for a long time. Then Franklin exhaled, turned, and walked back into the sitting room. "*Please*, Somiss?"

Sadima heard a door bang open. She braced herself when she heard footsteps, but Somiss looked sullen, not angry. "If we have to go, let's go," he said flatly, and turned toward the door. Franklin slung the food sack over one shoulder and they hurried to follow him. Somiss did not look back at them as he strode up the wide corridor and went out the street gate.

Franklin ran a few steps to catch up, and Sadima ran with him, irritated. Somiss was walking faster than she had ever seen him walk. "I have a place in mind," Franklin said. Somiss didn't slow or speak. "It's a place you will remember once we get there," he added. Somiss still didn't react.

Sadima lengthened her stride. "Where?" she asked Franklin, loud enough for Somiss to hear.

Franklin threw her a grateful glance. "Out of the city a little ways, into the—"

"Out of Limòri?" Somiss demanded, stopping and turning. "Franklin, no. I can't spend that much time away from—"

"You have to," Franklin said. "What good will you do if you die before the year is out?" He gripped Somiss's shoulder, looking into his eyes. "You promised—a whole day without once talking about the work."

Somiss shook his head. "I meant someday, not *this* day."

Franklin didn't release him. "You promised. A day without study."

Somiss shook his head again and Franklin nodded, at the same instant. They both laughed. Sadima saw their eyes meet and knew that something had passed between them, some old memory of a boyhood game, something from simpler, better times.

"I can't remember the last time I laughed," Somiss said quietly.

Franklin exhaled. "Nor can I."

Somiss looked up at the sky and blinked in the sunlight. Sadima watched him lower his eyes to meet Franklin's and she stepped back, feeling like an intruder.

"And you are far too thin," Franklin said.

Somiss frowned. "Am I? "

"I will buy a looking glass," Franklin said, "so you can see yourself."

"Polished metal won't show me anything I don't know," Somiss said. "I am thin. My sagging trousers mentioned it this morning."

Sadima laughed, then covered her mouth with her hand. She had never heard him make a joke. Somiss turned to look at her. "I'm sorry," she said quickly.

He shook his head. "It was a *jest*. You laughed. Franklin is the one who should apologize—he didn't even smile." The corners of his mouth lifted slightly, and the smile looked strange on his gaunt, bony face.

Then he started walking again. Sadima was glad when he moved away. She had never seen him outdoors, she realized suddenly. The bright sun turned his hair the color of autumn straw, and his eyes looked almost clear.

"That was a jest too," Somiss said over his shoulder. "About Franklin needing to apologize."

Franklin glanced at Sadima. Then he made a silly, high-pitched, obviously false laugh. Somiss chided him for laughing far too little and far too late. Franklin apologized profusely, explaining that he would have laughed sooner, but the joke hadn't been funny. Somiss reached out to nudge Franklin's shoulder, pushing him off balance.

Sadima stared, walking along behind them. She had never seen Somiss show any humor at all and Franklin only rarely—and she had never seen either one of them act like this. As they walked, they continued insulting each other like boys half their age. Franklin ran a few steps so Somiss had to catch up, then walked so slow Somiss had to push him along. Franklin kept looking back to make sure she wasn't being left behind. She waved him on, and he grinned. It was easy, now, to imagine them as children together, as almost-brothers.

"What?" she heard Somiss ask. "What are you saying, Franklin?"

Franklin leaned close to answer him and they both laughed. Sadima fell back a little farther, watching them as they led her along narrow streets into a section of the city she had never seen.

Then Franklin turned to the right and cut between two buildings, and they were suddenly crossing a wide expanse of empty grassland. On the far side, they stepped from the grass onto cobblestones so broad and flat, and a street so wide, that Sadima lifted her head to look up the hill to the houses it led to—and she realized that she could see all the way to the massive dark cliff that rose above the city on the North End.

Somiss and Franklin dropped back to walk beside Sadima as they started up the hill. The houses were bigger than any she had ever seen, set back behind iron fences and towering shade trees. Sadima wanted to stop and stare, but Franklin whispered in her ear. "This is near where we grew up. That's Ferrin Hill." He pointed to the west. "His family lives on the other side of it."

Sadima turned. The houses in the distance were even bigger than the ones that lined the street they were on— and they were much farther apart, each one surrounded by green lawns and flower gardens. "Does the king live up there?" she whispered to Franklin when Somiss had gained a stride or two on them.

Franklin shook his head. "The king has three residences— one by the sea, one in the mountains, and one on the far side of that hill, not far from Somiss's father's house. The king's is biggest, of course, but all the houses on the other side make these look small." Sadima glanced at him, sure he was joking, but he wasn't. Franklin walked faster, and they caught up with Somiss.

There were pools of water in some of the house yards. Sadima saw a pair of swans swimming in a slow circle. They were fat and snowy white and beautiful—and sad. There was something wrong with their wings—something a man had done to them. With a knife. They would never fly. Sadima looked at Franklin; he was clowning to make Somiss laugh, so clearly overjoyed that Somiss seemed happy . . . and tears filled her eyes. She blinked them back before he turned to look at her. She would not spoil this day for Franklin.

There was a deep and shady woods down the road, far beyond the houses. Paths ran through them in long, graceful curves. Somiss stopped abruptly and faced Franklin. "I know where we are going. It's that place we slept out when I wanted to run away."

Franklin smiled. "Remember the waterfall?"

Somiss nodded and they went on, walking faster.

It didn't take long for them to find the spot. They spread the food out across a flat rock at the edge of a pool that was rippled by a little waterfall at the far end. They all ate slowly, the summer sun warm and bright. Somiss finished what Franklin had laid out for him and asked for more. Franklin caught Sadima's eye and smiled, then mouthed a silent *thank you.*

Magpies chattered in the branches of the trees, and Sadima saw a squirrel racing along a wide branch. She felt his urgency, his hurry. She inhaled deeply, feeling the leaf-strained air flow into her lungs, circle, then come back out. That simple act calmed her heart and her mind. It was beautiful here. It was *quiet*.

After the food was gone, Franklin and Somiss stretched out on the grass, hands behind their heads, talking. Sadima took off her shoes and walked into the woods. She saw raccoons and a doe and a long, dark snake that was thinking about its burrow, cool and safe and not too much farther.

She sat a while in the woods alone, wondering how Micah was, if plowing had gone well enough. Laran's brothers would help now that Papa wasn't there to refuse it. And Micah would help them when harvest came. His children would have Mattie Han as their grandmother. Winterfeast would be a happy time in the little farmhouse now. Birthdays would be celebrated, not mourned.

Franklin and Somiss were still talking when she came back into the little clearing. And the conversation had become serious, she could tell.

"Will you come for a walk with us?" Franklin asked, looking up a few minutes later. Sadima realized that he had not noticed her leave or come back.

She shook her head. "I'll stay. I want to paint."

Franklin nodded and they set off, leaving her alone. Sadima felt almost giddy, arranging her brushes. It was wonderful to be outside, to paint. She chose an ancient tree with healed-over lightning wounds and an odd shape and began a portrait. It had finished drying by the time she heard Somiss and Franklin coming back. She had tucked the artist's paper back into her bundle and had her brushes and paints put away when they burst into the clearing.

"I found a staircase," Franklin said, "cut right into the rock."

"It's old," Somiss added.

"So old that the rain has rounded the edges of the steps," Franklin told her. "There are vines and moss all over it. We couldn't tell how far up it goes, but at least halfway, and—"

"The way the stone bellies out, you can't see the top part of the cliffs except from a long distance," Somiss interrupted.

"Ten or twelve people have told us a story about a stone city and we—," Franklin began. Then Somiss grabbed his forearm and he stopped.

"You both have to vow never to tell anyone else about this place," he said. "Never."

Franklin laid his hand on his heart. "I vow it. To the grave."

Sadima repeated the words, but she couldn't bring herself to put her hand on her heart. She saw Somiss glance at Franklin, and she didn't care. Couldn't they hear themselves? They both sounded like overserious little boys vowing never to reveal their make-believe kingdom to anyone else.

— 36 —

Franklin was often there when we arrived, but not always. Sometimes we all sat, uneasy and silent, for what felt like eternity before he walked in the door.

We smelled horrible—but I don't think anyone cared anymore. I didn't. I was almost happy, which sounds crazy, but it was true. I was beginning to believe I might live, at least a while longer. I was getting good at keeping track of the tunnels. And I was eating better. Much better.

I worked out ways to eat alone. Gerrard did the same. I smelled fish on his breath almost every day. But after Franklin's classes, we went to the food hall together as we always had, both of us acting as though I still needed to follow him. He would pretend to try to make food and fail, and I would make a few apples, then we would leave.

Gerrard and I never once talked about it, but we understood each other. We didn't want the ones who were unable to eat to know that we were eating. It was simple for me: I couldn't stand them knowing because I was ashamed of being too scared to help them. For Gerrard it was probably more complex, some strategy in the competition to graduate.

Then one day or night or morning or whatever it was, I noticed that Levin looked a little better. I caught his eye as he came into Franklin's class, and I touched my own belly as if to straighten my robe. He gave a tiny nod, invisible if you weren't watching for it. I let the corners of my mouth turn up so slightly that anyone not staring at my face could have noticed, and Levin blinked twice, then turned away. We were learning how to talk without talking.

I looked around the room. Jordan and Luke seemed less dazed too. Had Levin's roommates helped each other? Were they defying Somiss? My arms prickled with hope and fear. Then I saw Tally shuffling in behind them and my joy died. His eyes were half closed, his face drawn. I glanced away, my heartbeat thudding in my temples.

Shit. How could they be in a room with him, watching him get weaker—and not feed him? Or maybe he was refusing to accept help like Gerrard had? Or maybe they had tried and Somiss had scared them out of it.

Will came in then, leading the way. His cheeks had a little color—and he had gotten stronger, not weaker. But his roommates had not. Rob's skin looked stretched over his bones and Joseph walked slowly, as careful of his balance as an old man. The fourth boy looked worst of all.

I glanced away as everyone sat, wishing Franklin would hurry so we could do something besides look at each other. But then, instead of Franklin, Somiss came out of the wall like water seeping through cloth and stood before us. We all sat up straighter, turning to face him squarely. He looked into our eyes, one at a time. I felt my spine go stiff when he looked at me. When he had finished the circle, he cleared his throat. "Stop helping each other," he said in his graveled whisper, "if you wish to live."

I blinked and Somiss was gone, and Franklin was standing in the same place. He sat, sinking with his usual grace to the floor, crossing his legs so that the soles of his bare feet showed. "First pattern," he said. "Slow, slow, slow."

I closed my eyes wearily, obediently. All the patterns calmed me, but I especially loved this one, the first and simplest. I could feel the air sliding into my lungs as slowly as a snail crawled, then turning in a deep, wheeling circle to start back out. I could feel my thoughts slowing too, then fading into silence. It felt wonderful to stop being afraid. It was like floating on warm water.

"Open your eyes," Franklin said to us, his voice quiet.

But it wasn't *us*. It was me, only me, and when I opened my eyes, Franklin was sitting right beside me on the cool stone. He looked at me sidelong, and before I could say anything, he put his finger to his lips. "You can't see them, but they are all still around us." He spoke to me, but his mouth remained closed, his eyes on mine. I could see an ornate iron gate behind him—and trees beyond it. My heart ached for sky and wind and trees.

Franklin smiled. "It is better not to think about what you miss," he said, and this time I thought I saw his lips moving. "Are you eating?"

I started to speak and he held up one hand. "Just nod or shake your head slightly," he said, "as you do with the others." I nodded, the tiny motion all the boys used.

"Gerrard, too?"

I nodded again.

"I have been waiting for you," he said. "Both of you."

I wanted to ask him what he meant, but my thoughts were faint and slow, and before I could whisper my question, he was gone. The trees and the iron gate melted into nothing. I sat straighter, blinking, waking up. I was back in the chamber. Everyone was practicing the first pattern, their eyes closed. Franklin's face was as placid as a pond on a windless day. I felt a yawn rising in my throat and squelched it. I had never dozed off in class before, and I was grateful that Franklin hadn't noticed. I knew I'd had a dream, too, but I couldn't recall it.

I began the pattern, then found myself looking at the other boys. If I lived through this somehow, I would find a way to go home, and I would kill my father first, and then all of theirs. The thought came too quickly to stop, and my heart leapt and my hands made fists. Then I felt something like peace settling into my stomach and it scared me. I breathed with a ferocity of purpose, erasing my thoughts. All of them.

37

Sadima wrung out the wash rag and shivered, her wet skin chilled. She didn't have to go to Rinka's until noon, and she had a half day free of Franklin and Somiss. There was a tiny knot of worry lying in her belly. Still, she had used every drop of hot water to bathe. Her clothes were clean and hung to dry on the racks above the stove. She reached up to touch the hem of her better dress. It was damp, barely. She pulled it down and slid it over her head, then jerked her comb through her hair. Once she was finished, her wet hair braided neatly, she felt the knot in her stomach tighten.

Somiss had told her they wouldn't be back until midday, and he hadn't given her anything to fair copy while they were gone. He had seemed distracted and nervous. So she had asked Franklin where they were going—and he had lied. It was that simple.

Franklin had said he didn't know. But as they went down the stairs, she had listened. Somiss had asked Franklin if he knew the way. And Franklin had said yes, he was sure of it. Sadima's skin prickled. Where were they going? Back to the cliffs? Why? To search for a stone city from a winter-hearth tale? Probably. Why wouldn't they? It could prove the value of everything they were doing.

Ever since the day in the woods, Somiss had gotten better, sleeping and eating more—and he was kinder to Franklin. He even spoke to her now and then, and she wasn't sure whether she was glad or sorry. She also noticed him watching her sometimes, and it made her uneasy. Franklin had told her not to worry, that it only meant Somiss liked her, was accepting her. She hoped so. It was about time.

On an impulse, Sadima opened the doors to the little balcony and stepped out into the morning sun. The street wasn't crowded, so she threw out her bathwater, then just stood in the light, enjoying the fresh air for a long time. Then she went back in and cleaned the kitchen and swept the floors. When she was finished, she found herself standing in the hallway, staring at Somiss's door.

She reached out and touched the door handle. She slid her fingers around it and stood, wondering if he would have some way of knowing that she had opened it. She lifted her hand, then put it back, then lifted it again. If he did have a way to know, he would make her leave. She sighed, wondering if that would be the best thing anyway. But then she imagined never seeing Franklin again, and she stepped back.

The knock on the front door was careful, quiet, and it startled Sadima into gasping. Hands shaking, she smoothed her dress, trying to still her heart as she went back into the sitting room, chiding herself. Somiss would not *knock*. He could not see through walls.

Sadima opened the door. A heavy, round-faced woman blinked, then cleared her throat.

"I was told to ask after Somiss," she said stiffly.

Sadima nodded. "He is not here. Can you come back tomorrow?"

The woman shook her head. "Maude buys honey off me and she said to bring the old songs when we had time. I got an hour, no more."

Sadima opened the door wider. She introduced herself.

"Hannah," the woman said, clasping Sadima's fingers so hard that it hurt. "I know six of them old songs. Which one do you want to hear first?"

Sadima stepped back and Hannah came in. When she saw the table, she headed for it, pulling back a chair to sit down.

"We walk nearly three hours to get here," she said bluntly. "The ponies carry them honey tins, but we walk."

Sadima nodded. Weary legs were something she understood very well. "I'll never learn six in an hour, but I want to learn them all. I will pay you a half copper for each of them, if you'll come back until we're finished."

Hannah sat up straighter. "Done. I'll come back with what you don't get this time," she said. "Which one to start?"

"Tell me what they are for," Sadima said.

Hannah held up her hands, ticking off fingers as she spoke. "I got one for bellyache, one to lengthen a life, one for birthing, one to bring the seed up, one for a lame pony, and . . ." She stopped to think, then arched her brows. "And one that's a love charm. My mother says that's how she got my father. She would have got him somehow, if it hadn't worked. Stubborn woman, my mother."

Sadima smiled at the warm affection in Hannah's voice. "One of them is to lengthen lives?"

Hannah nodded. "My mother is sixty-four years old and she sings the little song to herself every morning. Her mother has made it to eighty-two, or so she says, and that's rare enough. They both say great-gram passed ninety."

Sadima hid her reaction. No one got that old. But women usually fibbed in the other direction, saying they were younger than they were. "Does the one for bellyaches work?"

Hannah laughed aloud. "I don't know. The little song takes your mind off it at least. My sister and I had easy birthings, and my mother was in there singing over us the whole time." Hannah smiled again. "I like all the tunes well enough. Bellyaches, then? Or what?"

"Long life," Sadima said, and Hannah sang the melody. Her voice was clear, and her pitch was as perfect as a meadowlark's. Then, without asking, she began over again. After she had sung the melody five or six times, she added the words.

It was a long song—much longer than Rinka's—and

Sadima wished she could write the words down the way Somiss did. She forced herself to concentrate, closing her eyes as Hannah sang the song over and over. By the fourth time through, Sadima joined her on the first verse and managed the first few lines before she got mixed up. By the twentieth time, she could sing all four verses so long as Hannah began each one. By the thirtieth time, she could sing the song through on her own. After she had done it twice, Hannah put her hands on the table and pushed herself upright. "I'd best go."

Sadima walked her to the door, then spent the rest of her time alone singing the song to herself as she worked. When the sun was close to its noon zenith, she opened the balcony doors again and watched the street. Franklin and Somiss did not come. She finally left for work, singing the song to herself as she walked.

Rinka laughed when she told her about meeting Hannah.

"The honey vendors. Yes, I know them a little—I buy from them sometimes. The whole family is a bit odd, but they are honest and they work hard."

"I hope you don't mind if I sing it a little while I work?" Sadima asked.

Rinka laughed. "Sing it a hundred times. Perhaps we will both live longer."

Later, when they were both working with a new batch of curds, Sadima thought again about Hannah, the way she had talked about her mother. She looked up at Rinka. "You are married?"

Rinka nodded. "I was. To a good man. He died five years ago."

"Would you tell me about love?" Sadima asked quietly.

Rinka looked up.

"My mother died bearing me," Sadima told her, and it hurt just to say it. "I have never asked anyone. . . ." She had no idea how to go on. But Rinka smiled. And she began talking in a low voice, sweet and heavy with both love and grief.

When Sadima asked her more questions, she answered bluntly, honestly, without modesty or embarrassment. "It's Franklin, isn't it?" Rinka asked her.

Sadima nodded. "How did you know?"

"When you say anything about him, even the smallest thing, your voice softens."

By the time Sadima got home from work, it was dark and Franklin met her by the street gate. "Somiss is in a terrible temper," he said, and Sadima knew this would not be the night to try to tell him what was in her heart.

"Where did you go this morning?"

Franklin shook his head as they went inside. "He forbade me to tell you or anyone else."

Sadima went up the stairs without looking back at him, then stopped at the top. "Franklin, your loyalty to him is—"

"I know it is hard for you to understand," he interrupted, whispering, coming up the stairs two at a time so that she would hear him. "Somiss is all I have."

"No," Sadima said. "He isn't." And for the second time, she kissed *him*. They stood unmoving after that, then Franklin brushed his lips on her forehead and stepped back. She saw a flight of feelings in his dark eyes before he turned and went in, tiptoeing. Sadima followed, watching him glance toward the hallway every few seconds.

She made stew and rekindled the fire. Then she told him about the song, and he brought out paper and pen and wrote the words down, using letters to build each of the words she had memorized. Sadima watched very closely. It was one letter per sound, sometimes two, once in a rare while, three. The letter that stood for the sound of hissing was shaped like a crawling snake. It was the first letter of her own name. And, she thought, the first and last of Somiss's.

"Thank you," Franklin whispered when they finished. He leaned closer to her, inhaled, then drew back and smiled, his eyes shiny. Tears? "You smell like soap," he said. "Did you use all the water?"

Sadima nodded. "I will get more first thing in the—"

"I think I will fetch some tonight," Franklin cut her off, gesturing in the general direction of Somiss's room. "He might want a drink later. Do you mind making the copies so I have a present for him if he comes out?"

Sadima sighed, then shook her head. "How many?"

Franklin hesitated. "Probably three. Two to mark up and one to save."

Sadima waited until he had gone. Then she stood at the end of the hall, listening. There was no sound coming from Somiss's room. Maybe he was asleep. Sitting at the table, she set to work—but she made four copies, not three. She hid the extra one in her paint box, folded small. When Franklin came back, he took one of the copies down the hall to show Somiss.

After Franklin had gone to bed, Sadima lit a candle, then sat on her pallet, staring at the extra copy. She knew the words, what they sounded like, each and every one. She whispered them, staring at each group of letters before she slipped the paper back in with her paints. It took a long time for her to go to sleep that night. It was a lie for a lie, in a way, a secret for a secret, but that brought her no comfort at all.

In the darkness, she was wakened by footsteps in the sitting room, then the rustle of paper and the dim flickering of candlelight. She stood and slid along the wall, listening. Holding her breath, she leaned just far enough to see, then duck back. Somiss? After a long moment, she heard his door close, and she lit her candle again.

Three copies of the long-life song were on the table now, in the stack of work Franklin had finished. Why would Somiss have brought them out now, in the middle of the night?

Sadima stared at the writing, then whirled around and went back to the kitchen for her copy. Trembling, she put them side by side. Somiss had recopied the song completely, three times over. All three of his copies were exactly alike but different from hers. He had changed it. Why? To keep the real song from her and Franklin?

38

It got harder to eat. Not harder to make the food,
I don't mean that. Making food got easier. I could make five
or six of my favorite meals without too much thought. It
was just hard to convince myself that I had the *right* to eat.

The starving boys were in the food hall every second
they weren't in class. Tally and all of Will's roommates sat
dull-eyed and sad on the benches, standing up now and
then to try the stone again. They were scarecrows.

It was torture for me to walk past them, make food, and
walk out, knowing their eyes were following me, their
mouths full of bitter saliva. I stopped eating. But after two
of Franklin's classes had come and gone, it seemed stupid.
My not eating wasn't helping anyone.

After the next class, I ran to the food hall. It was empty.

Sweating, glancing at the door, I made enough cheese and fruit to carry back. I gathered it all in my robe-front, then, holding the hem gathered up in one hand to make a sack, I ran back to the room, my legs bared the way Gerrard's had been that first time.

He looked up as I came in. I saw an odd expression on his face. He got up and washed his face and hands, then left. It felt strange not to follow him, but there was no reason to pretend anymore.

I laid the food out on my desk. There were no mice in the tunnels, no insects. Gerrard wouldn't touch it, and if anyone else somehow found our room and took it, I knew I would only be glad. So for a while I managed to eat without going to the food hall at all. I could not stop thinking about the starving boys anyway, but it was a selfish relief not to have to see them.

Coming back from the next class, for no reason I can name, I turned down a passageway I had never been in before and ran, just ran, straight down it, counting the branching tunnels I passed so I could find my way back. The floor began to slope upward and I ran faster, running until I had to stagger to a stop. Then I leaned against the wall, my chest heaving, staring at my own feet.

Running had peeled off the last of the scabs. The skin was mostly healed, just still pink and shiny. My feet had become tough as hooves. My skin had thickened where the robe rubbed. Nothing hurt. My eyes filled with tears. It felt unbelievably good to run, to feel strong again.

Going back into the room, I turned the fish-shaped handle

silently. Gerrard was there. He did not move, and he gave no sign that he had heard me enter. I lit my lamp and lay down on my bed to stare at the dark stone ceiling.

Six of us were eating. Six of us were getting stronger, not weaker: Me, Gerrard, Will, Jordan, Levin, and Luke. Maybe if I could talk them into helping, if we all hid food everywhere, we could get away with it. I could talk to them and . . . When? Where? The food hall wasn't safe, and I had no idea where their rooms were. I felt a clammy sweat rise on my forehead. Was that why the wizards separated us? Was that why there was always one to walk us to class—and never the same one? Shit. The academy was old. They had gotten very good at this.

I turned on my side, wishing I could talk to Gerrard, but he was sitting with his back to me as always, reading. And the wizards probably had some way of listening. Maybe they were always watching us. I shook my head, feeling foolish. Why would they bother? They knew how scared we were. I stood up and walked two steps toward the door to see, sidelong, if Gerrard's eyes were open or if he was deep in the silence inside his own skull.

But Gerrard was reading *Songs of the Elders*—the book in a language I had never seen. His lips were moving slightly, and as I watched, he turned a page.

I went back to sit on my cot, and eventually, I lay down and went to sleep. My dreams were ugly. I saw people begging for food, their faces hollow, their teeth black and broken.

When a wizard came to pound on the door, I got up and pissed and splashed my face and followed him down the corridor, glad to escape my dreams. When I got to class, Will and his dull-eyed roommates were sitting close together. Jordan, Levin, and Luke were there. But Tally wasn't. And Levin's eyes were red and hollow.

"Third pattern," Franklin said, and we all obeyed him, like whipped dogs. I closed my eyes and tried to erase everything. But this time, I couldn't. I glanced at Gerrard. Had he even noticed?

"Please lady, please lady, please lady . . ." The little boy's voice was rough and hoarse. Sadima watched him. He hadn't seen her yet. Now that she had a few coins in her dress pockets, she had not been able to ignore all the children's pleas. And this one had caught her heart. He had a cheerful demeanor, and a terrible scar. Someone had tried to cut his throat, the knife sliding up behind one ear as he fought for his life.

The boy's eyes hooked hers for an instant and he grinned, then started toward her at a stiff-legged trot. Sadima gave him a little nod, and then pretended to ignore him as she walked a half block farther. He followed, his hand out, keeping up his beggar's song. As they walked, she sorted through her pocket until she found a half copper to put in the boy's hand.

In an eyeblink, he tipped his palm so the coin slid off, dropping into his other hand, held low and close to his belly. His right hand still stiffly extended, still singing his plea, he slid the half copper into his trouser pocket with his left. Then he winked and followed Sadima another half block, pleading. She finally pretended to shoo him off, scowling as he winked again, then turned back, dragging his feet, his face contorted with feigned disappointment. He was very convincing. He was very clever. Once Franklin had explained it to her—that the older children would be watching to see if he got anything—Sadima had learned to play her part.

Quickening her step, fighting an urge to glance backward, Sadima left the beggar boy behind and turned down an unfamiliar street. She had been taking a different route home each day, walking farther and farther into the North End shop district before heading back to Market Square. The lettered signs gave her a chance to practice. She could sound out some of them now, and every day she memorized one that she couldn't read and copied the letters once she was home.

Then, when both Somiss and Franklin were in their rooms for the night, she used her copy of the long-life song to figure out the sound each letter made. A few words had defeated her, but not many.

Sadima glanced at the signs on the other side of the street. There was one with smaller lettering and more words than most. Sadima crossed between two merchant wagons. The second driver grinned at her and made a low whistle between his teeth. She ignored him, staring at the sign. Once she had memorized the letters, she glanced inside the half-open door.

It was a shop for the wealthy, no mistake about that. There were no shelves stacked with roughly made tunics and trousers, no bins of hand-shaped soap or piles of old clothing being sold for half pennies. There was only a heavy, dark-wood table with sweets and tea on it and a few chairs of wrought brass. The goods must be very valuable, locked in some back room. She wouldn't know what they sold until she sounded out the letters on the sign, if she could.

The sun was low in the sky as Sadima walked on. She cut across a narrow street, then turned at the corner and walked faster. She stepped off the boardwalk once or twice to get around groups of people who had met friends and stopped to talk.

Halfway home, she began wrestling with an idea. She had seven coins in her pocket this evening. Sales were increasing, Rinka said. People liked the twice-boiled cheeses. Somiss—and Franklin—would be expecting five coins.

It was getting dusky and chilly by the time Sadima real-ized she had gone so far north she had ended up on the wrong side of Market Square. She spotted Franklin, still sit-ting at his little table beneath Maude's awning. In the wan-ing light, she could see a woman seated opposite him. He was holding her hand, palm up.

Sadima looked at him and aimed her thoughts the way she would have with her goats, the way she had with Shy. *Franklin?*

"Wait for me," he called, looking up. Then he turned back to his customer.

Sadima shivered. It had worked. Or had it? Maybe he had just looked up by chance. She stared at him and said his name in her thoughts again. He continued talking to the woman.

Idling, watching the dwindling crowds, Sadima noticed a fancy carriage and recognized the woman sitting primly on the tufted velvet seat. Kary Blae. The dark-wood carriage didn't look so amazing now that Sadima had seen so many of them. But it was still very fine. A different pair of horses was pulling it, long-maned, shining black mares, perfectly matched. Kary Blae waved and Sadima waved back, amazed that the woman remembered her.

"Sadima?" She turned. Franklin was walking toward her, smiling. "What brings you to this side of the square?"

She blushed, unable to tell him the truth. If Somiss ever found out she was teaching herself to read, he would be furious. She shook her head and put her thoughts firmly on being chilly and a little hungry, in case Franklin was trying to listen to them. "I've begun walking different ways. The beggars are getting to know me for a soft touch now."

Franklin nodded. "I give them something now and then too. Be very careful that you don't tell Somiss."

Sadima sighed. "Would he really be so jealous of a half copper now and then?"

Franklin nodded. "With me, of course. With you? Probably. He thinks of everything we earn as his to use for the work."

Sadima felt her skin prickle, but she nodded, watching his face. He looked tired. She started walking, and he fell in beside her. Then he leaned close to whisper. "Did you see any king's guards this evening?"

Sadima glanced at him. "I don't think so. What do they look like?"

Franklin gestured, lifting one hand over his own head. "They are big men wearing dark tunics and helmets of polished nickel. They carry staffs and wear swords."

Sadima shook her head. "No. I saw no one like that on the streets. Why would there be?"

Franklin looked around. "Somiss said the king had sent guards to look for him."

There was something in his voice that told her he doubted it. "Is it true?" Sadima asked.

Franklin shrugged. "His father hates what he is doing, and—"

"So he says," Sadima interrupted, irritated. Was it impossible for them to talk for more than a moment without discussing Somiss?

Franklin frowned, and she looked away.

As they came out of the trees and started up the boardwalk, walking in silence, Sadima saw that the balcony doors were slightly ajar. There was a lamp burning inside. Was Somiss working at the table? There would be no chance to tell Franklin about her extra coins, then. Not tonight.

They crossed the cobbled street, and when Franklin held the door for her, she saw that his hand was trembling. Did he believe Somiss—and was he that scared of the guards?

"Franklin," Sadima began, but angry shouts cut her off. She turned. A boy of nine or ten was running down the stairs, his mouth bleeding through the fingers of his right hand. He pitched forward when he jumped down the last three steps, then somehow managed to stay on his feet. Franklin grabbed at him and swung him around, asking him if he was all right, but the boy broke free and kept running, sliding on the stone floor, almost falling again as he turned into the street. An instant later Somiss shoved past them, sprinting for the street gate, turning the same way the boy had.

– 40 –

Tally was not in the next class either. Nor was Joseph.
Levin's other roommates were there. So were Will's, but they
were barely able to walk. Will staggered along between Rob
and the only boy whose name I had never learned, one arm
around each of their waists. They were both so much taller
than he was that it looked impossible, but he was managing
to keep them both upright. I could see the strain on his face,
but I was too scared to stand up and help him.

Franklin was staring at the stone above our heads. Was
he trying to erase his thoughts? Did it work every time for
him? Maybe his dreams were as shitty as mine. I hoped so.
Or was he so used to this that it didn't really bother him
anymore? Or maybe, I thought suddenly, he was like the
ponies. Maybe he had no choice.

Rob staggered and fell to his knees. I started to get up and I saw Jordan and Leigh shift their weight and half rise. Then we all saw Somiss in the entryway and sank back down. Levin put his back to Somiss, and Jordan raised his chin so that he was looking almost straight up at the invisible ceiling arched above the reach of the torchlight.

Franklin didn't acknowledge Somiss either. He made us start in the third pattern, and began to speak in his calm, steady voice. I focused on his words the way a drowning man stares at a boat in the distance. Then, after we had done three more patterns, he spoke again.

"There are three gates inside your mind," Franklin said quietly. "Or more."

Our collective breath hitched, then fell back into unison. This was new.

"The first gate leads to your careless thoughts," he said, "the ones you have learned to quiet."

The words came into my ears, but they made little sense, and I don't think any of us understood at all. Or wanted to. No matter how hard I tried, I couldn't stop staring at the two weak boys, their heads down, their shoulders slumped, bones showing through their skin. And where were Tally and Joseph? Were they lying on their cots, too weak to move? Or were they dead?

Breathing with Franklin, I kept looking into the shadows, wondering if Somiss was still there, still watching. When class was over and Will waited for his roommates to struggle to their feet, not one of us dared lend a hand. We were all scared witless, shitless, heartless. I was so ashamed I felt sick. But I could not make myself go help. I glanced at Gerrard. His face looked as hard as the stone walls.

I walked back to the room slowly, thinking. That evening I went early to the food hall and stood alone in front of the huge gem. I closed my eyes and worked until the image was perfect. My hair damp with sweat from the effort, I finally put my hands on the stone and a complicated supper blinked into being. It was crab cakes, honeyed salmon, buttered sweet corn, and roasted potatoes with dill.

I sat without touching it, listening for footfalls in the tunnel. If Somiss wanted to kill me, he could, but I was going to feed *someone* supper. I glanced at the arched entrance, hoping that Tally would summon his strength and come shuffling in the door, or Joseph or Rob or Will's other roommate. I had found my courage, and somehow, my decency. I would give the food to whoever came in, and Somiss could eat shit and die for all I cared.

But no one came.

It was all right, I lied to myself. I was going to do this every day after class, and I would leave the food here, on the table. I would tell Levin I was doing it. And Will. So they could tell the others. I sat until I ached from the hard stone bench.

When I finally stood up, leaving the tray on the table, my filthy robe clung to my back. I reached over my shoulder to jerk at the cloth. The sour smell of my own armpit made me wince. We smelled like barnyard animals kept in a small and filthy pen. We were all cowards, especially me.

I had been able to eat before anyone else. Had I helped them? No. I felt tears jab at my eyes. I had been a coward too long, and it was too late.

Footsteps made me jerk my head up. Levin came in, eyeing the food I had made and had not touched, then walked past me without speaking. I stood, uneasy, knowing I should say something to him, should ask about Tally. But he was standing before the stone, and I could see his shoulders tense.

Levin took a long time to lift his hands and step forward. But when he did, there was a plate of food—broccoli and venison. He didn't bother with silverware—maybe he had tried and hadn't been able to make any. Or maybe he had never thought of it. He sat at one of the other tables and ate fast and in silence, without so much as glancing at me. Then, when he stood up, he met my eyes. His were glassy with tears. "Why would they do this?"

I shrugged and shook my head, meaning to tell him that I would leave food for Tally and the others every day, but I couldn't say it. I couldn't say it because I wasn't sure I meant it. Levin swept his tray and the plate onto the floor. The bits of food sparkled and disappeared. Then he left. I started to follow him, then slowed and went to my room. I barely slept that night, hating myself, the wizards, my father. But mostly myself.

At Franklin's next class, there were only eight of us again—Tally and Joseph were still missing. Will walked between Rob and his other roommate, struggling to steady them as they slid their filthy bare feet along the floor.

Levin's face was bleak, his eyelids rubbed raw. I just sat still, listening to what sounded like a sea storm roaring inside my head. I closed my eyes, and when Franklin asked us to breathe, I let the movement of my own chest rock me back and forth.

Leaving, Gerrard was the first one out as always. I managed to position myself behind Levin. He glanced back at me, then leaned close for an instant. "Tally died, Hahp. He *died*."

All the way back to the room, I tried to figure it out. This was the best I could do: The wizards were going to kill all but one of us. They would tell our families that we had become part of the academy. Which would be literally true. I shivered. There had to be a cavern somewhere, full of bones.

I dreamed about it that night. A stone room full of bones, all of them jumbled, some broken, a messy pile of boys' skeletons, indistinguishable one from another.

− 41 −

"**Should we go after him?" Sadima asked.**

"Not you," Franklin said, pulling her upstairs. "I'll come back as soon as I can." He opened the door. "Stay inside. Don't let anyone in. If anyone asks about Somiss, shout through the door that he left here days ago."

Sadima nodded and went in, closing the door and barring it, listening to Franklin's footfalls as he went back down the stairs and ran to the street gate. Trembling, she walked to the kitchen and made herself write down the letters she had memorized, using a single sheet of paper she had bought for herself. Then she pulled out the song for long life and turned, meaning to go sit on her pallet and sound out the words on the sign to keep herself busy. It was then that she saw the blood on the floor.

Sadima wrung out a washrag and wiped it up, then noticed more. And more. Her eyes stinging with tears, Sadima walked through the place, wiping up the spatters, imagining the scene. The boy had run one way, then back, then had crawled beneath the table. The spatters there became round drops, all falling close together as he hid, then scattered again as he turned, shrinking back from whatever side of the table Somiss was on. At one end, some of the drops were smeared in a long, straight line. Somiss had dragged him out and slapped him hard. There were pin-dots of blood in an arc on the wall.

Sadima washed out the rag, throwing the pink water to the street below when there was a long enough gap between passersby. Then she stood still, her arms crossed, turning one way, then the other, scanning the crowds, shivering, desperate to see Franklin. But he did not come.

Sadima went back inside. She straightened the table and set the chairs back. Her hands unsteady, she hid her papers. Then, for the first time, she glanced down the hall. Somiss's door was standing open.

Her first thought was to close it so he wouldn't have a second reason to be furious. Then she hesitated and stood, two steps away, glancing back toward the hall door. What if he remembered leaving it open and found it closed? Then she decided to look in, just for a second. But if he came in, angry as he was, and saw her in his room? Involuntarily, her right hand rose to cover her mouth.

Sadima made a sudden decision. She ran to the front door, opened it, and looked out. No one was coming. She closed the door, barred it, then whirled around, running back down the little hall.

Somiss's room was far bigger than Franklin's. There was a bed, the linens heaped, one corner of a blanket trailing on the floor. There was a table, too, centered against the wall beneath a narrow, shuttered window. There were stacks of paper on it, and burnt candle stubs. Sadima wrinkled her nose. The room smelled bad, and she could feel the grit of unswept dirt beneath her bare feet. She walked to the table and glanced at the papers, then turned to leave. She took two steps toward the door, then stopped to stare. There was blood on the sheets.

The sudden sound of voices on the stairs jerked her backward. She was out of the room, closing the door in a heartbeat. She slid the bar up and out of the way, then ran. By the time the apartment door opened, she was back in the sitting room, pretending to straighten the table.

"Why did you let the little bastard get past you?" Somiss was demanding, coming in the door. His movements were spasmed, tight with anger, his eyes narrowed. He seemed not to see Sadima at all as he walked past her to the kitchen arch.

Franklin met her eyes for a moment. "Stay clear," he whispered, while Somiss was faced away from them. Sadima nodded, but Somiss was already turning, pacing toward her. She pressed her back against the wall. It was still damp from the washrag.

Somiss shoved one of the chairs. It skittered on the smooth floor like a kicked dog trying to get away from him. She slid along the wall toward the kitchen, stopping when Somiss looked up. "You're the ones who let him go!" he yelled at her, then lifted his chin to glare at Franklin. "He ran right past you both. You didn't even try to grab him."

"He just looked like a beggar, Somiss," Sadima said. "And I had no idea what—"

"What?" Somiss interrupted, jerking around to look at her. "You could see he was bleeding and you heard me shout—did you think I had been playing hide-and-seek with him?"

Sadima eased one more sideways step toward the kitchen, then turned to stone when Somiss paced past her. His shoulder hit hers hard enough to hurt. He didn't notice.

"Are you sure it was—," Franklin began.

"Have you never looked in a mirror?" Somiss cut him off. "That boy was a Marsham."

Sadima slipped past him, exhaling when she finally passed through the arch and out of sight, into the kitchen. She stood still as a fence post, then, listening.

"Perhaps," Franklin said. "But you can't be—"

"I know what a Marsham looks like," Somiss spat. "My father buys ten or twelve of them a year."

"But what would a boy that age—"

"Don't be so thick-headed, Franklin," Somiss shouted. "My father sent him to *find* me." Sadima flinched at the sound of him hitting the wall with his fist. "The boy probably asked in the marketplace and someone showed him the way. Maybe Maude."

"Just calm down enough to—," Franklin began.

"Calm down?" Somiss hissed. "I should have killed him. *You* should have." There was a long silence, then the sound of a fist striking the wall again. "Before sundown, my father will know where I am."

— 42 —

The chamber seemed too big. Gerrard, me, Levin, Luke, Will, and Jordan—we barely looked at one another, sitting in our shrunken, sad little huddle of six. Or five, really— Gerrard always stayed off to one side, sitting as Franklin did, so loose jointed now that the soles of his feet faced upward. None of the rest of us could do it. I shivered. Where were Will's roommates? Weak in bed . . . or gone?

"Today we will approach the first gate," Franklin said. He started us off, working our way up through the patterns. It was automatic now, at least for me. I no longer needed to count or think about it at all. Most of the time I found myself only half listening to Franklin, slitting my eyes to stare into the shadows in case Somiss was watching.

"First pattern," Franklin said, and we all fell back into

the simple, slow-in, slow-out. I closed my eyes and relaxed into it, feeling the calmness seep into my body. I knew it was false, a lie, but I welcomed it anyway. When I opened my eyes, I saw Luke looking past me, his face hard, his upper lip lifted a little, like a dog snarling. I turned my head just enough to see Gerrard staring back at him. If we had been in a real school, I would be expecting a fight at the next chance.

My stomach tightened. Shit. How could they be thinking about who was going to—

"Close your eyes," Franklin said quietly, and I glanced at him. His own eyes were closed. Did he know we all watched the walls, trying to spot Somiss? Or maybe I had imagined him saying it. It would not be the first time. My own thoughts seemed louder than real voices sometimes. Franklin opened his eyes and I closed mine.

In the darkness behind my eyelids, I could feel the air as it slid in and out of me, wheeling the slow circle. My usual reverie began. If I was the one to graduate, first I would kill my father. Then I would run away where no one could ever find me again—not even the wizards. I did want to live. I did not want to become one of them.

"Move your thoughts from your mind into your belly," Franklin said.

I heard him, but it made no sense. I heard the others shifting on the stone. Gates and belly thoughts and breathing patterns. Was all of this a test? A joke? Were they going to kill all but one of us and then teach *him* the real magic? I stared at the darkness inside my eyelids again, trying to calm myself.

"Anger is a good place to start," Franklin said. "Angry thoughts often live in your belly."

I opened my eyes and found him looking at me. Then I blinked and his eyes were closed. I had no belly thoughts. Maybe anger? But feelings weren't the same as thoughts. Were they? I wasn't sure. But I found myself listening to my own thoughts as though I were a mildly interesting stranger. It didn't scare me. I was glad to have a conversation to keep from thinking about the boys who were not here. The stranger didn't want to think about them either. Was I supposed to hear the interesting stranger talking from inside my belly?

"Exactly."

I opened my eyes and saw Franklin sitting still, his eyes closed.

"Now move your thoughts to your belly," he said and I saw his lips move. "Close your eyes."

I heard the others fidgeting, scratching themselves, sighing. Someone coughed. I shifted on the stone, the robe rubbing the slick pink skin where the scabs had been. I wanted a bath and a soft shirt and trousers—and shoes. I wanted shoes. And I wanted to see the sky.

I thought about my father, and that began another of my familiar daydreams. I imagined him sitting in the grand leather chair in his office. I pictured myself standing before him in a black robe, his eyes flickering over my face, a little sweat on his brow. My father, with his arrogance and his bully's heart, would one day stand before me and sweat and he would be *polite*.

"Hahp," he would say to me, and his voice would be

quiet, respectful. "Will you stay for supper? It would mean a lot to your mother."

I imagined myself staring at him, refusing to respond to his question until he was uneasy, glancing past me, a little scared.

"If you cannot, she will understand," he would say, pushing his chair back to dismiss me. But I would just stand there, staring at him so that the sweat on his brow began to bead.

"It is good to see you," he would say, not knowing what else to talk about.

"How is Mother?" I would ask him, but I would already know. She would be happy, because he would have been kind to her, because he was afraid of me. And he would know that perhaps I would let him live, if she stayed happy.

"She is fine," he would say, carefully.

And suddenly I could hear my father's fear-tightened voice rising upward from my belly to my ears.

"Your brother will be here for Winterfeast," he said. "He said to tell you that he was proud to be the brother of a wizard." He paused. "As I am proud to have you as my son."

"What?" I asked him.

"I am proud to have you as my son. Very proud," he said, and his voice rose from my own belly.

"What?" I demanded, intent on making him say it again.

"You can go with the others, Hahp," I heard Franklin say.

I felt like someone had jerked me out from under water. I gasped, opening my eyes. I was the only one in the chamber. Franklin reached out and cupped my cheek in his hand. He smiled at me, the way a grandfather smiles. Then he disappeared.

43

"Does Rinka close her shop for King's Day?" Franklin
asked.

Sadima nodded, set down her quill, and stretched. Then
she leaned forward to turn up the wick in the lamp. "I don't
have to go at all tomorrow. She said there's a procession?"

Franklin smiled without looking up from his work, and
Sadima knew she had sounded both awed and eager, like
the farm girl she was. She lowered her head to hide her
blush. "How long before Somiss is back?"

Franklin shrugged. "I am not sure he will be here at all
today. He's a royal—the whole family walks behind the
king."

Sadima exhaled. "So is everything mended? His father
won't—?"

"Not today," Franklin said. "His mother wept and pleaded and convinced his father that Somiss will go back to wherever she said he was tomorrow after the feasts and stay out of trouble. She would say anything to make King's Day go smoothly. She always has clothing made for the event, carriages built; it takes months for her servants to plan her famous entertainments. It's very important to her and Somiss's father. Sometimes the king himself attends."

Sadima nodded, then bent back over her work, thinking. Almost two days without Somiss. There would never be a better time. She glanced up. "Has he ever said any more about that poor little boy?"

Franklin shook his head. "No. But I know he was at least half right. The boy was sent by his father. Some of the South End Marshams had to be bought off to keep the boy quiet. My cousins said Somiss's father had hired him to find me, to ask me what I knew about Som—"

"Your cousins?" Sadima interrupted.

Franklin took a drink of the tea she had made him. "Somiss's mother took care of it this time, sold a ring or something to pay the bribe. She doesn't want his father finding him any more than we do."

"Your cousins knew the boy?" Sadima repeated.

He set the tea down. "The Marshams are a big family."

Sadima looked into his eyes. "Somiss said his father buys—"

"Yes," Franklin said.

Sadima waited for him to say more. It took a long moment of silence before he looked at her. "My parents sold me to Somiss's father. The money kept them fed and warm for five winters."

Sadima watched as Franklin's feelings flickered through his dark eyes. "They *sold* you?"

Franklin shrugged, and she suddenly remembered the blood in the bedroom, on the walls. The bloody sheet was long gone. She had looked, first chance. Somiss hadn't washed it. He had gotten rid of it. He was a violent man. Had be been a cruel boy? Had he beaten Franklin? Would anyone have cared? "Somiss scares me," she said aloud.

Franklin shook his head. "You have to understand. A boy like him, brilliant and willful—and spoiled. Try to imagine never even having to wait for anything you wanted, what it would do to you, to the way you understood the world."

"Everyone waits for supper," she said, angry at him without knowing why. None of this was his fault. What kind of parents *sold* their children?

"No," Franklin answered, sliding a finished sheet to one side. He laid down his quill. "He never waited for anything. Meals were made and served all day long in case anyone was hungry. And if the cook had made crab cakes and Somiss wanted honeyed lamb, they would throw his crab cakes to the pigs, and six Marsham boys and four cooks would be running to find a lamb to braise. They would spit it live if it saved a moment or two."

Sadima blinked. He wasn't joking.

Franklin exhaled and flexed his quill-stiffened hand. "If he wanted a puppy, the servants brought one in moments.

If it was brown and he wanted a white one with long ears, twenty grown men and six houseboys leapt to go find a white one with long ears. If it took too long, or if he was in a bad temper over something else, they were beaten."

"And you were his companion and his friend," Sadima said wonderingly. "Did you ask for things and the servants would—"

"No," Franklin interrupted. "You don't understand. I was a puppy. He picked me out when we were very small. There were about twenty little boys, all of us scrubbed and scared. He found me amusing because everything in the house astounded me so. Then, later, he found he could talk to me about anything. His mind . . ." Franklin paused and gestured broadly. "Everything interested him. I was three when they told me I had to keep him calm, keep him happy."

Sadima was quiet, trying to imagine it. "Three? Did you parents just take you there and leave you and . . ." She trailed off because he was nodding. "Weren't they afraid that some harm might come to you?"

Franklin dipped his quill and went back to work. "Papers were signed. My parents were paid well."

"I was going to ask you something tonight," Sadima said.

Franklin kept writing.

"Please," she said quietly. He looked up. "I was going to ask if you would save money with me, secretly, a little here and there, so that one day we could buy a little farm some-where." She saw his eyes widen and kept talking before he could interrupt. "I have a different question now. What would you cost?"

Franklin frowned. "What?"

"If we saved our money, together, to buy your freedom, what would Somiss make us pay?"

Franklin was silent. He looked into her eyes for a long moment, then stared at the wall. "I don't think he would consider it," he said finally.

"You can ask him," Sadima said.

Franklin shook his head. "He won't. He needs me to help with the academy."

Sadima blinked. "Academy?"

He bit at his lip. "He forbids me to tell you. If you say anything—"

"Franklin!" Sadima said. "We could try. We could ask and—"

Footsteps on the stairs made them both fall silent. Franklin picked up his quill and went back to work. Sadima spread out her finished papers, then picked up the quill knife and sharpened her point. An instant later the door banged open.

Sadima flinched. But Somiss wasn't angry, he was excited. And he was carrying something beneath his arm.

"I was on my way to Ferrin Hill when a Gypsy woman ran across the street to give me this." He put a slim book on the table.

Franklin pulled the book closer and opened it. His eyes widened. "It's their tongue? So they do have a written form?"

Somiss nodded. "They do. It's a big secret. And this is a book of what she called 'the elders' songs.' Guess why she gave it to me."

Franklin shrugged. "The last time I spoke with Gypsies, I was in bed for a fortnight. I have no guesses."

"She gave it to me because she was angry at her father," Somiss said. "He arranged the attack."

Franklin's eyes narrowed. "But she's a *Gypsy*, Somiss. They barely talked to us, and none of them would even hint at having anything written down in their language. So why—"

"When we were in their camp," Somiss interrupted, "do you remember the child that nearly stumbled into the fire pit?"

Franklin looked puzzled, then nodded. "Oh. Yes. I caught him and set him back from the coals."

"That child is her son. She said she begged her father not to harm us. He wouldn't listen." Somiss laughed. "So she wanted to get back at him. Noble motive, is it not?" He held up the book. "She said she copied this from several other books, choosing the songs since that was what we had asked about first. She sewed the binding herself." He nudged the book with one index finger. "It looks it. But her father won't miss it—he doesn't know it exists."

"Can you translate it?" Franklin asked. Sadima heard the eagerness in his voice.

"I have to," Somiss said, opening to the first page. "It will take time. But all the rhymes and stories we have transliterated will probably give me a reference point. I will have to find more, and it might take a year or two, but I will manage it."

Sadima watched, wondering if the Gypsy woman was the one who had stared at Franklin by the well. If she was also an Eridian, she believed that the fruits of the mind were for all to share.

"Start copying it today," Somiss said. "The first thing we need is four copies—one of them to keep hidden and safe."

Sadima saw Franklin nod and knew that the safe place was a new one and was part of their shared secrets.

Somiss straightened and glanced at Sadima. He had no more expression in his eyes than he would have had glancing at a chair. She turned and went into the kitchen.

"I have to go," she heard him saying to Franklin. "My mother will want me bathed, shorn, perfumed, and wrapped in deep green velvet to walk behind the king tomorrow afternoon."

When Sadima heard the front door open, then close, she came back into the sitting room. Franklin sat staring at the closed door for a long moment. Then he rose and came back with a fresh quill and another inkpot. He got paper from the cupboard and sat down to work. Sadima watched him for a long time. Then she sat down.

"Consider what I said," she said evenly. He looked up. "Just think about it. You have kissed me and I have kissed you. I know what I felt."

"Stop," he said, without looking up. "The joy you bring me is something I can't have."

Sadima leaned forward and cupped his chin in her hand.

"That's a lie. You are just afraid. Promise me that you will think about it."

He was perfectly still for so long that she wanted to scream at him and shake his shoulders. But then, finally, he nodded. "I will."

"Where should I begin?" she asked, touching the book with two fingers.

They ended up working with the book between them, their chairs a hand's breadth apart, their shoulders touching. And when she went to bed, Sadima recited the long-life song, as she always did now, repeating it three times. Then, in the dark, she stole down the hallway and pressed her ear against Franklin's bedroom door. How many nights would there be when Somiss was not there? She opened Franklin's door silently and tiptoed in to stand beside his bed. There was a little moonlight seeping through the shutters. She reached out to touch him, to wake him so they could kiss, maybe make love, then lie beside each other until morning. One night at least, if never again.

The idea made her shiver with feelings she couldn't unravel and couldn't understand. But when she did reach out to touch Franklin, she only rested her hand on his foot as she recited the long-life song, twice, before going to bed. And every night after that, defying her fear of Somiss, she did the same thing.

44

Knowing that four boys were dying or dead had changed nothing for Gerrard. He did what he had always done. He came back from Franklin's class every day, studied, went to the food hall and ate, then studied again and went to sleep. He never spoke. But then, he almost never had.

In the silence my thoughts got louder. Nothing was hard for me now. I ate whatever I wanted to eat. And it was ridiculous, but I was good at the things Franklin was asking us to do too.

"Now move your thoughts from your belly to your toes," Franklin said one day. I opened my eyes, sure I had heard him wrong. I hadn't. He repeated it.

"Breathe," he said. We all obeyed, like the smelly, beaten-down, well-trained animals we had become. I closed my eyes again. Tally was dead. I assumed Joseph and Rob and a boy whose name I had never learned were dead as well. Will looked half-dead—not from hunger, but from sorrow. I pitied him, going back to an empty room after class. Levin's eyes were flat and without expression too, and I knew he was grieving. But Luke and Jordan were as angry as I was, I could see it in their eyes. I couldn't tell what Gerrard felt about anything, except that he meant to win, to live, to be the one the wizards chose.

Boys had *died*, and I was learning to hear my thoughts coming out of different parts of my body. We all were. It was all perfect, crapping, complete nonsense.

"Keep going," Franklin said. "And move your thoughts."

I imagined my thoughts moving from my belly to my toes. They slid down my legs like water. They settled into my bare, calloused toes. It was odd, hearing my toes thinking, listening to them. They had my voice, of course, and they felt exactly as I did. They were angry and scared in a dull-witted, exhausted way.

"Good, Hahp," I heard Franklin say. I stiffened, pissed. It had been a long time since he had spoken to me in class. Luke would transfer his rage from Gerrard to me if he thought I was the one to beat out, I wondered—that is to say, my toes wondered—if Luke wanted what I did. To graduate and then go visit his father. If Gerrard had been telling the truth, he was at least spared the desire for murder.

That thought set off the whole long daydream of going home in black robes. I couldn't seem to stop having it. I changed it a little each time, adding more of an argument, sometimes hitting my father, sometimes making him into a white pony with dead eyes.

The truth was simple: While I was imagining, I felt strong and steady. Was that what being a wizard was like? Feeling stronger and steadier than anyone else?

"That's part of it."

It was Franklin's voice, coming from my toes, and my eyes flew open. His were closed. Shit. I couldn't tell what was real and what wasn't. Maybe this was the test. Maybe the one who stood up and screamed that all this was crazy was the one they wanted. Whichever one refused to do all this silly crap would be the one to live, to become a wizard.

That last thought hung in the air above my feet, as though it was too novel, too amazing for my toes to contain. I felt it settle slowly back into my stomach, lying cold somewhere, and deep. It terrified me. Could that be the point of starving some of us to death? To make one or two of us angry enough and desperate enough to overcome our fear of this place, of the wizards, of everything? I dredged the idea back upward, toward my chest, then back into my mind. It felt cold there, too, but it couldn't hide from me. I opened my eyes a little.

The cavern was empty. No one was there but me.

I felt the stone move beneath me, a long, swooping sensation. And then they were back. Franklin was facing us. Gerrard was off to one side. Levin, Will, Luke, Jordan, and I sat in our usual haphazard half circle.

I only pretended to follow Franklin's instructions for the rest of the class. I sat behind my closed eyes in the silence. How long would it be before I was crazy? Maybe that was the second test, I heard my toes thinking. The one who didn't die trying to make food and who didn't go crazy.

"Hahp," I heard Franklin say. "Forgive me."

My eyes opened. He was gone. The other boys were standing up, stretching and shaking their heads like swimmers trying to get water out of their ears. I stood up too and saw Luke looking at something. I turned to follow his gaze.

Somiss was standing beside the door. He wasn't bothering to hide this time. So Levin and I didn't exchange even the tiny whispers we sometimes risked. His eyes met mine for an instant, and I imagined that I could hear *him* thinking. He was as frantic as I was to find some logic, some sense in all this. I bit my lower lip and followed the others.

Somiss stared at us, one by one, looking into our faces as we passed. I met his eyes for an instant and felt it like a blow, then I turned my head and walked faster just to get by him. Once I was out in the tunnel, I ran.

Gerrard wasn't in the room when I got there. I pissed, splashed water on my face, then clawed my hand through my long, filthy hair. I turned when Gerrard came in. He glared at me and I thought he might speak, might actually say something. But he didn't. He picked up the thick history book from the corner of his desk and sat down cross-legged, his back to me.

I sat on my bed, exhausted. It wasn't until I swung my feet up to lie down that I felt the sharp corner of the history book. It was lying on top of the thin blanket, in the exact place where I lay my head every time I slept. I had not put it there. I felt the question settle like a stone on my chest. Was someone coming into the room when we were gone? Was someone still here? I stood up to look under my cot, then sat on the edge again, looking up into the shadows that clung to the ceiling.

— 45 —

Alone, every night, once Franklin and Somiss were both in bed, Sadima pulled out her copy of the song for long life and whispered the words she had memorized, following the text as she went. The letters all meant something to her now—each one had its own sound. She could cobble together the words on most of the shop signs she saw. The shop with the dark-wood table sold gold and silver jewelry. The next one she picked sold silk and lace. The one after that had turned out to be a seamstress's shop. Small wonder the wealthy women of Limòri dressed so well.

But this morning Sadima had no time to practice reading—and no opportunity. It was King's Day. At home, in Ferne, her brother and Laran would be rising early, cooking all day, then going to Mattie Han's with baskets of food. Or maybe Mattie and her children and grandchildren would come to the farm. Sadima tried to imagine the sad little house full of noise, of children's laughter. She could not.

The sound of a door opening in the hall made Sadima tense reflexively, even though she knew Somiss was at his father's house. Franklin was still yawning, blinking in the lantern light as he came in.

"I never manage to rise as early as you do."

Sadima smiled at him, fetched the tea she had made, and waited until he'd had a breakfast of bread and butter. Then she couldn't hold her tongue any longer.

"Did you think about it?" she asked, knowing it was unfair—he was barely awake.

He shook his head. "Sadima, we would be old before we had enough coins. And if I tried to run away, he would find me."

She felt her anger rise at the finality in his voice. "You don't know that," she said quietly. "You are just afraid he might not even try." The instant the words left her lips, she regretted them. Franklin stood and took his plate to the kitchen. When he came back, he sat down and began to copy. Sadima stared at him for a long moment, then began her own work.

The Gypsy symbols were intricate, and she was so much better at them than Franklin. She would help him finish copying the book, then she was going to leave, to make her way back to Ferne. Mattie would take her in. Then she would find a way to open a cheese shop in town. She would think of Franklin often, with sadness and love.

Thanks to him, she knew that there were other people in the world like her. That was enough. She would learn not to listen to animals' thoughts and would concentrate on more useful skills. And she would do what Micah had done. She would find someone to love.

Feeling lighter because she had finally made the decision, Sadima worked steadily, automatically, her thoughts spinning images of King's Day in Ferne. Her brother playing with children, Laran perhaps pregnant. Both of them happy, laughing. Sadima squeezed her eyes shut to stop the little blur of tears. It was King's Day and she would not be with her family. Instead, she was copying symbols for a man she hated, sitting across from a man she loved, who would not love her back.

Franklin shifted in his chair.

"How old is he?" Sadima asked, forcing her voice to stay even.

Franklin cleared his throat. "Somiss? Twenty. A year younger than I am."

"No." Sadima said, irritated. "The king."

Franklin shrugged. "Last time I bothered to watch the procession—which was three years ago—his hair had gone white as snow."

"I wish I could see him," Sadima said. "I don't think anyone from Ferne ever has." She stared at Franklin's bent head, at his hand on the pen.

He glanced up. "They walk in a long circle around Market Square. When you hear cheers, just stand out on the balcony."

Sadima blinked and tried to smile at him. "The king will be that close?"

Franklin laughed gently and set down his quill. "You are so . . . lovely. You get excited about the simplest things and it makes me feel like there is still good in the world—though I know Somiss would disagree."

Somiss again. Sadima felt her smile fade.

Franklin didn't notice. "You should go down to the square early and wait with the crowds beneath the trees. It's fun."

Sadima looked into his eyes. "Come with me."

He shook his head and gestured at the book. "Somiss wants this done quickly."

"If we can get most of the book finished before the procession," she said, leaning toward him so that their shoulders touched, "will you come with me?"

Franklin looked at her and finally nodded. Then he went to get a second inkpot and new quills to trim. Sadima pulled the book toward herself and turned a few pages, then a few more, being careful. Franklin had loosened the binding stitches to lay it flat. She kept turning. Many of the pages were not entirely full of writing. If they hurried . . . Near the end, her eyes stopped and she stared at the page, then turned it back. The front side was covered with the Gypsy symbols. The other side was full of the letters they usually used. She silently sounded out four words. *Healing can be done . . .*

"Franklin!" she called out, standing up. "Come look at this!"

Moments later he was beside her, holding the rough-edged book, his hands shaking as he turned the pages back and forth.

Sadima thought carefully about what to say, about how she could hide her growing ability to read. She waited until Franklin raised his eyes to look at her.

"It's different languages, isn't it? Those letters aren't Gypsy symbols, they're the ones we always use." She pointed.

He nodded slowly. "Yes. Oh, Sadima, if this is so, if these are translations . . ."

"If they are, Somiss has you to thank," she said. "Your kindness provided this."

But Franklin wasn't listening. He was sitting down, his eyes darting back and forth as he read. "If this is a translation, this one is to heal wounds. Sadima! This is wonderful."

He laid down the paper, then lifted her off her feet, turning a circle before he set her down. "Can you imagine it? When someone is sick in South End, anyone who has learned the songs will be able to help. Farmers will be able to raise a good crop every year. No one will starve through the winters. No one will ever have to sell a child, and no child will ever have to lose her mother. Then this will . . ." he began, then stopped, his voice thick. "It will all have been worth it, Sadima."

Sadima reached up to wipe a tear from his cheek. She knew what he meant. He meant his whole life, everything he had suffered at Somiss's hands. If it ended up saving lives and feeding people, he could bear all the pain.

"That's the secret. That's what Somiss wants to do," he whispered. "Open a school that teaches the songs to children."

Sadima kissed his cheek, overcome by the intensity in his eyes. Maybe he was right. And maybe she should stay.

Franklin was loosening the binding. There were five pages written that way—back and front. Sadima watched him making a tiny mark in the upper right corner of each sheet as he freed them from the binding.

"See?" he said when he looked up. "The numbers are one through five. In case the ordering matters, we won't mix them up."

Sadima nodded, staring at the little symbols. Numbers. She had seen shopkeepers here use them to add and subtract. In Ferne people used hash marks, lining them up in fives.

"I'll do the hard ones," she said quickly. "The Gypsy words."

Franklin smiled at her and touched her cheek. "You just want to go see the king."

"With you," she said. Then she set to work.

They finished the translations first and set them aside. Then they went back to the rest of the book. They were still working when she heard the crowds gathering. They were nowhere near finished when she heard the people begin to cheer.

Sadima sighed.

Franklin laid down his quill. "Go out on the balcony, at least. You'll see him better from there anyway."

Sadima went into the kitchen and opened the double doors. The king was just coming, his golden carriage making a slow turn at the corner. Sadima could see his glossy white hair and the jeweled circlet on his brow. His guards walked both before and after his carriage, their eyes on the crowds, their swords half-drawn. Behind him came the queen and the crown prince, a thin boy of ten or so with dark hair and long legs. The queen was young, lovely, her gown the color of a full moon. The sleeves were enormous, puffed out at the shoulder, but tight around her forearms. The prince stood to wave, using a cane to steady himself.

"Is the prince lame?" she asked Franklin over her shoulder.

"They say it was an accident," he said. "A horse fell beneath him, trapped his right leg. But he has limped like that since he was a toddler, Somiss says. He is kind and slow-witted. It worries the royals a great deal. The old queen bore no children at all, and this new one has had only one. If she cannot bear a son fit for the throne, there will be fighting, plotting—Somiss's mother will certainly try to put him forward."

Sadima blinked and turned toward him. "Somiss could be king?"

Franklin shrugged. "He would have as good a claim as ten or fifteen others."

Sadima faced the street again. Just behind the queen's carriage was the beginning of what had to be the procession of royals. They were all riding in fancy carriages, the wood inlaid in patterns or painted in arcs of bright color or plated with silver. The horses' coats were shining, their hooves oiled and polished.

And the clothes! Not just the women, but the men, too. Sadima had never imagined that there was so much silk and velvet in the world. The colors were deep and rich, dark greens and reds and blues. Did the colors mean something?

Sadima was about to turn to ask Franklin when she saw one upturned face below. Somiss. She froze. He was staring at her, fury in his eyes. He jerked his head sideways and lifted one fist. Sadima ducked backward and out of sight.

"Have you had enough royal pomp and ceremony for one evening?" Franklin asked as she came back in. He was smiling. She smiled back, knowing she should tell him— but she didn't. She set to work and hoped Somiss wouldn't be too angry by morning.

— 46 —

After Franklin's class, I went to the food hall. My legs
and arms felt heavy, slow. It scared me. Was I getting sick?
As I came into the hall, I saw Gerrard, bent over a tin bowl
of fish stew, using a plain tin spoon. I stared at him a
moment before I turned to leave, then I stopped.

Since Somiss had noticed the silver spoon, we had made
sure we weren't in the food hall at the same time. But if
Somiss hadn't punished either one of us for it yet, there
was no reason to think he ever would. And I wanted supper. Eating was like sleeping. It felt good.

I walked toward the stone and saw Gerrard turn a page
in the textbook he was reading. He didn't look up at me.
He either didn't care if I was there, or he was too absorbed
in studying to have even noticed me.

I decided to make griddle cakes—Gerrard had already seen me make them and he wouldn't . . . what? Be as pissed off as he would if I made honeyed ham, buttered beans, and fresh oranges while he was eating his hundredth bowl of fish stew? The truth was I didn't want him angry with me if I could help it. So I focused my thoughts on griddle cakes, then stepped forward and touched the stone.

And nothing happened.

Sweat rose on my forehead, and I heard Gerrard laugh. But when I swung around to tell him to shut up, he was reading. Had I imagined it? I faced the stone and tried once more. Nothing. Then I heard the laugh again. But Gerrard was sipping soup, his eyes on the book.

My legs suddenly light with panic, I paced the perimeter of the big room, peering into the shadows between the torches. There was no one there, and Gerrard was still reading as though I was invisible, as though I wasn't there at all. Had Somiss made the stone stop working for me? Could he do that? Was this the punishment for making Gerrard a spoon? I forced myself to walk back to the stone. Sweating, my knees shaking, I imagined apples, wet with dew, myself in the orchard, hiding, eager, excited to see magic. Then I touched the stone.

A basket of apples snapped into existence.

I leaned on the pedestal, my palms on the cold stone, tears in my eyes, weak with relief. Then I remembered Gerrard and stood straight, turning to glance at him. He was still absorbed in reading. Still shaky, I decided to come back later. I set three apples aside, then put the basket on the floor and watched it sparkle and disappear. Then I picked up the apples and walked back to the room. The door sounded too loud when I closed it. I sat on the edge of my cot, rocking back and forth, trying to calm down. An argument began inside my skull.

What if I couldn't make anything but apples again? What if I couldn't even make apples? Images of the starving boys came into my mind, shuffling, their eyes dull. If I couldn't make the stone work, I would starve. No. I wouldn't. I could make food. I just hadn't been able to at first because I was nervous with Gerrard there. That was all it was. I was scaring the piss out of myself over nothing. I had made the apples. I would go back later and eat.

For an instant my thoughts paused and the silence was wonderful. But it didn't last. Who had laughed? Franklin? I had imagined him talking to me before, saying things that were impossible, things that made no sense. I dragged in a long breath. No, I hadn't imagined shit. Franklin had tricked me into seeing things, hearing things. It was some kind of weird magic. Maybe.

Or maybe I was just going mad.

Gooseflesh rose on my arms, then on my scalp. I bent forward, trying not to vomit. I was so sick of being scared. Maybe we had been through the worst. Maybe it would just be like a school now. "Or maybe this was the easy part," I said aloud.

The sound of my own voice startled me. It had been a long time since I had heard it. Since before the boys had starved? I saw their faces again and stood up, breathing the first pattern.

After a long time, I began to calm down. I was just scared, and I had every right to be scared. I was not going mad. And I might live through this. I might. If I studied harder and . . .

And then I heard the laugh behind me. Louder this time. I jerked around.

No one was there.

I ran.

I ran all the way back to the food hall. Gerrard was still sitting at the table, still reading. He looked up when I came in and stared at me as I came at him. "I heard someone laugh," I said, without knowing what I was going to say. "In here, then in our room. Someone laughed." Then I shut my lips and waited for him to hit me, to threaten me—

But he nodded. "Me too," he whispered, his teeth tight together, barely moving his lips. After a pause, he said two more words. "Thank you." Then he gestured slightly, motioning me to move away, not to put either one of us in more danger.

I walked past him, fighting tears, feeling joyous. I wasn't imagining it. I was not going mad. And Gerrard had been scared by it too, or he wouldn't have thanked me. We had talked and Somiss had not appeared to kill us both. A moment later I tried to make griddle cakes, and the stone worked perfectly. And when I went back to the room, the history book was on my bed again. I stared at it, my stomach tight. But this time, I picked it up and started reading.

— 47 —

"Is he still in there?" Sadima whispered as she eased
the door open, her arms full of grocer's packets. Franklin
nodded, then went back to his copying. He didn't seem
upset. So Somiss hadn't said anything about her being on
the balcony yet. Maybe he had only been irritated, not
truly angry.

Sadima carried the food into the kitchen, then turned
to look at Franklin again, really seeing him this time. His
shirt was dirty, streaked with dark soil. Had he emptied
the ash box or simply rolled in the gutter? Or maybe
Somiss had him cleaning out some old building that
would become the school he wanted to open. She didn't
ask. It was their *secret*.

"Has he come out at all?" she asked, not because she

cared, but because she wanted to talk to Franklin. Somiss had been keeping him so busy she barely saw him.

"Once. To tell me to make six copies of each page, laid out like this," Franklin said. He put his fingertips on the bottom corners of the paper and reversed it.

Sadima blinked and walked closer. The ornate Gypsy symbols were written in blue or black ink, all of the words containing both colors.

"The words in the old language should be pronounced about like the ones we have been hearing people recite," Franklin said, then looked up until she nodded. "So using our best song versions, we can begin to learn the Gypsy letters. Then Somiss hopes to correct mistakes in the songs we have collected from people. There almost have to be distortions from generations of being handed down without being written down."

Sadima nodded. "So it won't be as easy as you hoped. But why two colors?"

He yawned. "It's complicated. First, Somiss can't see a direct translation. He thinks the wizards themselves changed the wording or maybe the spelling long ago. Who knows how the Gypsies ended up with the songs, but Somiss now thinks they have made new copies, over and over, for hundreds of years, like you do, without knowing what they were writing."

Sadima pulled off her shawl and sat across the table from Franklin, wishing she could tell him the truth about her learning to read. She didn't want secrets between them. She reached out to pick up the wick trimmer and saw to the lamp. It burned brighter. Franklin smiled at her, and she noticed his hollow, red-rimmed eyes. "You need to sleep. Are you eating?"

He nodded. "I am, but Somiss isn't. He's desperate to make progress." Franklin paused, then leaned forward to whisper, "He's convinced his father will start looking for him again."

Sadima nodded wearily and stood up. Somiss. His father. She walked into the kitchen and washed her face and hands, put the beef roast she had bought into the oven, and built up the fire. She cleaned up slowly, staying out of the sitting room as long as she could. Then she came back and sat down opposite Franklin again. "How can I help?"

He looked up. "I finished the copies. Now I have to do this." He handed her a piece of paper.

Sadima stared at it. He had made a list of the Gypsy symbols. He had written some of them in black, some in blue. She looked up. "What do the colors mean?"

"Somiss marked up the first set of copies, counting the letters. The ones in blue occur most often," Franklin said. "He is hoping some or even most of them are vowels."

Sadima blinked, and he apologized. "Vowels are the letters you voice." He sounded out the word "stick," exaggerating the *i* sound. Sadima nodded. She had figured out that only some of the letters used her voice. Now she had a name for them. *Vowels.*

"The word '*nanolas*' appears five times in the first song in the Gypsy book," Franklin was saying. "Somiss found it in some of the nonsense songs we transcribed too—pronounced a little differently by each family. But in the Gypsy book, in the old language, there are no repeated words at all."

Sadima felt her heart sink. She had thought Somiss would have his school open soon, and that once it was open, Franklin might see that Somiss needed him less.

"By counting and comparing the blue letters," Franklin said, "Somiss is hoping he can narrow down the word matches by matching the number of vowels."

Sadima nodded, understanding. But what if this didn't work? Maybe Somiss was not going to be smart enough to figure it out. Then all of this wouldn't be worth anything. Hiding her uneasiness, she set to work copying.

When the moon came up and shone through the little kitchen window, Sadima stood up to stretch and went to stand on the balcony. She took deep breaths to rid herself of the smell of burning tallow.

"Eat, then go to bed," Franklin called from the sitting room.

She turned to face him. "I can work a while longer."

He stood up and came to stand beside her, looking up at the sky. "You're twice as fast as I am. You have already done your half and more."

Sadima felt the warmth of his arm around her shoulders. The stars were bright and the moon was the color of heavy cream. "Maybe someday," she said quietly, "Somiss won't need you so much."

Franklin tipped his head, looking at her with an intensity that made her heart quicken. She lifted her chin and met his eyes. Here, in the soft night air, in the soft light of the moon, he didn't look tired and preoccupied. He looked handsome and kind, the way he had the first day she met him. She wondered what she looked like to him. Then Somiss's door banged open.

Franklin was back inside and in the sitting room in an instant. Sadima came in too but stayed in the kitchen and pretended to be wiping the wooden table that served as a cutting board.

"Isn't she back yet?" Somiss asked. Sadima walked to the arch between the kitchen and the sitting room to see him frowning at Franklin.

"I am," she said quietly. "Supper is almost ready." He looked at her, his eyes glittering with the odd energy that seemed to come to him when he fasted. He nodded slightly, then turned back to Franklin. "Have you finished?"

Franklin pointed. "Sadima has done her share, but I have more to—"

"Then have her start on yours," Somiss cut him off. "It is impossible to know how much longer we will have and—"

Sadima had turned to the stove, but she looked up at the sudden silence and saw Somiss glaring at her. In three quick strides he was in the kitchen, pushing past her to close the balcony doors.

"Don't ever open them again."

Sadima nodded, scared by the wildness in his eyes.

Somiss leaned toward her. "I saw you on King's Day," he whispered. "Gawping at us like the field girl you are. It is possible my father's men have seen you walking with Franklin."

Somiss reached out and pulled a handful of her hair. Sadima stood wide-eyed, like a kitten that comes upon a snake in the grass. "Anyone would remember this," Somiss said, tugging hard enough to make her wince. "Cut it short," he said. He glanced at Franklin. "See that she does it."

Then he left, snatching up her finished sheets and Franklin's. When he slammed his door, Sadima flinched, her whole body jerking at the sound.

— 48 —

I began sitting as far away from Franklin as I could,
so the uneven half circle became an uneven triangle. Luke
glared at me the first time. He probably thought I was imitating Gerrard. Maybe I was.

Franklin kept having us move our thoughts around. It
had become easy for me. So easy that I began watching the
others. Will was struggling. The pain of it was all over his
face. Levin seemed relaxed, which I hoped meant he was
getting good at it too. Gerrard's face was unreadable, but I
had spent so many hours staring at his back I knew he was
having trouble too. His head was a little too high, his spine
was too straight. Luke and Jordan both seemed at ease while
we were practicing—but maybe they were pretending.

"Move your thoughts to your shoulders," Franklin said.

So I slid them upward from my belly and listened to them as they moved through my flesh. They were uneasy thoughts. Would the next life-or-death test be thought-moving? I wanted to believe that so much that I felt my eyes water.

Halfway back to the room after class, the faces of the dead boys drifted into my thoughts again. So I ran. I was almost all the way to the food hall before I thought about where I was going. Then I stopped. I wasn't hungry, and I knew I should go back and study. Gerrard was reading the books like his life depended on it, and maybe he was right. Maybe we would have a test, and anyone who flunked wouldn't be allowed to eat. Or perhaps the water spigots would stop working for them. Or their beds would be full of snakes.

I started walking again. I would eat, then go study. The food hall was empty. I made two loaves of fresh bread, a few apples, and a dozen rounds of cheese.

Then I went out, carrying everything in the front of my robe. But I didn't turn toward my room. I went in the opposite direction. Could we be punished for going some-where on our own? No one had ever said so, but I knew that didn't matter. They could do anything they wanted with us. No one would know, and my father, at least, wouldn't care.

I made turns at random, keeping track. It had become automatic, and I had refined the pattern. Conjunctions didn't count at all. Nor prepositions. And I had started using words that began with *l* or *e* for left turns, *r* or *i* words for right turns.

P words were for the tunnels I passed without turning. So this one went: *Long evenings roll past in a regal romantic pageant, puzzling and really interesting.*

I wondered, only once, what would happen if Somiss found me. It scared me so much that I moved my thoughts to my feet. The distance helped. I could hear them, but they were not so loud. I began the sixth breathing pattern and kept walking.

The farther I went, the fewer torches there were. I passed at least a hundred big, empty rooms of stone—all lit by a single cold-fire torch—and I just kept walking. Eventually, the tunnel narrowed. I turned again, then once more. All the tunnels were narrower, and the ceilings were lower. The entrances to the chambers I passed got smaller too. I found a long, straight passage and followed it. As I walked, the stone itself became rougher, as though these tunnels had been carved out with picks, not magic.

I went as far as I could before my fear swallowed my courage. Then I stopped and started back, searching the walls, walking very slowly. Finally, still in the narrow tunnels, I spotted a chamber with an entrance so small that I would have to crawl into it. In the sparse light, it looked like a shadow in the rough stone, not an opening. Perfect.

There was no torch inside, but just enough light came in from one of the few torches in the corridor that I could see a little as I sat there, knees bent, the stone cold again my back.

After a while, I made a neat pile of the apples, cheese

rounds, and bread. Then I just sat there again, unable to make myself stand up and start back. I soaked in the massive, heavy silence that oozed out of the stone. I finally smiled when I heard my belly thoughts tell the truth. I was happy. The crapping wizards had *no idea* where I was.

49

Two days later, standing outside the door, Sadima hesitated, touching the dull gray cap she was wearing. Rinka had given it to her and had shown her how to twist her hair into a tight roll that wound around her head. Franklin hadn't asked her to cut it, but she had seen the agony in his eyes. Somehow, she had to get him to leave with her. Somiss was not going to save the world. He didn't care enough about anyone besides himself to even try.

Sadima reached for the door handle and turned it silently. The sitting room was empty. Papers were stacked on the table—and Franklin's ink pots and quills were lined up. She glanced down the hall. Both bedroom doors were closed.

That told her nothing about Somiss, but it meant Franklin was probably telling fortunes or off on some secret errand. He had set aside one of his shirts for whatever dirty chore Somiss had him doing. He changed when he got home, Sadima had noticed, and he washed it himself.

Moving quietly, Sadima went into the kitchen to dip a cup in the oaken barrel. She drank, then set the cup on the sideboard and leaned over the still water, trying to see her reflection. The light was wrong—the sun was already low in the sky, coming through the little window in dusty bands. She wanted to open the balcony doors, but she was afraid to. She moved to one side, trying to see better. Did the cap make her look like a boy?

"It looks very pretty."

Sadima jerked straight and turned, almost bumping into Somiss. "I just didn't want to cut it. Franklin doesn't know—"

"I assumed that," he interrupted. He waved two sheets of paper at her. "Bring me copies of these as fast as you can write." His eyes flickered across hers.

Sadima nodded, and he set the papers on the sideboard. Then he took her shoulder and pulled her closer, turning her around so that she was faced away from him. He bent to whisper, and she could feel his breath on the naked nape of her neck. "You will keep it like this when you go out?"

Sadima nodded, trembling between fear and rage. She tried to step forward, to get his hands off her shoulders, but he held her still.

"You won't ever forget?"

She shook her head.

"Good." She felt something—his fingertips? his lips?—brush the back of her neck, then he was walking away from her, heading back to his room. "Sadima?" he said over his shoulder.

"Yes?" she managed.

"If you leave us, Franklin will be very sorry."

She started to smile, then he spoke again.

"I will make sure of that."

Sadima blinked, stunned into stillness until she heard his door close. Then she slumped into a chair. All his life Franklin had borne punishment he had not earned. Somiss knew she could not add to that. He *knew*.

Sadima went to sit at the table. It took some time for her hands to steady. Then she picked up a quill and used the little knife to trim it into a point. After she had the copies finished, she picked them up and walked down the hall.

Standing before Somiss's door, she made a decision. She would work to keep Somiss calm—but she would talk Franklin into leaving with her. She had to make him see how evil Somiss was—no. He already knew that better than she ever would. What she had to make him see was that he could leave.

The faint sound of a voice startled Sadima out of her thoughts. She exhaled. Somiss was reading out loud. She hesitated. What if her knock startled him? She listened through the door as he recited the song for long life. But it wasn't the same as the one Hannah had taught her. Not quite. The first verse was slightly different. The second stanza had a line she hadn't learned at all. Was this version from the Gypsy book? Then his voice dropped, and she couldn't hear anything but murmuring.

She waited until he fell silent, then she waited a few moments more. Only then did she tap the door with one finger. He did not answer. She bent to slide the papers beneath the door. Somiss didn't call out a thanks, but Sadima heard the rustle of the papers as he picked them up.

She made supper, letting the simple task ease her heart. The smell of chicken baking filled the place, and Sadima found herself humming as she worked, moving the finished gravy to the cooler side of the stovetop, then peeling parsnips to steam with butter and a little honey. She could feel the cold air of the evening seeping beneath the balcony doors.

When Franklin came in, his cheeks were pink from the night air, his shirt dirty again. Sadima turned to face him, standing just inside the kitchen arch. He stopped and tilted his head to stare at her, a slow smile curving his mouth as he looked at the cap.

She laughed. "Somiss said it's all right." He looked so relieved that it touched her heart. She wanted to tell him the rest of what Somiss had said, but not yet. Not until they were safe away somewhere Somiss could never find them.

50

I fell into a pattern. I left class and then sprinted to the food hall. If it was empty—and I walked the walls and looked into the shadows to make sure—I would make more food, then carry it to the little chamber I had found. It soon held stacks of beeswax-coated cheeses, apples, and smoked meat. Once it was half full, I started hiding food other places too. If they starved us again, and if I was very careful not to be discovered, I would have a chance of living through it. And, I told myself, even if they killed me there would be a boy someday who would live because he found food I had hidden.

I named the first little cavern Hope Hall, and it became precious to me. I went back whenever I could. Sitting against the stone, I would go through Franklin's patterns until even my quiet thoughts would drift into silence. Then there were only images, quick snippets of Celia hugging me, a pretty serving girl, the smell of my mother's chambers after her bath, memories of girls who smiled at my brother at the Winterfeast galas, their silk gowns whispering secrets when they leaned close to him.

Sometimes I would touch myself—the idea that the wizards could not find me was as exciting as anything else. Afterward, I wondered about the wizards who led us to class every day. Did they do this? How could they *not*? Had any of them tried to make a woman in the food hall? The double meaning in that made me laugh aloud. Then I stopped laughing.

Could I make something besides food? Could I make whatever I could imagine with enough detail? I crawled out of Hope Hall and was walking back up the tunnel before I realized it. When I got there, Levin was sitting at one of the tables, eating with his hands—still no silverware. We looked at each other. His eyes were red—was it still grief? Or too many hours reading the history book?

It was boring—I usually fell sleep when I tried to study the amazing accomplishments of the Founder. His translation methods were detailed in the book and hard to understand. They included counting vowels and comparing hundreds of versions of the old songs—and repeating certain words thousands of times to himself to see how the words might have been changed over time, all the while dodging his own royal family. They were all jealous of him and his genius.

Then a Gypsy woman had fallen in love with him when he saved her child from death, and she had stolen an ancient book from her father to give the Founder. I was beginning to think the old language the history text talked about was the one *Songs of the Elders* was written in. If the Founder had worked so hard to translate the language, why did we have to learn it?

I realized suddenly that Levin was looking at me. I glanced at the walls, then back at him, lifting my eyebrows a little. He shook his head, the slight movement that we all used. So no one was here but us.

"Are you all right?" I asked quietly, before I knew I was going to say it.

Levin made a small gesture with one hand, a vague come-closer motion that I obeyed, walking at an angle so that I could turn and head for the stone if anyone came in. "Luke hates you," he whispered once I was close enough to hear him. "Be careful."

I nodded—one of our tiny, barely perceptible nods. "Why?" I whispered.

Levin glanced around. "Your father cheated his."

We hadn't exchanged this many words since the first few classes. He was risking a lot to talk to me. I walked away, grateful and furious.

This was perfect. Crapping *perfect*. My father had forced me to come here, knowing he might never see me again. And now my most dangerous classmate hated me because my father was dishonest.

I heard muted footsteps and knew that Levin was leaving.

I wanted to turn and call out a good-bye, thank him, say something. But of course I didn't. Instead I stood and stared at the monstrous, faceted stone in front of me without really seeing it. There had to be a way out of here. Maybe, if I walked far enough down the right tunnel, I would emerge into sunshine.

The thought made my whole body quiver. Then the sense of it struck me. There had to be a way out. There might be fifty. There had to be air vents, and there were drains that carried our wash water away. Was that why they kept us scared and hungry and filthy? So we wouldn't look for a way out?

I pushed one hand back through my hair and realized how matted it was, how dirty. I had come here intending to make a pillow—but now I wanted to make something else.

I concentrated, remembering the color, the scent, the feel of the soft, cream-colored soap that was made by my father's servants. Then I stepped forward and touched the stone. There was a flash. I grabbed the soap and spun around, walking fast. I passed Gerrard, going the other way, and I hid it in the folds of my robe. He barely looked at me, but as soon as I had made the first turn, I ran the rest of the way.

The water was icy and the rough washrag hurt as I scrubbed, rinsing the cloth clean over and over. It was harder to wash my hair, and I had no comb, so dragging my fingers through the tangles was painful. And none of it mattered. It was glorious to wash my stink down the drain.

When I was finished, I felt like I was alive again, myself

again. But when I turned back to my cot to wash my robe out, it wasn't there. I stared at the folded green one that had taken its place. Did the wizards know what each one of us had made? That tightened my stomach. Did they know about all the food I had hidden, then? Would they punish me for it even after they had rewarded me for making soap? Or would this robe dissolve my skin or burst into flame or . . .

My thoughts were shouting again, and I calmed them with the third pattern. Then I reached out, very slowly, and touched the green cloth. It was softer than my old one, and it was clean. I slid it over my head and was standing there running my hands over the fabric when Gerrard came in.

He looked at the robe, then cursed and went back out, slamming the door so hard that the sound echoed off the stone. I took one step, feeling like I should follow him and say something. Then I stopped. What would I say? That I was sorry? The soft, clean cloth brushed my ankles, and I realized that my old robe had been this long when I had gotten it. I remembered tripping on the hem. When I had taken it off, it had hit me midcalf. Had I grown that much? Shit. How long had I *been* here?

51

Sadima had talked Rinka into working bits of olives and red peppers into the cheese, and people loved it. Rinka's business was growing, and she paid a bit more each week—it was nine coins now. Sadima always gave Franklin four of them and kept the rest. She had bought a good hairbrush and a second pair of shoes, to wear in the shop. She left them in the back room every night and walked home in her first pair so that Somiss wouldn't know. One evening, on the way home, she made a decision.

She had already begun hiding her saved coins in a washed honey jar, hanging from the flue key on the back of the kitchen stovepipe. She loved Franklin. And she could not leave, with or without him. Not yet. But she could continue to prepare. She made a habit of coming in quietly from work every evening and listening carefully to overhear Somiss reading the songs aloud before she began copying.

Franklin always left a stack of finished copies from his early-morning work, and there was almost always a stack for her to work on once she got home. Sometimes there were interview notes and new songs—or a new version of one they already had—sounded out and written down. Hannah had come back, and there were many others.

Sadima began making an extra copy of each new document, hiding the papers in her shawl-bundle until she could carry them to work the next day. She knew what Somiss would do to her if he discovered her secret, and she did it anyway. She was afraid of him—and she was afraid for Franklin—but Somiss could not be trusted as the sole keeper of the old songs. Rinka's Erides was right. No one person ever should be.

The hiding place had been easy. Rinka had not minded her storing a few things in the back room. It had started with the shoes and the new shawl. Now everything was in a beat-up cheese box Rinka had given her. Sadima placed the growing stack of paper in the bottom. Covering it was the painting she had made of the old tree, and the oldest of her dresses—threadbare and unwearable now, but full of memories of home, so she had kept it.

One day Sadima came home from work to find Somiss leaving. She lowered her head to avoid his eyes, and he passed her with less interest than he had for the rail beneath his hand, the stone beneath his boots. He didn't so much as nod at her.

Hoping that Franklin was home and that they could have at least a little time together, Sadima hurried up the steps. But he wasn't. And that presented an opportunity so rare she felt almost giddy. She ran to stand by the little kitchen window, setting the carry-sack full of the day's groceries on the sideboard as she went. Cracking the balcony door, she watched long enough to be sure that Somiss was striding out of sight. Then she filled a pot with hot water from the kettle, throwing in two handfuls of barley, a peeled onion, and the venison she'd bought.

Trembling, she opened the front door and checked the stairs, then looked out the balcony again, barred the door, and flew down the hall. She knocked on Franklin's door and called out his name. Then she opened it to be sure. Only then did she go into Somiss's room.

There were so many stacks of paper Sadima wondered if she would ever find the Gypsy songs. Then she remembered the little numbers Franklin had written in the corners. She began at one end of Somiss's work table and leafed quickly through each stack. Halfway through the piles of papers, Sadima spotted the tiny numbers in the right-hand corners and moved the lamp closer to count the pages. There were ten. These were the originals.

She ran to set them on the sitting-room table. First she pulled Somiss's stack of daily work close and copied a single page, then a few lines on a second page, and put them aside. Then, her hand flying across the paper, Sadima copied the Gypsy version of the song for long life, then the translation. The instant she was finished, she hid it in the kitchen with Hannah's version, then ran back to the table and started on the next one. She had finished all but one of the songs when she heard voices.

She jumped to her feet, hid the last two sheets in the kitchen, then ran down the hall and replaced the Gypsy songs on Somiss's work table. She whirled around and closed the door behind herself and managed to unbar the door before Somiss tried it. She was back in her chair as it opened. Forcing herself into calmness, she rubbed her eyes and pretended to yawn as Somiss and Franklin came in.

Neither spoke to her, but Franklin smiled wearily. Somiss went straight to his room and Franklin hesitated, then followed him down the hallway. Sadima added carrots and celery to the broth to make a real soup. Then she worked feverishly to copy more pages before Franklin reappeared.

Late that night, she practiced the version of the song for long life from the Gypsy book until she knew it by heart. She sang it all the way to work the next day, then all the way home. That night, as usual, she lay awake until she was sure that Franklin was asleep, then crept into his room and stood at the foot of his bed. He was curled up like a child, one hand outflung as though he had reached for something in a dream. Quietly, quietly, she sang over him, the whole song three times through. Then she kissed his cheek. He stirred but did not wake as she tiptoed out.

52

Gerrard did not speak to me, look at me, or wait for me the next time a wizard pounded on our door. He was already up, his piss taken, his face washed—and he walked out the door while I was still peeing. I finally ran out the door just in time to see them make the first turn. Sprinting, holding the long robe up and away from my legs, I managed to catch up.

Walking into class, I saw everyone blink, then stare. I could imagine their thoughts. I wanted to shout at them that I had no idea what the change of robes meant. Was soap hard to make and the clean robe was a reward? Or did the green robe mean I had broken the rules and would be the next one to be killed in some slow, ugly way?

Or was it simply to make sure that they all resented

me—that not even Levin would ever talk to me again? That seemed most likely. And if so, it was working. One by one, the others turned away, aligning themselves so that they didn't have to look at me at all. All but Luke. He made a point of staring.

I half expected Franklin to say something about it, but he didn't. We just went through the patterns several times, with him correcting us slightly. Then we moved our thoughts all over our bodies. I risked glancing at Will, whose face was even more strained than usual, and Levin, who kept glancing at me, then away before our eyes met.

Then I spotted Somiss watching from the shadows and felt clammy with fear. Was he here to say something? Do something? But when Franklin ended the class and walked out, Somiss disappeared.

We stood up. I was farthest from the entrance, and I felt five pairs of eyes on my back.

"Hahp will come with me," a voice said.

We all jerked around to face the door. There was a wizard coming in. I had never seen him before, I was sure— I would have remembered his scar. The wide purple-pink line ran across his throat at an uneven slant, then upward to disappear behind his right ear. His eyes were as black and as cold as the stone floor. I felt a sheen of sweat between my shoulder blades.

"Go," he said, gesturing for the others to leave. I was trembling, and I half turned, considering running. If I could make it as far as Hope Hall, maybe I could live long enough on my hidden food to find a way out of the crapping tunnels.

I glanced toward the door. The others were gone, but Gerrard had hung back, was glancing over his shoulder, curiosity on his face. Not fear, not dread, not pity. Curiosity.

"My name is Jux," the wizard said. "Franklin says you are ready to go on."

My heart stopped, then started again.

I felt my eyes water and blinked back tears of relief. Or was he lying to keep me from running?

"Franklin is rarely wrong," Jux added.

I managed a weak nod to let him know I had heard him. But if he expected me to speak, I could not. I could barely stand.

"Follow me," he said, and somehow, I did. He walked as fast as any of the others, maybe faster. We turned to the right down a corridor that was narrower than any I had ever been in, including the ones around Hope Hall. Rain, I thought to myself, choosing an *r* word, and began paying close attention, memorizing the turns.

Then the floor began to slant upward. We turned again and entered a tunnel so steep that I was winded by the time we came to what I thought was the top. But it wasn't. It was a tight hairpin turn that led upward again. Three times we turned, and the last slope was so steep that I could feel my legs aching with the effort.

Jux did not once look back to see if I was keeping up. He went as fast uphill as he had on level ground, and as we stepped out of the steep, narrow passage, I was stunned by a sudden smell of . . . grass? The air was better here, fresher.

Were we close to the top of the cliff now? Were there passages here that led to the outside?

"Here," Jux said. There was a round door made of what looked like copper. He opened it and I followed him into sunshine. Sunshine. But we were not outside. I could see dark stone overhead. There had to be long slits in it, though I couldn't see them for the trees. Trees! We were standing in a sunlit forest beneath a black stone sky.

"Over here," Jux said, and gestured as he led the way.

I followed him, my heart flying. The sun was out, it was daytime. The world outside was still there, and there was a chance that I might see it again one day.

"The first enclosure," Jux said.

I blinked, trying to understand what he meant. He gestured impatiently, and I finally saw the shine of glass. There was a glassed-in area that enclosed a tall tree and a few bushes of different kinds.

"Go on," Jux said. "Through the door."

It was only following his gesture that I noticed there was a door at all. It was glass too, handle and all, finer and clearer than any glass I had ever seen. I hesitated and swallowed hard. "Do you want me to go inside?" I managed.

He made a shooing gesture and I pulled on the handle. The door was heavy, and if there were hinges of any kind, I couldn't see them. Still, it swung open.

I felt a sudden bump on my back that made me stumble, and I whirled around to see Jux closing the door. "There is a snake," he said. "Its venom can kill you." And then he turned and walked away.

I turned in a slow circle. The enclosure was about the size of a stable box stall. A horse could have walked a stride or two in any direction, no more. I could pace four or five steps. But I didn't. There were snakes at home, in the woods. I knew enough to spend a long time making sure there was nothing within or beneath a log that was near one wall. Then I sat down and tipped my head back.

If there was a glass ceiling, I couldn't perceive it. The sun was warm and the air was soft and scented. I started the first pattern to keep from scaring myself into pounding on the door and begging to be let out. Maybe there wasn't a snake. Maybe it was like our room that first day—just a trick. Or maybe the snake would appear and scare me to death, then disappear.

After a time, a tiny rustling sound made me turn my head to stare at one of the bushes. I sat up straighter. The snake eased out of the leaves and slid toward me. I moved my hand, hoping to startle it into hiding again, but it only lifted itself off the ground and swayed back and forth, looking at me.

"Please don't hurt me," I heard myself whisper over the thudding of my pulse.

The snake lifted itself a little higher and hissed. I held still as stone. Franklin had thought I was ready to go on, Jux had said that. Go on to *what*?

The snake coiled, watching me. It was as thick as my forearm, and a little hood rose from its head. It looked like it knew it could kill me. I closed my eyes and waited to die. Would it strike if I didn't move? If I did? Would it hurt? Would I die slowly? My thoughts were shrill and loud, and out of habit I moved them to my feet to lessen the noise.

I heard another rustling sound and opened my eyes. The snake was still staring at me, but it was a little closer now, its body wrapped in a tighter coil. It was beautiful, in a terrible way, I heard my feet thinking. The snake slid forward a hand breadth, opening its mouth. I stared at it, seeing every scale, the tiny, nibbed texture of its split tongue, the segmented plates on its belly, the perfect curve of its fangs.

My fear of dying made me see it as clearly as I had seen Celia's griddle cakes. Were its thoughts in its belly? I heard myself wonder. Or in its skull? Where did mind stop and belly begin, on a snake? Or me? Why couldn't it tell I wasn't a threat?

I felt my thoughts sliding to the very tips of my toes, arching, reaching as the snake came closer. Then, abruptly, for a split second, I saw myself through the eyes of the snake. To him, I was a sprawled giant, huge, terrifying, unpredictable.

It made me dizzy to see myself like that. My breath went out in a rush, and I had to fight to keep from falling to the ground. I could feel the snake's fear and hostility, its resentment of me; it slid closer still, and I felt its tongue flicker across my bare toes, saw the tips of its fangs, wet with venom as it slid across my foot and lifted its head to strike. I moved a single thought from my body into its body. It was like shoving a boulder uphill, but I felt it roll.

I mean you no harm.

The snake drew back and swayed again. Then it turned in an arc as graceful as time passing and slid silently back into the bush.

I vomited.

One morning Rinka's sister was back, bringing the
babe with her. They hung a hammock-cradle from one of
the roofbeams and took turns rocking the infant when
she was fussy. Sadima loved having Sylvie's tiny daughter
grasp her fingertips. She loved the baby's smile. It made her
wonder—how had Micah felt, raising her? Had he held her
as tenderly as Sylvie held her baby, singing and rocking, staring down into her face with love in his eyes? Micah would
have his own children soon, Sadima knew. She tied the
cloth around a batch of curds and worked faster.

"You can work less now," Rinka said that afternoon.
"The olive and pepper cheeses are selling so well that I
can't let you go like I planned. Sylvie and I would never
keep up. But you can work less."

Sadima was re-tucking her hair and adjusting her cap. This was exactly what she had been hoping for. She turned. "Six days in seven?"

Rinka smiled. "Or five. Sylvie will be here." She tilted her head. "I'll pay you the same. It's your cheese that has made things so busy."

"I'll take two days, then?" Sadima asked. "And come in again the third?"

Rinka nodded.

Sadima thanked her warmly, then started home. This was perfect. She had finished copying the whole Gypsy book and many of the songs. She had nearly thirty-five coins saved in the honey jar. And now she would be able to help Franklin get caught up with the copying—and she would have a day free to meet him in the marketplace. They had to talk.

She intended to tell him that she had copied the whole Gypsy book, and most of what was on Somiss's desk. She wanted to convince him that they could open a little school somewhere in the farm country, that they could teach children the rhymes. He would leave with her. He had to. If he didn't, Somiss would kill him one day, with overwork or his fists or with fasting. And she could not stay to watch it happen.

Coming home, she read the shop signs out of habit, gave the beggar boy a whole copper and smiled when his eyes got round, then bought a pheasant at the butcher and vegetables from the grocer who had opened his store for her the first time she had gotten paid. He always smiled when he saw her. And he liked the cap.

She made pheasant stew for supper, dropping dumpling batter into the boiling broth. Franklin came in as he had every night for so long, bone-tired and dirty. She gave him a bucket half-full of warm water, then followed him to his room. He poured the water into his washbasin, then turned and saw her behind him. His face tensed.

Sadima lifted her chin and spoke very quietly. "Rinka doesn't need me every day now. Her sister is back."

Franklin glanced past her, and she knew he was worried that Somiss would come out of his room and see them together, talking. "I want to take a few hours and go for a walk together tomorrow," she said. "Just say yes and I'll go finish supper."

Franklin's shoulders sagged. "I can't, Sadima," he whispered, then paused. "I just can't."

There was so much pain in his eyes that Sadima stared at him, wishing she could hear his thoughts. "What's wrong?" she whispered. "What does he have you doing?"

Franklin glanced past her again, and Sadima nodded. She understood and turned to leave. When she glanced back, Franklin was already facing the basin, pulling up his shirt. There were long red scrapes on his back, like he had been dragged over cobblestones.

— 54 —

After Jux's first class, I made my way back down the steep tunnel, stopping to rest twice. My legs were shaking. The air in the tunnels below felt heavy and smelled awful; it was like walking into a dirty kennel. When I got to the room, Gerrard wasn't there and I couldn't smell fish, so he was probably at the food hall. I was hungry, but I was also exhausted. I sat on the edge of my cot, weak-kneed, remembering the snake's thoughts, the slow, cold simplicity of its mind. It had been real, not imaginary—I had exchanged thoughts with a snake.

Letting me out, Jux hadn't said a word about the vomit. Or anything else. I sat very still, letting hope form in my heart. I might be the one to graduate. Without meaning to, I began the daydream about going home to see my father.

I stood up abruptly to stop my thoughts, then leaned over to pull the history book off my desk and found my place. The next chapter wasn't about the Founder. It was about the songs that magicians from the first Age of Magic had passed down by memorizing the words of their magical chants, then setting them to simple tunes. They had taught their children the songs, and their children had taught their children, and so on. So for all the centuries when there was no magic in the world, when kings ruled completely, scraps of it were saved.

I looked up from the book. It was hard to imagine a world without magic. My father bought magic for *everything*. No Malek ship had been caught in a storm. He paid for good weather and he paid to have water run through the pipes in our house; he paid for the streams and fountains in Malek Park, for the ponies to fly and a thousand other things.

Everyone did, unless they were too poor.

I flipped through the rest of the book. There was a long section that talked about how bad the world had been when kings were allowed to force young men into their armies and go to war. I knew what war was from other history books, in other schools.

Toward the end, a heading caught my eye: FORBIDDEN PRACTICES. There was a list beneath it. Two lists, really, in a boxed table. The first column named the offenses. The second named the punishments, which were all alike. Death. I stared at the list. It was short. Four items:

**Carnal Acts
Silent-Speech
Teaching Magic Outside the Academy
Betrayal of the Four Vows**

I started to flip more pages to find the Four Vows, but I heard the door handle turn and Gerrard came in. He glanced at me, then went to his cot. As he placed his books by his right hand and settled into a cross-legged position, I was overwhelmed by his smell.

His back was toward me, which I was used to, but his smell was more than I could stand now that I no longer stank and my lungs had been cleaned out by the fresh air in the forest chamber. And maybe, after facing the snake, Gerrard didn't scare me as much as usual either.

"I made soap," I said, "because I was sick of stinking. I washed. When I turned around, the green robe was lying on my—"

"I know," he cut me off.

That stopped me. "How?"

He didn't answer.

I stood up and went to the door. Then I turned. "How? How could you possibly know?"

He was silent, his back straight and his shoulders squared, and anger rose in my throat. I was so shit-sick of staring at his back. "You're a liar," I heard myself saying. "You're a crapping liar and a coward."

He whirled around to stand up, but one foot snagged in his blanket and he stumbled, catching the edge of his desk for balance. "Don't," he said, finally getting a solid stance.

"Don't what? Am I breaking one of the Four Vows?" I wasn't sure why I said that. Maybe I was trying to prove that I studied too, which was ridiculous. I hadn't even read the whole book.

Gerrard's face went rigid. He stared at the wall above my head, then he lowered his eyes to meet mine. "I've been trying to make soap." His eyes shone with sudden tears and he wrenched around to hide his face. And something dawned on me. I had made foods I had known all my life. I had made soap I had used all my life. He was still making the same bowl of fish stew and I knew why. When he was little, had he ever used soap? Then I had another thought. He had let me follow him through the tunnels for a long time. If he hadn't helped me . . .

"Under my mattress there's a bar of—," I began.

"I don't need your fucking soap," he interrupted. "I'll make my own and—"

"I just meant you could smell it, touch it, memorize it," I whispered. Then I went out the door and headed for the food hall. I ate slowly, then walked to Hope Hall and spent time just sitting, trying not to think about anything at all. When I finally went back to the room, Gerrard was still sitting in his usual position, legs crossed, practicing the fourth pattern. His history book lay open beside him. He was more than halfway through it. He didn't speak, so I didn't either. I lay down and tried to keep reading. But my eyes were closing, and I finally gave in to sleep.

My dreams were full of starving boys who shuffled their

feet when I tried to lead them up the steep tunnel. I pulled at them, clutching their robes, crying, hauling them along, but the tunnel would not end. It went up and up, and I woke in a cold sweat, my heart thudding inside my chest. It was dark in the room. Gerrard was sleeping—I could hear him snoring softly. And then a wizard pounded on the door.

— 55 —

Sadima woke before dawn, as she always did. She lit the lantern and built up the fire, then began copying. By the time Franklin rose, the day's work was more than half finished. He shook his head, smiling, and went into the kitchen. In minutes Sadima smelled the warm odor of potatoes frying in grease. She looked up to see Franklin leaning against the wall by the arch, watching her.

"If I were as good as you are, we'd be done by noon every single day." He shook his head. "I try."

Sadima smiled at him. She couldn't say what she wanted to say. Not with Somiss just down the hall. "I need to talk to you," she whispered.

Franklin's shoulders dropped. Then he lifted his head. "All right."

Sadima's heart leapt. "When?"

"Somiss has to go talk to someone today," he said very quietly.

Sadima nodded, and neither of them said much more as they ate, cleaned up, then went back to copying the pages Somiss had laid out. Sadima put their finished copies beneath the ones yet to be done. She saw Franklin glance at her and knew he understood. There was no reason to prompt Somiss into giving them more work. And he would, if he knew they were very nearly finished by the time he got up.

Once Somiss was dressed and gone, wearing a hat that he pulled low on his forehead, Sadima got up and opened the balcony door just far enough to peek out. She watched Somiss veer to the left, then start up Carver Street. If he went far enough that way, he would be at the docks.

"Do you know where he's going?" she asked Franklin as she came back in. "And please don't lie to me."

Franklin looked down, then up at her again. "I do. But I can't tell you."

Sadima exhaled. "You have to."

He shook his head. "Somiss told me—"

"Don't tell me what he said. I asked *you*," Sadima snapped. Then she slapped him across the face.

Franklin winced and turned, but he didn't raise his hands, and when she stepped back, her chest heaving, she knew why. He was used to this. He had spent a lifetime learning not to get angry at people who shouted at him, who hit him. She felt her eyes flood with tears.

"Tell me," she said, lowering her voice almost to a whisper. "If you care about me at all, you have to tell me where he is going, what he's planning."

She saw tears well in his eyes too, but he shook his head.

"Does it all have to do with the school?" She said it in a normal voice, not a whisper, and she saw him glance around. "Please, Franklin?"

He looked into her eyes. "If I tell you, he will hurt you."

She leaned closer. "And he told me that if I left, you would be sorry, that he would see to it. Can't you see what he's doing?"

Franklin nodded. "Of course. But you should go, Sadima. Go back to Ferne. I am so sorry I ever asked you to come here."

"I'm not," she said in a small voice, and she knew it was true. "I just want you to leave with me. Have you thought about it?"

He didn't answer. She started to tell him that she had copied the songs, about her dream of them opening a school together, really doing what Somiss pretended to be doing—but the fear in his eyes stopped her. Franklin was so scared of Somiss. Maybe he would tell him what she had done? "We could buy a little farm," she said, her throat tight. "We could have children." She saw joy in his eyes for an instant, then it was gone.

"He would find us. Or some constable would. I belong to his father, Sadima. They would offer a reward."

"Then we will go far, far away. Not back to Ferne or

anywhere nearby." She put her arms around him, and they stood close together. Then there was a shout in the street and he stepped back, pulling out his chair before he realized which direction the sound had come from.

"It's just a vendor," Sadima said.

He nodded, but he sat down and picked up his quill. Sadima watched him work for a few minutes, torn between hitting him again and simply getting her things and leaving now, this morning. But she didn't do either. Instead she sat down and finished the pages before her, then reached for some of his.

"No," he said, stopping her hand. "You go to Market Square. I'll finish up. You shouldn't have to do it all."

Sadima waited for him to look up and meet her eyes. When he didn't, she got her shawl and went out. She walked in circles for a long time. And when she got back, she could hear Somiss in his room, reading aloud. And Franklin was gone. She stayed awake as long as she could, but she didn't hear him come in.

56

Jux came for me after Franklin's class again. I followed him up the steep passages into the forest chamber. I was so scared I barely noticed the clean air and the sun. After the snake, what would they do, bring me a bear?

"Make them leave it alone," Jux instructed me, pointing.

The enclosure was bigger this time. I stared at the line of ants on the ground at my feet. They were roiling around a glob of honey he had dropped a pace or two from their nest.

"By moving my thoughts into them?" I asked, but he was already walking away.

"If you can't," he said over his shoulder, "you will be starved. Or hanged." He turned far enough that I could see him grin. "Probably starved."

I stood, staring after him, trying to remember if I had

ever seen a wizard grin. Or even smile. I was pretty sure I hadn't, not in my whole life, and it made me uneasy. Was he joking? He had looked like he was joking.

I began the first pattern, lulling myself. Then I tried doing on purpose what I had accidentally done with the snake. It didn't work. The ants were so small, and all of them were moving. It was impossible to make my thoughts jump from my toes into their minds. If they had minds. It felt like beating on a locked door.

After that, I lay on my belly, moving my fingers forward slowly until they were crawling across my hand like it was just another stone on their way to get the honey. I forced myself to concentrate again. I formed a simple thought: *Leave the honey alone.* I moved it from my head to my shoulders, then to the back of my right hand, the one the crapping ants were crawling across. I felt the thought go out of my skin into them. But even though the twenty or so ants that received the thought veered off and went away, none of the others did. I started sweating. There were thousands of them. How could I possibly give the thought to all of them?

I started over, letting them cross my bare leg. I managed to make a hundred or more veer off, away from the honey, but it was like a drop of water in an ocean. And I realized that the line of ants was widening now. More of them were being sent to get honey. If I didn't stop them soon, I never would.

I took off my robe and lay belly-down beside their trail, then moved my fingertips into the ant path. It took a long time to divert the horde up my arm and down my back. I sent the thought into them and felt them scatter, aimless again, as more marched onto my fingers. It tickled, maddeningly, but I forced myself to stay still. The third time I sent the thought, I felt a stinging pain in my armpit. The aimless ants had moved beneath me and I had shifted my weight just enough to injure one.

The second bite broke my concentration and I flinched. Instantly five or six more ants bit me. The bites burned and I jumped up, brushing at the ones on my arms, helpless to do anything about the ones on my back. I saw welts rising on my skin and I moved backward, stumbling over a pale stone in the sand.

But it wasn't a stone.

It was a skull, almost polished, not a shred of flesh or hair clinging to the bone.

"Go," Jux said, startling me. He was suddenly standing just outside the enclosure, shaking his head, disgust on his face. "Just go." Then he blinked out, disappeared like Franklin and Somiss did. It was even more unnerving in the late afternoon sunlight.

I picked up my robe and left the enclosure, shaking it out, then dragging it across my back like a towel, then shaking it out again. I walked back to the round door, still slapping at the sting of new bites as I descended the steep passages. I walked fast, passing our fish-handled door and going straight to the food hall, a wad of dark green fabric in each hand as I pulled the cloth back and forth across my shoulders, trying to kill the last of the ants.

I stood in front of the stone and gathered the image of Celia's yam pie in my mind. When I put my hands on the ice-cold gem, there was a little flash. The pie was steaming hot. I blinked back tears. I could still make the stone work.

I walked to the table, using my robe sleeves as pot holders. Then I realized I needed a fork and went back to make one. Before I could even begin to concentrate, I heard footsteps. I turned and saw a wizard I had never seen before coming toward me, walking fast. My stomach dropped.

"Hurry," he said, and gestured, then turned and walked away. I ran to catch up. He led me on a route so complicated I got mixed up on the turns. My skin was on fire. It was hard to walk.

It was a small chamber this time, and everyone but me was already seated around a carved, green-brocaded parlor chair. Somiss was sitting in it, his back to the entrance. Will looked terrified. Levin and Jordan gave me stiff little nods. I avoided Luke's eyes. Gerrard didn't seem to notice me at all. I sat behind him and instantly smelled soap—perfumed soap. I remembered his story about the woman who had bought him the fish stew. Then I saw what I had missed in the flickering torchlight. He was wearing a green robe.

"That's everyone?" Somiss rasped. He hadn't so much as bothered to count the dead? No one answered him. He seemed not to notice. "You will soon be asked to recite the first song perfectly," he said. "You will go hungry until you can."

I heard Will make a sad little sound, and I glanced at him. When I looked back, Somiss was gone. The chair was gone. We were alone with one another, with our silence, with our fear. Will stood and ran out of the chamber. I could hear him choking back sobs.

57

Sadima worked five days. Then, on her next free day
she pretended to go to work early, before either Franklin or
Somiss had come out of their rooms. She found a wide-
trunked oak placed so that she could hide and still see their
street gate, and she settled in to wait. She shivered and
pulled her shawl close against the chill.

It wasn't long before she saw Somiss leave the apartment alone. He was wearing the same hat and a dark
woolen jacket she had never seen before. He walked west
to Carver Street and turned up it without glancing back.
She watched him as far as she could—he turned right at the
fourth or fifth corner.

A longer time passed before Franklin came out, carrying
a cloth sack over his shoulder. He was wearing a hat, but

he had no jacket as he headed east, the bag swinging with his stride. Sadima bit her lip. Somiss had them all in disguises now. He didn't care if Franklin was chilled to the bone so long as no one recognized him.

Sadima waited a moment or two, then followed, staying as far back as she could without losing sight of Franklin. As she walked, she promised herself she would just see where he was going. Then she would turn back.

Franklin walked fast, with his shoulders hunched and his free hand in his pocket. Sadima found herself struggling to keep up. Twice she thought she had lost sight of him for good; then she managed to spot him again. And as he kept going, she realized that he was more or less following the route they had taken the day they had all gone to the country together.

He led her into the North End neighborhood, and she fell back even farther. There weren't nearly as many people on the road, no city crowds to hide in. When she saw him leave the road to follow the curving paths they had walked together, she waited until he was well ahead before she continued. The bag looked heavy. Tools? Was Franklin making a camp? A place for Somiss to hide from his father's men?

She shook her head. Franklin and Somiss weren't little boys running away from home now. They couldn't possibly think they would be able to live outside all winter. Then she remembered the old steps they had told her about, the cliff. Maybe they had found a cave, or some piles of fallen stones like the circles around Ferne. But unless they had found an abandoned house with a good roof, they would freeze out here when the snow came.

Sadima walked slower as she got closer, and she kept to the edge of the woods, ready to hide if Franklin came back up the path. Whatever he was doing, maybe she could figure out a way to simply encounter him on the way home without admitting she had followed him. If not today, tomorrow. They could have at least a little time together, alone. Sadima blushed. What was she hoping for? A kiss? Why would one more kiss make anything different, anything better? Franklin would not leave Somiss.

Sadima shook her head. Somiss was not a brilliant man. He was still just an over-smart boy who enjoyed angering his father and bullying Franklin almost as much as he liked pretending to be important and heroic. Why couldn't Franklin see that?

Sadima stopped in the center of the path, startled out of her thoughts by the faint sound of high-pitched shouts. Children's voices?

– 58 –

It was strange to see everyone in the food hall at the
same time, but we all had come to answer the same question. It didn't take long. Somiss had not been making an
idle threat. None of us could make food.

I went back to the room, fighting the familiar lump of
fear in my belly. I could go to Hope Hall and have some
kind of dinner, but they might be watching now. What if
I got caught? I wasn't anywhere near hungry enough to
take the risk. Not yet. I scratched at my ant bites and
arranged myself on the bed with *Songs of the Elders*.

Gerrard came in and sat with his back to me as usual.
I saw him pick up the history book and felt gooseflesh
rise on my arms. Why? Had he already learned the first

song? As if he had heard my thoughts, Gerrard looked over his shoulder at me, then went back to his reading.

I made a show of closing the book of songs and reaching for the history book. Then I felt like a complete horse's ass. He couldn't see me, and he wouldn't care if he could. Still, I flipped through some pages as though I was looking for something, just in case he turned around, and I came across the Four Vows. They were taken only by graduates, the text said. I guess they wanted us to know, just in case any of us lived long enough to care. The way the words stacked up made the point as well as anything. These awaited the lucky graduate:

The Vow of Lifelong Cloister
The Vow of Lifelong Silence
The Vow of Lifelong Celibacy
The Vow of Lifelong Poverty

That was the reward for graduating? Vowing to give up everything that mattered to most people? I shoved the history book aside and opened the song book. The first one was a page long—the words were all complete nonsense to me, unlike any language I knew or had ever heard. *Songs?* Would we be singing them eventually?

I waded through the first verse, guessing at a pronunciation for every single word. I had always hated memorizing things—poems, the names of kings and their heirs, whatever I was assigned. I wasn't good at it. Or at ant herding, obviously. My whole body itched and ached from the ant bites as I studied, trying to make up and memorize pronunciations for the first verse at least.

After a long time, I stopped reading and looked up at the shadowy ceiling, rubbing at an ant bite on my neck. Maybe the wizards would take the green robe back as well as starving me. Would they give me my old one again? Or would I have to be naked until I could memorize a nonsense song, talk to ants, and *fly* by flapping my own ears. I closed my eyes, suddenly weary. It was all starting over again. Boys would starve, and I might be one of them this time.

When the wizard pounded on the door, I jerked awake, and the song book slid to the floor. Had it been a whole hour, even? It had felt like minutes. Every part of my body was tired. He led us to a different chamber with a different ornate chair in it. Somiss appeared a moment later. He made us all recite, stopping us to correct pronunciation as we went. Most of the boys managed only the first verse, or less. We all had to start at the beginning over and over, completely lost after each and every interruption from Somiss to correct our cobbled-up pronunciations. No one did very well, not even Gerrard.

Somiss dismissed us with an annoyed wave of his hand.

"Will we be able to eat once we can say it all, or do we have to have the pronunciations all correct too?" Will asked in a near whisper.

Somiss didn't answer. He disappeared.

I went back to the room and stayed awake as long as I

could, studying the song, trying to remember at least some of Somiss's corrections. But the words blurred in my mind first, then in my vision, and I closed the book. I just wanted out. I wanted to go home long enough to say good-bye to my mother. Then I would run away, or just kill myself. Nothing seemed impossible or scary to me now. Anything would be easier than this.

Sadima left the path and crept forward. Was there a family walking in the woods this chilly morning? It didn't seem likely. And now she couldn't hear anything but the birds. She spotted Franklin moving along the foot of the massive cliff. As she watched, he set down the sack and pushed a curtain of vines to one side. A cave? He went through the opening, stooping low to duck under the over-hang.

Sadima stood still, glancing back toward the path. It was time to go. But she didn't. Keeping an eye on the cliff base, she made her way deeper into the woods, then circled back. When she found a tall, dense pine close to the base of the cliff, she tied her shawl tightly around her waist and started climbing. Once she was high enough to see, she stopped and worked herself into a tolerable position. Then she watched the entrance of the cavern closely, listening. But there was only silence now.

By the time Franklin came out, Sadima had unwrapped her shawl and found ways to pad her hands and feet. She watched him as he pulled the vines back to cover the opening and walked away, his head down, the unfamiliar hat obscuring his face. He still had the bag, but it was clearly empty now, lying shapeless on his back. Even so, he walked slowly, like there were weights on his feet, his dirty shirt clinging to his skin.

Sadima watched until he was almost out of sight. Then she climbed down. She stretched and walked a little to ease her legs, then stood still, knowing she should just leave. But what were they planning? Neither one of them had any idea what it would take to live like this. And they would die trying to learn. If they were provisioning a cave, she wanted to know now. She needed a chance to talk Franklin out of going along with something this dangerous. Glancing back up the path once more, Sadima hid her shawl behind some serviceberry bushes, then ran.

It took a little time to find the opening. The vines spilled down off the rock for a long ways. When she finally found the entrance, she realized she wasn't tall enough or strong enough to push the vines back. She had to part them, then wriggle through.

She ducked beneath the overhanging stone, then straightened up. It wasn't a cavern, exactly. It was more like a tunnel. There was no light except for the little that filtered through the vine, but that was enough to see that Franklin had left a lamp here, where he would need it next time. The striker was lying beside it. Hands unsteady, Sadima lit the wick and walked forward, tucking the striker into her bodice.

The passageway was straight and long, and she stopped twice to look back, feeling trapped by the darkness before and behind her. This wasn't a natural cave. What was it? She kept walking, her careful steps almost soundless on the cold stone, wishing she had brought her shawl. It was even colder here than outside.

Abruptly the tunnel ceiling lowered, and she had to bend nearly double to keep going. She felt the stone rub her back and remembered the scrapes on Franklin's skin. He was much taller than she was.

When the passage widened, Sadima stopped again, holding the lantern. The ceiling sloped upward from where she stood. Cautiously she went forward, holding the lantern at arm's length.

This was a natural cavern, she was pretty sure. It felt enormous and dry as bones—and it was much warmer than the tunnel. She exhaled. If they could find a way to get food and to vent smoke from a constant fire, they *might* be able to live here.

Sadima turned around, wondering what had been in the sack and where Franklin had left it, but she was too scared to go much farther without more light. It was as though the narrow tunnel had disappeared behind her. It took a long, scary moment walking back toward it before the lantern light fell on the opening.

Sadima gathered her skirt in one hand, ready to duck back into the passageway. But then she heard whispering. She lifted the lamp, but the light didn't penetrate the darkness much beyond the reach of her hands. The whispering stopped. "Who is there?" she asked, her heart racketing in her chest. The whispers came again, then one little voice. "Lady? Is there more food?"

Sadima walked forward, her mouth open with cold dread, her eyes filling with tears when she saw the bars of the cage. It was full of boys. "Who brought you here?" she managed to whisper, fumbling with the iron lock on the door, then dropping it, realizing that she had no way to unlock it.

"The one with ice for eyes," a whisper came from somewhere among the boys.

Sadima felt a swoop of nausea at the smell as she moved closer. There was a slops bucket somewhere. "Why did he bring you? Do you know?" Several boys shook their heads.

"They will feed us," one of them added. "But we have to be quiet." There was a general murmur of agreement. She lifted the lamp again and saw the littlest of the boys pressed against the stone wall that served as the back of the cage. He lifted his head, and she saw the scar that ran across his throat. Oh no. *No.* What was Somiss doing with these children?

Sadima straightened, horrified, overcome, sick to her

stomach. "I will come back," she promised them. Then, before any of them could say anything more, she turned and ran.

Desperate to get out, she scraped her back twice against the unforgiving stone and nearly forgot to leave the lamp and striker inside. She clawed through the vines. Finally outside, gulping down fresh air, running to get her shawl, she wanted to cry, but she could not.

~ 60 ~

Franklin made us run through all the patterns. Then he had us move our thoughts to every part of our bodies. Almost. He always skipped our penises. It had made me smile the first time I had noticed it. Now I remembered the celibacy vow. Had my father known that, too?

Franklin suddenly stood up. "You have been here a year," he said. "This is our last class and our first. Keep practicing."

Then he walked out.

We all stood up slowly. Last and first? What the crap did that mean? I glanced at Levin. He looked dazed. Everyone did. A year? Was that possible?

No one spoke, not even a whisper. I looked for Jux as I went out, but he wasn't there. I had no idea what that meant, but it scared me. I went back to the room and read the first song over and over again, then tried to recite it, quietly, putting in all of the pronunciation corrections I could remember. How many days before I could recite it perfectly? Five? Ten? Thirty? My stomach rumbled.

A sudden pounding on the door startled me into jumping up. A wizard leaned in to gesture at me, then at Gerrard. When we got to the slanting tunnels—by a route far different from the one I had learned—I knew where we were going. Climbing the slope, I wondered why the route to Franklin's class had changed every day, but the route to Jux's class hadn't—until Gerrard had joined us. Now I knew two routes to get here; he knew only one. What possible reason could there be for doing that? Maybe there wasn't one. I wanted to believe that.

Two wizards met us just inside the round door. Jux led me in one direction. Gerrard's teacher took him in another. I glanced at Gerrard's stiff back and wondered if he would meet the same snake I had. If he did, I hoped he would be all right. Jux positioned me at another anthill. It took me a very long time to come to the simple solution: I moved my thoughts to the honey, not the ants. Once the honey itself seemed to be telling them it was poisonous, the ants backed away. The instant I stopped sending the thought, their instincts took over, and they relied on the smell of the honey or whatever ants usually relied on to tell them the truth.

It was another lucky accident. I had been trying to move my thoughts to a single ant near the honey so that maybe it would warn the others. They wouldn't hold still long enough, so I used a slender stick and mired one of them in the honey. Then I aimed my thoughts at that one—and missed.

When Jux came back, I showed him the honey trick, proud of myself. He smiled, then shook his head. He reached down and scooped up a handful of sand, which he poured over the honey. Then he looked at me like I was a half-wit. "Magic is not to be wasted."

I had to fight down my anger. "I though we had to—"

He snapped his fingers to stop me midword. "No one gave you any rules."

I bit my lip. He was right. But I wanted to ask him if what I did wasn't better. It had certainly taken more time, had been harder to figure out than a handful of stinking sand. Why would I use my hand and dirt when I was here to learn magic? I started to speak, but he shook his head. "Go."

Gerrard was already back in the room. He didn't say a word to me about the snake or anything else, but when he stood up to piss, I noticed a dark red-black stain on the hem of his new robe. Blood? I tried hard not to wonder. I studied the song until the wizard pounded on the door.

On the way to Somiss's class, I walked last, behind the wizard and Gerrard, my mouth dry with nervousness. This time Somiss laughed at three of us—Will, Luke, and Jordan. He made us all tongue-tied with his ridicule and the constant interruptions to correct the pronunciation of almost every word. I glanced away and noticed that

Gerrard's lips were moving. He was whispering along with each of us. It was so smart and so simple. I began doing it, hoping it would help.

Gerrard was last. He recited the whole song, and Somiss corrected only ten words when he was finished. Ten. No one else had managed more than ten correct words in the first verse. I stared at him. The wizards were crazy. If they had let us help each other, we would all have been able to graduate—and no one would have died.

That night I studied in spite of the ache in my belly and the hot itching of my skin. Gerrard stripped off his robe and used his bar of soap to wash the hem. I glanced up several times and saw a pink tinge in the suds. Had he killed the snake? How?

In my dreams that night, there was a boy who looked like me, but taller and with wider shoulders. He lay in a dark place, waiting, his skin itching and burning with some terrible disease, for a wizard to pass by.

I don't know if he killed the dream wizard, because a real one pounded on the door. I got up hungry and tired. Were they cutting down our sleep?

Running blindly, jerking her shawl free of the bushes, then stumbling back toward the path, Sadima didn't see Franklin coming until she slammed into him.

"Sadima," he said, grabbing her shoulders to keep her upright. "Sadima, wait. Please. I want to—"

"What are you doing with those boys?" she shouted at him, beating at his chest.

"Wait," he pleaded with her, trapping her hands. "Sadima, I saw your footprints at the turnoff, so I came— Stop. Just listen to me," he said when she wrenched sideways, trying to break his grip. He got his arms around her, pinning hers at her sides.

Clenching her teeth and her fists, Sadima threw herself backward with all her strength, and he was startled into releasing her. She staggered a few steps, then caught her balance and came at him again, a low, agonized sound coming from her lips. She just wanted to hurt him, to wake him up, to make him realize what Somiss *was*. "How can you help him do this?" she asked him, over and over, hitting him, sobbing. "How can you?"

Franklin's face was contorted with emotion. Anger? He raised one fist. Startled, she turned to run, but it was too late. He grabbed her from behind, and she fought to free herself. "You don't know anything about me," he said, dragging her close, his weight on her back, his mouth against her cheek. "You think you do, but you don't."

"I know you're a coward," she spat, straining to stand up straight, to turn, to free herself. "You'll let him hurt those boys because you are too scared of him to even—"

"No!" He spun her around to face him. She shoved him backward, and he stumbled to one knee, then pitched to the side, dragging her with him when he caught at her forearm.

They hit hard, and Sadima heard his breath explode from his mouth. She tried to roll free, to get up, but he held her against his chest, muffling her voice, pressing her face into his shoulder, making her listen.

"I am the only thing that stands between those boys and death," he said, close to her ear. "Can't you see that? Somiss listens to me. I know how he thinks. I know how to calm him down." She fought to get loose, but he held her tighter. "Sadima, if you want to help those boys, pretend you never saw them. Leave if you want to, but don't say anything to Somiss or anyone else. If you do, *you* will have killed them all."

Sadima felt her muscles go slack. She could hear his heart beating. "Come with me," she said, lifting her head. "Come with me right now. We can free the boys and take them and—"

"And then he will find more boys!" Franklin cut her off. "It won't stop him, Sadima. Nothing ever does. I should have—" He stopped midsentence and loosened his hold on her, looking into her eyes. "I should have killed him when we were boys. But I *couldn't*." His eyes held a lifetime of regret. "And I can't now. Someone will, someday, but it will not be me."

Sadima felt her rage turning into something softer and infinitely heavier. She laid her head on Franklin's chest again, and for a long moment they both lay still, breathing almost in unison. Then he let go of her. She stood up but did not run. Franklin got to his feet, and they just looked at each other.

"If you stay," he said slowly, "I will love you forever. If you leave, I will love you forever. But I can't go with you, not until he is dead. If I do, I know what will happen."

Sadima shook her head. "How can it be worse than this?"

Franklin's eyes were full of pain. "It can. And I will tell you someday how I know that. If you stay."

Sadima stared at him, unable to speak, trying to think.

"He is brilliant," Franklin said. "And he will rediscover magic and he will change the world. It will be for the better—if I do what I have always done."

Sadima reached out to touch his cheek. "You can't stop him from—"

"He trusts me," Franklin cut her off. "He almost loves me."

She blinked, finally understanding. "And no one else."

He nodded.

"So you think that if you leave him—"

Franklin was still nodding. "Yes. There will be nothing left to hold him to anything human. You know he is already hiding much of what he has learned?"

Sadima nodded. She heard a magpie jabbering. Then she listened to the wind touching the treetops.

"Don't you want to do something that matters?" Franklin asked. "You talked about people understanding animals' hearts. And magic is bigger than that. A thousand times bigger. Do you want to live your life on a farm, Sadima? Really?"

She swallowed. Then she spoke slowly, staring at the trees. "I will stay if you promise me something." She met his eyes.

"What?"

"That you will let me kill him if it comes to that."

Franklin stood still as stone.

"If you can't promise, I can't stay," she said.

Franklin looked up at the sky, then at the grass beneath his feet. Then he nodded and they shook hands, like two merchants making a bargain, but they did not let go, not until they were back on the road where someone might see.

At the next recitation, I made it all the way through
the song and had fifteen corrections. I was so relieved that
I smiled, then noticed Luke glaring at me. I didn't blame
him. He had missed thirty or more words. Will did even
worse. His eyes were starting to look hollow again—and so
full of fear. I felt terrible for him—to be that scared and
completely alone with it. Jordan and Levin did better too,
missing fewer words, making it to the end. Then it was
Gerrard's turn. He did it. Perfectly. I tried not to hate him
when he walked past our door and went to the food hall—
then came back later, smelling of fish stew.

When Jux pounded on the door, I was studying the first
song. Gerrard was sitting on his bed. He stood up too, but
Jux motioned for him to stay behind. I glanced back at

Gerrard as we were leaving. He didn't look angry, he looked scared.

I had to sit in a glass enclosure with Servenian humming-birds. They were in a little cage inside the enclosure. I was told to let them out. That was it. No other instruction.

I had never seen hummingbirds before—or any bird like them. I sat still, my arms crossed as they realized the cage had been opened and came out one by one. There were six. They all flew the length of the glass enclosure.

I stood and waved my arms, trying to get them to slow down, but it only scared them. The fastest one walloped itself against the glass, dropping to the ground. I ran to pick it up, but it was limp in my hand, its neck broken. Then I realized I had startled the others. One more hit the glass and died. I picked it up too and held both of them in the palm of my left hand. They were so tiny, so beautiful. And I had killed them.

I sat down and held still. The others slowed their flight instantly. Three more bumped the glass but seemed all right. Then they flew in a group to one side, trying to find a way out. Or so I thought. After a long enough time, I realized that there was a honeysuckle vine growing just outside the enclosure. Freedom wasn't the goal—they were hungry

It took a long time for me to notice the opening in a corner of the glass enclosure. It was very small, just big enough for the hummingbirds to pass through. None of them had found it because it was on the opposite side from the honeysuckle. They seemed very hungry. "Let them out," Jux had said, and I had assumed he meant the little cage. Was I supposed to let them out of the glass enclosure?

I kept watching, and it seemed to me that the graceful little birds were getting weaker. Would they drop from exhaustion? There was no place for them to perch, to rest. But if I just opened the door and let them out—and was wrong? I fell into the fourth pattern and moved my thoughts into the biggest hummingbird, seeing the world through its eyes for an instant before my thoughts pushed its thoughts aside. I made it wonder if there was a way out on the other side.

It took about ten minutes for it to find the little gap. When it did, it flew out, whipping into a steep turn to circle the enclosure and get to the honeysuckle on the other side. One of the others had seen it leave and flew to the corner— then found the way out. By the time Jux got back, they were all outside, eating.

"Why did they want out?" Jux asked when he came back.

"To eat," I answered.

"Why did you help them?" he asked tersely. My chest tightened. Had he meant only the little cage? Was helping *anything* against the rules? Was I supposed to have known that?

Then Jux winked. "Go."

Later Gerrard and I were led to a new chamber. Somiss had another chair, grander, bigger, its silk cushions the color of sapphires. There was a torch stand beside him. His eyes reflected the cold-fire like little mirrors. We sat on the floor in front of him. The chamber was cold. Why?

"You," he said, pointing at Will. "Recite."

Will stood up, and the torchlight hit his face. He was shaking. Somiss made him start over on the first word and corrected nearly every word that followed. It was horrible to watch. Luke did better, and so did Jordan and Levin. I didn't. I had been watching crapping hummingbirds instead of studying. I mispronounced more words this time, and I got stuck in the middle of the last verse and had to start over. And Gerrard recited the *second* song and missed only seven pronunciations.

When he was done, Somiss made a gesture of dismissal and his chair lifted into the air. We all stared as it disappeared into the darkness beyond the highest reach of the torchlight. Leaving, no one spoke, though I saw everyone glancing at Gerrard.

I walked straight past our room, heading for the food hall. Then I passed it and headed for Hope Hall, running to make the first turn in case someone came up behind me. Once I was in the narrow passage, I slowed again, my mouth watering, my stomach churning.

But Hope Hall was empty. Not a crumb of bread, not a grain of sugar, not even the warm smell of the cheese. Nothing. I went to two of the other places I had left food, then gave up and just sat down, shivering against the cold wall.

When I finally went back, Gerrard looked at me like he was about to say something, but then he didn't. I studied the song as long as I could stand it, too light-headed to concentrate. When I went to sleep, my dreams were about hummingbirds falling to the ground and fluttering, too weak to rise, and a wizard with icy eyes was stepping on them, crushing the life out of them.

— 63 —

Sadima had been lying awake on her pallet for hours when she heard the door rattle, then open. She could hear Somiss's voice and knew instantly that something good had happened. Once he and Franklin had gone to bed, she got up, meaning to recite the song for long life over Franklin as she did most nights. She hadn't told him yet about the changed songs, about her copying everything, but she would, soon.

She passed through the arch, took a step into the dark sitting room, and ran into Franklin in the dark. They were both startled, and he held her until her fear dissolved. Then she shivered, and he held her closer against the chill of the evening while he told her that they'd had a meeting with some Eridian Elders. "I think they will help us," he said, whispering.

"Help? You mean give Somiss money?" she asked.

"Yes," he answered quietly. "At least that. Maybe more. I'll tell you the rest tomorrow."

Sadima nodded. He kissed her forehead. "Thank you," he said, and she understood him. She had done for him what he had done for her when he came to Ferne. He was no longer alone.

She stood still, listening to him walk down the hall. Once he was in bed, she lay on her pallet, listening to the night sounds in the street. What would this mean? Would the Eridians want to give all the songs and all the knowledge to everyone? If they could make Somiss do that, the world might benefit from his work after all. Unless he changed things by a letter or two, left out vowels in the songs, and switched verses. Sadima frowned. Maybe Rinka would know who should be warned. And if he—

Sadima's thoughts stopped when she smelled smoke. She got up, sure she had closed the flue too far when she banked the fire for the night, but she hadn't. Coughing, she pushed open the balcony doors and went out to get a lungful of fresh air. The odd flickering light that rouged the cobblestones below made her blink. Then she leaned over the railing, trying to see. The flames were halfway up the wall.

"There he is!" someone rasped from the street.

"That's just the girl," someone answered. "Watch the door!"

Sadima whirled around and ran down the hall. Feeling her way in the dark, she found Franklin's bed and shook him awake. "Fire! Someone set the building on fire!"

Franklin stumbled upright and pulled on his pants. "Did you wake Somiss?"

"No!" Sadima told him, and ran back to the kitchen. She dressed, got the honey jar, then gathered the rest of her belongings, glad that the papers were safe at Rinka's. Hands shaking, she made a bundle of her shawl and tied it tightly around her waist. Then she ran back up the hall and stood in the doorway. The weird orange light was brighter back here. Somiss was trying to gather up his papers, dropping some from beneath his arm as he tried to pick up a second stack.

"Use the bedsheets!" she shouted at him. He turned to stare at her. She dragged the linens onto the floor, spreading them out. Then she turned back to Franklin. "Get shirts, shoes, and jackets for both of you," she said, close to his ear. "Hurry!"

She ran to the sitting room and got the papers off the table, then helped Somiss stack his work onto the sheets and tie them into bundles. It took moments, no more, but the smoke was thicker when they had finished. They were both coughing, their eyes running with tears.

"I heard someone say to watch the door," Sadima told Somiss. "How can we get out?" He pointed upward. There was a workman's hatch in the ceiling of his room.

Sadima watched him shove his desk beneath the hinged door to open it and knew he had realized it might one day be a way to escape—maybe he had planned on it. Franklin ran back in, coughing and flushed, carrying their shoes and clothing tied up in a sheet.

Somiss went first. Then Franklin hoisted up the sheet-bundles that held his papers, and Somiss jerked them through the opening. Franklin insisted on lifting Sadima upward next. She grabbed Somiss's hands, and he hauled her through the hatch door and set her on her feet, then turned to help Franklin. There were shouts in the street now. Sadima heard a woman screaming angry curses and hoped it was their landlady, safely out of the building.

"This way," Somiss said. "Be careful. Some of the slates are loose."

Franklin and Somiss each carried two sheet-bundles. Sadima walked between them, Franklin walking closer where the roof got steeper. Then, when it flattened out again, Somiss threw his bundle across a gap onto the roof of the next building, then jumped the gap. Sadima gathered her courage and her skirts and followed him. Then it was Franklin's turn.

When they were all three across, Somiss led off again. Sadima was sure he had walked this route at least once before. He crossed the neighbor's roof, then they jumped downward, onto a building that was only two stories high. From there, Somiss guided them to an outside stairway that took them down to the ground. He opened the latch to let them out. The owner had clearly never thought that intruders might come from above.

Once they were in the street, Somiss ran, keeping to the

shadows. Glancing back, Sadima could see the flames and the orange globe of light that extended upward from the building. There were shouts and screams, and a dray team with water barrels in a heavy wagon clattered down the street. Sadima caught her breath as they hid behind a carriage and watched the wagon pass, the driver whipping the team, half standing on the buckboard.

The carriage horses snorted and sidled, uneasy because of the smoke and the commotion. "Look at this!" Somiss said, then laughed, gesturing at the open carriage. He threw the sheet-bundles in, then lifted Sadima, shoving her over the rail. Franklin was climbing in as she found her feet and stood up, her side bruised. Somiss was fiddling with the reins as the horses whinnied and shook their manes. He pulled awkwardly at the tether knot, and Sadima realized he had probably never driven a carriage team in his life.

She started forward to free the reins just as he grabbed the whip and slashed at the horses' backs. Already terrified of the smoke, the startled horses lunged into a gallop. The carriage lurched forward, and Sadima fell. She wrenched around and saw Franklin half over the carriage rail. He had been climbing in; now he was hanging on for his life.

Sadima fought to stand, using the passenger's bench to brace herself, then grabbed his shirt, pulling him forward in awkward hitches, slumping beneath his weight so that they fell to the floorboards, holding each other when the carriage caromed around a corner, two wheels bouncing off the ground, then crashing back. Sadima tried to untangle herself, to turn so she could try again to take the reins, but Franklin held her tight.

"Let me go!" she shouted into his ear. "Let me go or he will kill us all!"

Franklin loosened his arms and she managed to stand, swaying, but was jerked to one side when Somiss heaved on the reins, turning again. On the next straightaway, she crawled to the back of the driver's bench, then reached out, clawing air as she tried to reach the reins, screaming at him that she knew how to handle the horses. But he shoved her back, and the carriage tilted again, one wheel in a ditch, slamming her sideways.

Sadima struggled up and faced front again, feeling the horses' terror of the smoke and the whip as Somiss lashed them onward. Then Sadima recognized the street and she sat down, knowing that the horses would be able to stay on the wide, straight road they would soon be on.

But on the last corner, turning onto the wide lane that went through the North End, Somiss waited too long, then jerked on the inside rein with his whole weight. Sadima felt the carriage tip again, this time rising so high on the right side that she felt the balance shift. She shouted at Franklin, but it was too late to do anything but hang on.

— 64 —

I failed the next recitation test—by five words. Only
five. Gerrard passed the second song. No one else came close.
But Somiss had a surprise for us. "You waste my time," he
rasped. "Study for three days on empty bellies. Then you can
all try again."

Three days. I heard Will make a sound of anguish. No one
spoke. No one cursed or argued. And then Somiss was gone.

Gerrard would be all right, of course. For the rest of us—I
started to count the days, then stopped. It made no difference.
However long it had been, it would be three more days now.

We all stood up. Luke stumbled as he left, but caught himself before he fell. Levin and Jordan walked close behind him.
Will shuffled out alone and I watched him go, feeling weary
in a way I cannot describe. I walked to the food hall afterward

and tried to make a simple broth. I knew I couldn't, but I needed to try. When I touched the stone, of course, nothing happened. Levin came and tried, then wandered out. I just kept standing in the corner, watching, swaying back and forth in a rhythm that seemed to calm my fear a little. Not much.

I kept thinking about Will. There was no one in his room to encourage him, or even break the silence now and then. He was in there, alone, without classes to go to for three days, only silence and his own thoughts. And would it really be three days? Or three hours? Or ten days? None of us had any way to know anything but this: The wizards had done this many times. It had become routine to them, watching boys die. I hated them so deeply, so completely, that it scared me.

Walking back to the room, I tried to talk myself into believing that I might make it. How long had I gone without eating before? I had lost weight, but not nearly as much as Tally and the others had. And I would probably pass the recitation next time. But what if I didn't?

I opened the door and went in. The room smelled like soap and fish, which seemed almost homelike to me. Gerrard was sitting cross-legged, his face to the wall. He was reading the history book. I sat on my cot, then lay down, turning toward the wall so Gerrard couldn't see.

Once I felt steady again, I got the song book from my desk and stared at the title, the only words on it that weren't written in the strange language. I opened to the first song, then the second, then, without thinking about why I was doing it, I flipped through the pages. The second song was about the

same length as the first, but then they got longer. Much
longer. Toward the back of the book, they were ten and fifteen pages long.

I felt faint as the reality seeped into me. I was going to die
here. Even if I passed the song test next time, I would be able
to eat for only a few days, then I would have to starve for six
or nine or twelve more. And there would be a day when the
songs were too long and I would never eat again.

"Gerrard?" I didn't know I was going to say it, and the
sound of my own voice startled me.

He turned.

I had no idea what to say next. I hadn't meant to speak at
all. "I hate them," I said. And it felt so good to say it out loud
that I repeated it. Twice.

I expected him to turn away, angry, warning me to leave
him alone, but he didn't. He said this: "I have to graduate. I
have to."

I nodded. "You will. You will be the one."

To my amazement, his eyes got glassy. "Jux disagrees. And
so would Franklin if you asked him. I can't," he began, then
hesitated. "I can't move my thoughts. I can't make anything
but fish stew."

"And I will never learn the songs," I told him. "I hate the
wizards," I said once more. "Thank you for letting me say it
before I die," I whispered. "I hate them all."

"So do I." Gerrard stood up and came closer.

I glanced at the ceiling. "Are they watching us?"

He shook his head. "Not in the rooms. Franklin still forbids it."

"But what about the laugh? You heard it too."

"Jux is crazy," he said flatly, as though it was an answer. He took another step toward me. Then he stopped. "If I help you," he whispered, using barely enough breath to shape the words, "will you help me?"

I nodded, astounded. "Yes."

"And then will you help me destroy this place?"

I knew he couldn't possibly keep a promise like that, but I put out my hand, and he gripped it. The touch of flesh on my flesh, his skin on my skin, jolted me into feeling a kind of hunger I hadn't even recognized. How long had it been since I had touched anyone?

We held our handclasp a moment longer. Then he sat at his desk and opened the book of songs. He began reading aloud, very quietly, slowly, precisely, with his back to me. I listened to him the first time through, then recited it with him the next. By the third time I could feel myself learning it in a way that reading it silently, stumbling over the words, I could never have managed.

On the tenth time, he stopped reading after the first few words, and I recited it, alone. I reached out and gripped his arm for an instant, then sat back on my cot to practice silently. It had been so long since my thoughts were thoughts, not screams. I was still scared, but somehow the knives had gone out of it.

Later I ate fish stew and then slept without dreams. And when a wizard finally woke us, we pissed and washed, and Gerrard waited for me to finish before he opened the door.

— 65 —

Sadima staggered upright, calling Franklin's name.
There was no answer. She turned, one hand pressed
against her forehead, trying to make sense of what she was
seeing in the moonlight. The horses had dragged the tilting
carriage onward a long ways, then had plunged to a stop in
front of a pasture fence after it finally overturned, throwing all three of them into the air.

"Franklin?" Sadima's whole body hurt, and she felt a
sharp pain in her right ankle with every step. "Franklin!"

"Get the papers!" It was Somiss. He was pulling at the
sheet-bundles, trying to free them from the wrecked carriage. The horses dragged it forward and he shouted again.
She could see blood trickling down the side of his face. It
looked black in the moonlight.

"Where is Franklin?" she yelled at him. Somiss pointed, and she turned to see a shape sprawled in the road.

Sadima ran to kneel beside Franklin. He stirred, and she patted his cheeks and rubbed her hand across his chest, trying to rouse him. He opened his eyes and groaned. "Is Somiss all right? Are you?"

"I am," she said quickly.

"Somiss?"

"He's picking up his papers," Sadima told him. "Where are you hurt? Can you sit up?"

He nodded. "I think so." He turned to lay flat. "It's not nearly as bad as being beaten by Gypsies."

Sadima smiled and held his hand tightly. "Whoever owns this carriage will send the king's guard before long," she whispered. "And we will—"

"No," Franklin said in a strained voice as he tried to sit up. It took three tries. When he could, he pointed at the elaborate design painted on the broken carriage gate. "See the crest? It belongs to Somiss's father. He won't tell anyone. He can't let anyone know we got away."

Sadima helped Franklin to his feet, and together they limped across the road. She calmed the horses, then led them into the woods, dragging the wrecked carriage as close to a little pond as she could. She and Franklin unhitched the carriage and pushed it in, then unharnessed the horses and spooked them into a gallop back toward the city.

Somiss carried all the sheet-bundles, and he was laughing, his eyes as wide as a child's as they started down the path. Sadima suddenly remembered, and she turned to face him. "Where are we going?" she asked, and felt Franklin touch her shoulder in gratitude.

Somiss threw his head back and stared at the open sky for a few heartbeats before he answered her. "To the ancient home of magic," he said quietly. There was awe in his voice. "If it is what I think it is, it will take me a hundred years to find everything they built, everything they had taken from them."

"Here?" Sadima asked, feigning astonishment. "Isn't this near where we came? Is there another city out here?"

"Inside the cliff," Somiss said. "It's in the Gypsy songs." Then he set off, the sheet-bundles huge and ungainly on his shoulders, a wild grin on his face. Franklin dropped back to walk beside Sadima. The night was cold and the stars glittered as they followed Somiss into the darkness.